INVASION OF THE BLANCHE

Corey Mariani

AUTHOR'S NOTE

In the following manuscript, I have attempted, with the aid of whorls, to recount my part in the strange and otherworldly events surrounding the Humboldt County Christmas Flood of 2013. Where there were no whorls to guide me, I relied on my memories, grafting to them with all the grace I could muster. To my estranged siblings, if you exist, you are in existential danger. Knowledge of your enemy is herein.

CHAPTER 1

RHODODENDRON PILOT SCARF.

Lou and I hopped out of the truck. The air was cold, the sky overcast. I rubbed my bare arms to create warmth. My coat still hung in some closet at the Lodge.

In my mind, I repeated the words *Rhododendron Pilot Scarf* over and over, a Pictionary poem I'd used to graft to reality itself. I'd tried to encompass my surroundings, my current mood, my outlook on life, my thoughts on mortality, people, green beans—everything. I'd tried to condense the entirety of my existence into one phrase: *Rhododendron Pilot Scarf.*

Lou had asked me to do it. The morphine could wear off any minute, allowing Naomi's wanda poison to take over my mind again. I'd been given several poisons by Naomi's mummers, causing mixed metaphors in my mind, which was especially dangerous. The grafting was supposed to help keep me grounded. *Rhododendron Pilot Scarf, Rhododendron Pilot Scarf.*

While we walked, Lou said, "Let me do all the talking when we get to the house. I've given this whole Jehovah's Witness spiel a ton. I got it down. Once the otalith becomes angry, we gotta stay in her presence, like at least within fifty feet of her, for a minute to make sure we absorb enough of her cackle."

My morphine must have been wearing off because my thoughts took on the shape of one of Naomi's metaphors again:

The houses were cheese curds. Lactic acid and cows lived in them, watching daytime TV and fermenting. Lou was mountain lion, listeria, lactose, and cattle dog. I feared him and hungered for him. The cows respected him. They would respond to his barks, his attacks.

I was having these thoughts, but they weren't consuming me.

Yet.

I still had control. I kept repeating my Pictionary poem, *Rhododendron Pilot Scarf.* It seemed to give me power over the metaphor, seemed to anchor me to reality.

Lou and I walked four blocks through the quiet neighborhood, turning twice along the way before he pointed to a two-story yellow house with a running fountain in the front yard and the top of a greenhouse peeking over the backyard fence. We climbed the porch steps and stood side by side. Lou rang the doorbell, but I heard mooing.

Rhododendron Pilot Scarf.

Rhododendron Pilot Scarf.

Lou gently pushed me back, saying, "She spits when she yells." After waiting fifteen seconds, he hit the bell again—

mooooo—*Rhododendron Pilot Scarf.* This time noises came from inside, sounded like slippers sliding across hardwood floors. The largest woman I'd ever seen opened the door, six-six at least, with broad shoulders, broad nose, and broad forehead. She wore a white T-shirt and Dallas-Cowboy pajama bottoms. She looked sleepy and confused.

Lou gave the pitch: "Good day to you, sister. We are here to share the message of the Bible for you today. I would like to read Second Corinthians for you: 'Praise be to the God and Father of our Lord Jesus Christ, the Father of compassion and the God of all comfort, who comforts us in all our troubles, so that we can comfort those in any trouble with the comfort we ourselves receive from God.'"

The woman waited patiently for Lou to finish, then she smiled and said, "See ya," and closed the door.

Now it was Lou's turn to look confused. "I don't understand. That always works."

I didn't have much time to brainstorm with him over what went wrong. The morphine had almost worn off completely now. *Rhododendron Pilot Scarf* was barely working anymore. Everything was cheese-related again. I refused to take another dose of morphine to bring me back from the brink. I stepped off the porch and walked along the front of the house until I found a hose behind a rose bush—milk truck tank, food-grade sanitary hose. A spray nozzle was attached to the end. I lifted the hose off the mount, turned on the water, and dragged the hose by the nozzle back toward the porch. The hose just reached the walkway.

"Ring the bell again," I said, barely hanging on to my sanity, the metaphors coagulating in my mind as they had outside the Lodge.

Rhododendron Pilot Scarf, Rhododendron Pilot Scarf, Rhododendron Pilot Scarf.

"Relax," Lou said. "I got this. Put the hose away."

I raised my voice. "I don't have time for this. Ring the bell."

Lou put a finger to his lips, shushing me.

I responded by yelling a line from one of the many cheese documentaries Naomi had forced me to watch with her: "A hot curd makes for a hard cheese!"

Lou threw up his hands, and I yelled the line again for the whole neighborhood to hear. When the large woman opened the door, she looked irritated, but we wanted her that way. I hit her directly in the chest with a pressurized stream of water/milk. "I baptize you in the name of Jehovah," I said, "and in the name of cheese everywhere."

Her face twisted with rage as she strode past Lou and leapt off the porch, a giant woman moving with the speed and grace of a cat. I tried to scramble around in the yard, hoping to avoid her attack while absorbing her cackle, but she was too quick. She slammed into me with her lowered shoulder and sent me flying. The ground, in collusion with my elbow, knocked the wind out of me, and I rolled over in pain, gasping for air. The otalith was already crouched over me with a raised, open palm. I threw up my arm in time to slow the slap down a bit before it struck the side of my head. Still, it rocked me. As she reared back to slap me again, Lou got behind her and put her in a full nelson hold. She roared, stood up, and spun, flailing Lou's legs out like stretched fresh mozzarella. After several spins, the otalith stopped, rested her hands on her knees, sweating and breathing heavily, Lou still on her back.

Afraid she'd calm down before Lou and I absorbed enough of her cackle, I goaded her again: "Accept Jehovah into your heart and you will be forgiven this transgression. Say it now. Say, 'I accept Jehovah into my heart.'"

The otalith growled and bucked back, then forward. Lou lost his grip and was flipped over her head onto the ground. I found the Bible in the grass and winged it at the woman, hitting her in the head. "Fun fact: The Greek titan Cyclops was a cheese maker." She growled again and turned from Lou to come after me. This time she was tired, and I was faster. I managed to stay out of her reach long enough for Lou to get up and grab her shirt.

"Run," Lou said as I heard the shirt tear. "We've got enough. Run."

I bolted down the street as fast as I could, my mind now completely clear of Naomi's metaphors. When I looked over my shoulder a half-block later, Lou was right behind me, and I was relieved to see the otalith ten paces back from him, already slowing. At the end of the block, she stopped and yelled, "If you ever come back I'll kill you!"

We kept running and didn't slow down until we turned the second corner and the truck was in sight. Lou had grass stains on his pants and shirt, and his lip was bleeding. We were both breathing heavily. I vibrated with adrenaline.

"What the hell was that?" Lou said. "It's going to be ten times harder to harvest from her now. I'm going to have to use a disguise."

"I'll do it," I said.

"Oh yeah?" He nodded with a patronizing expression on his face.

"Whatever it takes."

When we got back to the truck, Lou grabbed four lice cages from a box in the bed and attached them to his arms and legs. I asked where my cages were, and he said I didn't get any this time. I needed all the otalith cackle that was inside me to combat the wanda poison. He promised the cages on him would produce enough to keep Em's nightmares away for at least six months.

CHAPTER 2

LOU WAS UPSET AFTER our fight with the otalith. As he drove, his curses and complaints about my lack of respect and professionalism mingled alternately with the clicking turn signal, roaring gas pedal, and screeching brakes.

I had never met my father, and never had a father figure in my life—the closest thing had been May's high school sweetheart, who liked to get me in headlocks and let me punch his palms. I had been yelled at and even beaten by my mom's boyfriends, and by my two foster-dads, but I'd never experienced anything like this. There was genuine concern in Lou's voice and even fear for me and my family. He was scolding me. I'd never been scolded by an older man. Truthfully, it warmed my heart.

Then he gave me an ultimatum, which wasn't so heartwarming, but I understood it all the same: If I didn't agree to be his pupil and obey his orders, within reason, from here on out, he didn't care what agreement he'd made with Kaliah, he would drop me off on the side of the road right now and wish me good luck.

I wasn't stupid. I knew he was my lifeline. I accepted his conditions, and right away he began giving his orders. He insisted I move in with him so that my training could start immediately after breakfast each day. He told me that no one—not me, not him, not my sister—under any circumstances, could ever go back to my apartment to collect my things. And I especially couldn't go back to Naomi's. Even with otalith cackle as a defense, she was too dangerous. If I saw her on the street, I was to run the other way.

"I have to go back," I said. "My family's sourdough starter is there."

"What?" Lou squawked. "You're kiddin' me right?"

"One of the prisoners that were with your son told me it was important. They said, 'The secret to defeating the Memoirist lies beyond the cheese danish in the whorl of the sourdough starter.'"

"You can't trust that. Are you crazy? Even if that's true, it's too dangerous. You're lucky your wanda didn't poison you with Shakespeare metaphors. You get the Death-is-an-undiscovered-country routine and before you know what hit you, you're slicing your wrists up like they're onions. It's too dangerous, Doughboy."

Despite the risks, going back to Naomi's was one order I had to disobey. What the prisoner had told me was true. I knew it. But I didn't try to explain that to Lou. He wouldn't understand. The sourdough starter had been in my family for over two hundred years. The bread made from it was unique.

Generation after generation had kept it alive, replenishing it, feeding it flour and water after each use. In the 1800s, when it was taken in a stagecoach robbery, my great-great-grandfather formed a posse of his cousins to retrieve it. He killed a man for it. Or so I was told. I always thought it was strange how much importance my mom put on the starter, but now it made sense—kind of.

In hindsight, I wished I had done more to convince my sister to keep her portion of the starter alive. She and I had been a little complacent with the family heirloom for years. It had almost died once.

I wondered how long she would keep her bakery shuttered and Em out of school. I worried she'd get antsy after a while, refuse to stay at Lou's, and go back to her life despite the danger to her and her daughter.

She'd overcome a lot of things in her life by facing them head-on: our mother's addiction, her own addiction, the absence of her father, the death of our sister, having a batterer for a husband. She fought. That was what she knew. And now I was asking her to hide.

Lou lived in the hills above McKinleyville, down a secluded gravel road, behind an iron gate, surrounded by forest. He had a huge, box-shaped house, two stories tall and eight windows wide, with a wraparound porch. The front lawn was the size of a soccer field, and it was green, weed-free, and encircled by the driveway.

"You're rich," I said.

"Ha," Lou said. "You should have seen me before my second divorce."

As I walked through the front door, a stench like ripe roadkill assaulted my nostrils. "Do you have a dead body in here or something?" I said.

"Sorry about that," he said. "May and Em went out to dinner and a movie so I had the house to myself. I'll get rid of it."

"Get rid of what?"

"Durian. It's an exotic fruit. Puts off a smell like rotten meat. All halamites love it. Strong smells are intoxicating to us. We're like dogs that way. That's one of the reasons I like your sister so much."

"Did you just say my sister stinks?"

"Parts of her stinks. " He had an innocent look on his face. "To me anyway. But in a good way."

My mouth dropped open as I considered his statement, and a moment passed before I was able to form words again: "You don't have a thing for my sister, do you?"

"What if I did? You don't think I'm good enough for her?"

"I think you've been divorced three times."

"Yeah, but guys like me settle down at this age." He waved at the air as if he could physically wave away my concerns. "My next wife's gonna last me till I die. Trust me." Then he turned his back on me and walked away through the living room.

I called after him: "You should use those exact words when you propose to my sister. She'll love it. Trust me."

After Lou discarded the durian outside and opened a few windows, he gave me a quick tour of the house. He was one of those clean and tidy bachelors. The floors and surfaces were clean. The furniture was sparse and utilitarian. And there was no clutter that I could see. He had a home gym, a library, and a room dedicated to his collection of guitars and concert posters. Hanging in the hallways, stairwell, and other shared spaces were large photographs of Manhattan landmarks and framed eight by ten glossies of Liza Minnelli, Billy Joel, Frank Sinatra, and other celebrities I assumed were also from the east coast. All of the glossies were signed. Lou boasted that he'd rescued Frank Sinatra's son from his second kidnapping, the one the public didn't know about because it had been masterminded by a powerful wanda.

There was one framed photo of family on the wall, what looked like a senior portrait of Lou's son, Frank DiStefano, named after "Ol' Bue Eyes himself."

After the tour, we went down to the kitchen, where Lou prepared a small antipasto plate of prosciutto, Asiago, French bread, and pepperoncini. Lou was half Italian on his mother's side. I avoided the cheese, afraid it would somehow trigger another metaphor fit.

When we'd finished, I asked Lou if we could start my training tonight, which surprised him. I think he was a little tired from the day's activities, but he agreed to at least get my assessment out of the way.

He took me to the basement—which had not been a part of the tour. He had a training room here. Mirrors were everywhere, hanging and free-standing. Small, clear spray bottles filled with different colors of liquid were arranged on a Lazy Susan on a desk in the corner. A freezer chest, a table, and a utility sink were in the other corner. Between them was an old TV on a stand. In front of that, two chairs were separated by a small table, and to my right was a punching bag. To my left was a shelf full of Kaliah's totems from the case we'd gotten from Kmart: shoehorn, oil can, pocket purse, toy boat, candy dish, antique spectacles, small stuffed fox, and short samurai sword.

I spotted the shower curtain, neatly folded, on the bottom shelf. Its patterns were unmistakable. I walked over and grabbed it. "Do you have any bloom?"

"You're not ready for that," Lou said as he came over. He took the curtain from me and placed it back on the shelf.

"I've been in its whorls before."

"Kaliah told me. And I bet you left plenty of corruptions behind. You're not ready. One step at a time. Here." He pulled out one of the chairs. "Take a seat."

I sat down and looked over the shelves of totems for the shampoo, but I didn't see it. Lou went to the freezer, cracked a tray of ice, dumped the cubes into a pink tub, filled the tub with water, then brought it over and set it on the table next to me. The cubes clinked against each other and crackled as he said, "The mind distorts reality to avoid pain. It can be insidious, even genius with how it does it. When a shaka discovers a totem, their cackle goes crazy. It should be very painful, but the mind somehow avoids some of that pain by making you feel disgust for the source of it. Sometimes, rarely, a shaka will find a totem that gives them a mystical experience as a distortion. This is called gleaning the ghost, and the totems found while doing that are called Omen Totems. It's when your shanika's ancestors are trying to tell you something. That's why you're not ready for that shower curtain. You don't want to get in that whorl with your rekulak and start corrupting things any more than you already have before you get a chance to learn all you can."

Lou went to the TV stand, took a VHS tape from a drawer, shoved it into the VCR, and turned on the TV. "Put your hand in the bucket," he said.

"Why?" I said.

"You wanted to start training. This is training. It's called the trout test."

I submerged my hand into the cold water. The ice cubes bobbed around and bumped into my wrist. A close-up of a clear creek appeared on the screen, running over rocks carpeted with algae. Judging by the quality of the video, this had been shot sometime during the 1980s. Lou hit pause, and said, "Soon the cold water is going to start hurting, but don't take your hand out. Just wait till the video's done. I want you to count how many cutthroat and rainbow trouts are in the video. Can you handle that?"

I nodded, and he pressed play. Soon, the first trout jumped over the rocks, struggling to swim upstream. I couldn't tell what kind it was, but I counted it. The next one passed, and I tried to study it for differences, but there were none that I noticed, except for maybe the size. As the cold became painful, it excited the cackle inside me, and the voices started, all muttering at once, broken up by the occasional shout. But I continued to count. The pain got worse. The voices grew louder. I counted. Finally, the video ended.

I took out my hand, shoved it into my armpit, and rocked back and forth, hissing a little because that seemed to help.

"How many rainbow trout did you see?" Lou said.

I had counted seventeen fish total, but I hadn't been able to tell which were rainbow trout and which were cutthroat. "Three cutthroat," I said, guessing. "And fourteen rainbow."

"Nope."

"How am I supposed to tell them apart?"

"That's for you to figure out."

"It's impossible."

"Do you see why you're not ready now?"

I demanded that he let me try again, and he acquiesced. I put my other hand in the bucket. He pressed play. This time I tried to focus on the fins because I knew some fish could be identified that way. The pain and voices came back, and I tried to study the fins, but the trout moved so fast, and when Lou stopped the tape again, I still had no confidence in my count.

"Eleven cutthroat," I said. "Six rainbow."

Lou shook his head. "Not very good, Doughboy. We're calling it a day. You're tired."

You're tired, I thought as Lou turned off the TV and emptied the bucket into the sink. I wasn't ready to call it a day yet.

He went to the desk and pulled out a small bag of dried peppers, a VHS tape entitled "Kung Fu for Beginners," and what looked like a homemade coffee table book, then set them on the table. "These are for you," he said. The coffee table book was grey and unmarked. I picked it up and flipped through it. Titles like "Affectation Potpourri" and "Conflation Coping" caught my eye.

"That book will tell you everything you need to know about cackle poisons," he said. "Read it. Memorize it. I'm telling you, with the right spray bottles, you can conquer the world. And that tape, I want you to watch it every morning. And after that, exercise—run, stretch, and do push-ups, and run some more. And follow along with the Kung Fu tape. Don't cut corners, because if you do, and you end up riding the ghost of some expert martial artist in Kaliah's line, you'll either die trying to do the moves, or you'll be so sore you won't be able to get out of bed the next morning."

"What about these?" I said, holding up the peppers.

"Eat two before every meal," he said. "We need to build up your pain tolerance. When the bag is gone, we move you onto serranos, then cayenne, and so on."

CHAPTER 3

L OU GAVE ME SOME clean clothes and a toothbrush, pointed out the spare bathroom and where the clean towels were, then showed me my room and how to use the TV mounted to the wall at the foot of the bed. Taking a shower felt amazing, but it had no right to. Kaliah was a prisoner, at the mercy of her abusive ex-boyfriend, Kayak Brad, and the lives of my sister and niece had been completely upended. Em couldn't go to school, see her friends, and May couldn't run her business until I could make things safe, until I could make sure Blanche Duluth and her followers wouldn't hurt them again.

Lou seemed like a good guy, seemed like he knew his mobiak magic, but he didn't have enough urgency. I needed to stop the Blanche now, before my sister lost her business, before Kaliah lost her mind. I didn't have the luxury to train for years, to master my magic. I needed to make leaps in my training, take risks, do what I could as soon as I could

When I got out of the shower, a Bruce Springsteen song was blaring from down the hall, a little muffled by the closed door of Lou's music room, but not much. Inside, Lou played along with an electric guitar, inserting blues licks here and there in odd places.

I dressed quickly, skulked down the hall past the music room, and tiptoed down the stairs to the basement.

The last time I ate peppers before grafting had been a disaster. I'd been stuck in the whorl for far too long. But I knew what a drop of bloom did so I looked around for some. None of the spray bottles on the Lazy Susan were labeled. One was blackish-brown, like bloom, but I didn't want to risk testing it. Most likely each bottle contained something that would drive me temporarily insane in a unique and potentially useful way.

I started opening drawers. At the bottom of the third one, I found a pencil box labeled "Training Bloom." Inside were several small bottles with squishy, eye-dropper lids.

I opened one and squeezed a drop on my finger. As the pain-voices spread, I softly stepped across the room, plucked the shower curtain from the shelf, unfolded it, draped it over the table, and with my Pictionary poems, grafted to the pattern that held the meeting with Sheryl Glanton's: "Elderberry Shimmer Stone. Tank Top Summer Bridge, Hamster Sawdust."

And I was back in Sheryl Glanton's living room, sitting between Kaliah's murdered bond, Diane, and Sheryl's intact totem library of award-winning quilts. Sheryl was in her chair. Nothing had changed about her. She still had the quilt in her lap. Price is Right still played on the TV. But now a man crouched by Sheryl, partially hidden by her lazy boy. He stood, and I saw his face.

It was my face.

He moseyed across the living room and into the kitchen, casually, like he was going for a snack. It was the corruption I'd left behind from the first time I'd entered this whorl. It disturbed me to see him here. All sorts of thoughts crossed my mind. How much of me was in him? Was he happy? Did he resent me for leaving him behind?

But I didn't have time to worry about him. I could already feel myself corrupting this whorl again. I hurried and made the foundation gesture for Skepticism, which I'd discovered the last time I was in her, and I followed the pain from there, listening to Sheryl's set up Diane's murder with her fake concerns over what was happening at the Humboldt Historical Society.

Then we got to the part I came for: the ledger.

Sheryl handed it over, and this time I looked past the post-it note that read, "For the Memoirist," and I studied the names. The action derailed me from the pain of the whorl, so I only had so much time before I was kicked out. I read the names one by one, repeating them back to myself. Then I came across one I recognized: Frank DiStefano, Lou's son, the one I'd saved from the Zaditorian bite.

A cow mooed from the kitchen, and I knew what came next. A pool of scrill spread across the floor and up the walls, glowing blue. The rekulak shot out of it, crashing its massive head into the ceiling. Debris rained down. The Rekulak opened its jaws and doused me once again with its blue, foamy poison, the graft failed, and the whorl faded into the background of Lou's basement.

My skin was covered in scrill. It was under my clothes as it had been the first time I'd been drenched with it. Some of it was falling off onto the floor. While I looked around for something to clean it up with, footsteps sounded on the stairs, and Lou called out before I could even see him, "I can smell what you did Doughboy."

He opened the door and shook his head, then turned around and went back upstairs.

I followed. "Hey, I saw your son's name on a ledger."

"A ledger? *No way, dude.*" The guy was mocking me with a horrible California accent. "I'll have to talk with him about that."

"I'm serious. Why was his name on there?"

He stopped at the top of the stairs and loomed over me. "I don't know what you think you saw in that whorl, but you can't rely on it because, I don't know, maybe you don't know what you're doing. You can't just go in a whorl, corrupt it, and think you got the truth. Didn't we agree on something? I could've sworn we did. Oh yeah, you said you'd do what I say, and in exchange, I'd help you."

"That was before I knew you'd send me to bed before eight o'clock. You want me to train more? Then *train* me. Don't send me to bed to watch TV."

"I'm done with you." He strode across the room. "You somehow screwed this thing up before we even got started." He went out the backdoor and slammed it behind him.

A minute later, while I was washing my face in the kitchen sink, I heard him come back in. I dried my face with a towel and hurried to the living room as he opened the front door. A sheet of blue, almost-dry scrill slid off my arm and landed with a wet thump on the white carpet. I stepped in front of it, hoping he wouldn't notice. A briefcase was at his feet. Bruce and Pam, the mummers from Naomi's harem, stood beside him. He was putting a coat on Bruce like a mother preparing her child for the first day of school. From the vacant eyes, serene smiles, and silence of the two mummers, I gathered they were still under the influence of Lou's potion he called Affectation Potpourri.

"Where did they come from?" I said.

"The mother-in-law out back," Lou said. "What? Did you think I would let them go free?"

"Are you taking them somewhere?"

Lou sneered at Bruce and Pam and pointed a thumb at me. "A regular Einstein, this one." The Mummers just continued smiling, and Lou turned back to me. "I'm done with you, Doughboy. First, you mess with my otalith? Then you screw up the only clue you have that can get you out of this mess? You don't listen. I'm can't help you. I'm going to break Kaliah out of jail. Then my debt is paid, and you're her problem again. In the meantime, you and your family can stay here. That's what kind of guy I am."

"I'm going with you."

Lou rolled his eyes. "Nope. Someones gotta stay here and make sure Em gets her medicine. You can't trust your sister to do it yet. The otalith tincture's in the cupboard above the freezer in the garage."

"How are you going to rescue Kaliah by yourself? You needed help just to get your son out of Arampom before, and now the whole lodge is there. There's got to be way more security now."

"I didn't have two mummers full of wanda poison before.

Now I do. Simple as that. I'll be back with Kaliah by tomorrow morning. Then you guys are on your own." He leaned close, grabbed a hunk of scrill from my arm, and smeared it on his face and hands.

"What the hell?"

"I smelled nemaloki cackle the last time I was in Arampom. Every mobiak who's heard a nursery rhyme knows scrill is the cure for that. Save the rest in a jar. If you need the gate code, it's on the fridge."

Lou herded Bruce and Pam outside like they were lobotomy patients, then he slammed the door shut.

After finding a jar and scraping the scrill into it with a rubber spatula, I started training. I burned my mouth on a few peppers. I took the trout test a handful of times without success. And I spent some time practicing foundation gestures and expressions in a mirror. Then I did my best to follow the workout tape Lou had given me. I ran. I did pushups, sit-ups, and yoga—a lot of yoga. I was attempting to maintain a pose that had me balancing sideways on one foot and one hand when my phone rang. The number belonged to my sister, but she wasn't the one on the other end of the line: "Well hello to you too, Charlie," a man said. "Do you recognize my voice? I'm the one who gave your niece the candy."

I stopped breathing.

"Hello?" Warren said.

"Where's my sister?"

"She's here. And so is little Emily. We're waiting for you." Then I heard my sister's voice: "Charlie?"

"May? Are you guys okay?"

"Yes."

"I'm on my way."

"Okay," she said. Her tone was calm and defiant, as expected from her, but I could tell by her one-word responses that she was barely holding herself together. Hearing her vulnerable like that was an assault on the most tender region of my mind. She had always protected me, always been like a mother. Now she needed my help.

Warren came back on the line: "Remember to come alone, will you? Because if you don't, I'm going to cut Emily's little toes off, and then I'm going to feed her soul to a mummer I know."

CHAPTER 4

TRIED TO TELL him not to hurt her, that I would be there soon, but he had already hung up.

I yelled, crouched down, and squeezed my head, breathing fast and heavy. Had Warren hurt May or Em? Was he alone? Or were the other Friends with him? If I did exactly as he asked, would he hurt them anyway? If I didn't do what he said, what would I do? What if I paid someone to punch me again so I could reenter Kaliah's fighting whorl and try to ride the ghost again?

I called Lou, but his phone went straight to voicemail. I called again. Voicemail. He was in the mountains already, I assumed, outside of service range. I tried to guess what he would do, what Kaliah would do. Warren had already infected Em with Ghost Heart, a dreadful and incurable disease. He was capable of anything. I couldn't trust him. If I complied, if I followed his instructions, he could still torture Em, and I would be powerless to stop him. I agonized over the decision. Fight or comply. Fight or comply. I felt doomed either way.

Then Lou's words came to me: "With the right spray bottles, I could conquer the world."

I ran to my bed and grabbed the book of cackle poisons he'd given me. I took several deep breaths, calming my body so I could focus on the text. I have time, I kept telling myself, I have time. My adrenaline was flowing, and though I read quickly, I retained a remarkable amount, skimming through page after page, only lingering on poisons that seemed relevant to my current crisis.

After thirty minutes, I'd discovered two poisons I was sure could help me. I ran down to the basement, to the room of mirrors, and identified the poisons I needed by their color. I took the green and orange bottles from the Lazy Susan and ran back up the stairs. I was prepared to hitchhike if I had to but was relieved to find two cars and another truck in the garage, their keys hanging on the wall. I pressed the unlock button on one, and the truck honked.

On the way to town, I worked out a rough plan in my head and ran through it over and over, trying to think of what to do if this happened or that went wrong. The drive took five minutes. I parked behind the grocery store a block from the bakery, hopped out of the truck, and began walking. My plan was simple and straightforward, but I still kept repeating it in my mind, terrified I would forget some crucial aspect.

My fear got so bad that my legs began to periodically convulse. I decided to jog it off.

There were snow clouds, illuminated by the moon, spread

high across the sky like ripples in sand at low tide. The winter air seized and released my lungs, seized and released, as I jogged down the sidewalk with the potions in my back pocket. I passed a Christmas tree lot, where a few families milled about in scarves and puffy jackets. I felt awful for what I was about to do to them.

My sister's Rav4, Warren's BMW, and a red BMW I didn't recognize were the only vehicles parked in front of the bakery. I approached from the back, where there was only one window, small and frosted, that looked out from the bathroom upstairs. The bathroom light was off.

I found the green poison in my pocket and sprayed it into the air three times, careful not to get any of the mist on me. Otherwise, Warren, who was a halamite like Lou, would smell it. He would probably smell it anyway, but at least this way he wouldn't smell it before its target audience. I noted the time on my phone, then leaned against the back wall and listened to my thumping heart for seven minutes before walking around the building and through the front door.

The lights were on inside. May and Em sat at a table with two large men—the soccer dads, the Zaditorians. I'd hoped they wouldn't be here, but there was no turning back now. The book hadn't mentioned anything about the potions working on them. I pictured their hideous body parts sprouting out of those other-worldly bubbles. I remembered their tape-worm arms and how fast they'd moved. If they transformed, they would destroy my sister's bakery. We could run from them. I'd done it before. But we'd have to get lucky.

A woman I'd never seen before, with a He-Man haircut and coat-hanger shoulders, sat at the table beside my family's. She wore a Christmas sweater. Em was playing a game on my sister's phone. Warren Rochester stood on the opposite side of the room on a portable, green putting mat. He held a putter over his shoulder. A cell phone holster was attached to his belt. Several golf balls were arranged around the hole at the end of the mat.

Everyone looked at me when I entered. My sister made a sympathetic face, like my dog had just died. But what did she have to be sorry about? I was the one that was sorry. I made the face back at her.

"I told you he would come," Em announced. "You should have left when you had the chance."

I was charmed and surprised by her bravado and confidence in me. I had to smile, despite the circumstances.

"Good evening," Warren said, smiling from ear to ear. "I'm glad you could make it. My people tell me you're alone, so that's good."

I wondered if he was bluffing, if there really were more of them I hadn't seen who had monitored my approach. Had they seen me spray the poison?

"I'm alone," I said. "I'm here. You can let them go now."

Warren prepared to take another putt. "When the storm comes, the ducks have to share the duck pond with the sea gulls."

"What does that mean?"

"I said I wouldn't torture them if you came. I didn't say anything about letting them go. I apologize if you misunderstood. But hey, at least now they won't be tortured, right?" He pointed to the strange woman, who held a cell phone up to her ear and muttered something. "This is my bond, Caroline Granger. You haven't met yet. She's wonderful. Quiet, though, and wary, kind of like a rescue dog you take home for the first time."

Caroline rolled her eyes and Warren laughed.

"What do you want?" I said.

"Well, let's see," Warren said. "I want to play Augusta before I die. I want to become locally renowned for my mosaic artwork. I want a bigger boat. I want I want I want. But mostly I want to keep wanting what I want. You know what I mean?"

At the back of the kitchen, the door to the upstairs apartment opened, and Sheryl Glanton, the quilt lady, came out. She wore a flour print A-line dress, and her hair was bleach blond now instead of brown. A large beach bag hung from her shoulder. She walked toward me, stepping along an imaginary tightrope, with her chest out and her chin up. She set her bag on the table where everyone was sitting, obstructing my view of Em. Then she looked at me for the first time.

"Look," I said. "I know I forgot to tell you where your quilts are, but you didn't hold your end of the bargain either by telling everyone they could find me at Kmart. So you can't really blame me there. If you hurry, though, you might still be able to get your quilts back. I mean, there's a chance, as long as you let my family go."

"I am not Sheryl," she said. "I'm merely using her body. It's her punishment for not being completely open and honest with me."

"Who are you then?"

"Such an intimate question. Maybe I should let you interview me."

"We don't have time for that," Caroline said, her arms crossed over her chest, not even bothering to look up from the table she was scowling at. "I have a question for Charlie. Your niece isn't showing any symptoms of Ghost Heart. Where are you getting the otalith cackle?"

The person in Sheryl's body said, "Caroline," in a way that was a rebuke. "I think young Charlie Allison will be the one asking the questions for now. He is my official biographer, after all. He needs to start sometime."

Caroline shook her head but said no more. Warren had stopped putting to watch the interaction with a smile on his face. He seemed to live in a state of perpetual amusement.

The person in Sheryl's body placed a hand on her chest and said, "I present to you my name, Blanche Duluth, knowing that faces are nothing more than tools."

CHAPTER 5

LOOKED AT MY sister and said, "It's going to be okay."

She looked aggressively confused but acknowledged my reassurance with a nod.

To Blanche/Sheryl, I said, "I don't understand. You want me to be your official biographer? Is that what all this is about? Is that why you've been doing all of this?"

"I want many things from you, Charlie?" Blanche/Sheryl said in a way that made me shiver inside. She pointed a palm at a table by a window. "Sit."

I sat at the table, and Blanche/Sheryl sat across from me. She lazily batted at the air by her ear as if there was a fly, and the two Zaditorians came over and stood a few feet away like our own personal waiters.

"What have you done with Sheryl?" I said.

"She's here with me. She's fine."

"How are you doing this?"

"Let's start with something interesting. I discovered a long time ago that humans have cackle too. They just don't have that much. Their cackle is how I survived all these years, hopping from one human to another. If I'm careful, I can . . . occupy them for a great deal longer than I can a mobiak, and be relatively safe from Arawok's vomit reflex while doing it. You know, humans can even travel to whorls, as long as they have a connection to the infinite. Mobiaks were like them once. There was no such thing as whorls for our kind until the First Sojourner. She made our link to the infinite, and now her blood flows through every mobiak, although in tiny amounts. But you, you have so much of it. You can do for humans what the First Sojourner did for us mobiaks."

"Are you talking about the rekulak?" I said. "You can have it. Just let my family go."

"I'm sorry but it's not that simple." She looked up at the bearded Zaditorian, "I think Number Three will do for the young Charlie."

He pulled an envelope out of his inside jacket pocket, handed it to me, then took out a phone and pointed it at Blanche/Sheryl. He was the one who'd produced the milk that had saved my life. I couldn't look at him without picturing the disgusting spider-like nipples I knew he had under there somewhere.

The other Zaditorian, the bald one, took out two phones, held one out in front of him, pointing at me, and held the second up and back as if to capture both Blanche/Sheryl and me in a shot.

"Are you filming this?" I asked.

"Of course," Blanche/Sheryl said. "These men are from

Zaditor, where there's no need for cell phones, but they're learning. Aren't you boys?" They said nothing. "Not everyone can capture memories with whorls. It would be elitist of me not to document this with video for the less endowed." She brushed the air with her fingers in my direction. "Please read the script."

Over the last half week, I'd built up a tolerance to the absurd, but this was too much to take in stride. "What the hell is going on?" I said. "Is this really what you people want from me?"

Blanche/Sheryl slapped the table and spoke through her teeth: "I have granted you a privilege. Your niece and sister are watching. Don't disappoint them."

Interpreting that as a threat, I opened the envelope and pulled out the pages inside. Lou's potion needed a little more time to set in anyway. I began to read. My mouth was dry from fear, my speech was stilted and monotone, and I swallowed a little too often. The room was quiet otherwise. "'My guest for this evening,'" I read, "'is a world-renowned and award-winning author, most famous for her memoirs, *The Groundskeeper's Daughter* and *Pancake Whore*. Blanche Duluth, welcome.'"

I looked up from the pages to see Blanche/Sheryl nodding at me with a satisfied smile. "Thank you for having me."

"'It's an honor,'" I read. "'First, I want to get this out of the way, because I'm dying to know: Are you writing again?'"

Blanche/Sheryl let out a short puff of laughter and said, "You might as well ask me if I'm *me* again, writing is so integral to my identity. But the answer is yes, oh thank God, a thousand times, yes, I am *me* again. I am writing, and in such a joyful way now. I'm in such a good place. I feel so blessed. The words are just pouring out of me."

"'I am so happy to hear that. That's so exciting. What are you writing about, if you can even tell me?'"

Blanche/Sheryl wiggled a little in her chair. "Well, I don't want to spoil the surprise, Charlie, but I can tell you my next memoir will touch on my travels through the so-called 'magical' stomachs of Arawok. And they really are so magical. I don't think the people in this stomach realize just how magical they are. And of course, it will touch on my encounters with my less digested selves, who are just delights, each and every one of them. I also talk about the dark periods, of course, trying to reestablish myself in my native stomach. I inhabit mostly barrens. Arawok doesn't seem to notice them as much. But I'm in constant fear of regurgitation. It is no way to live."

I scanned ahead. There were three more pages of script for me, and Lou's potion would be taking effect by now. If I wanted some questions answered, now was the time. "This is ridiculous," I said. "Where's my mom? You're her bond, right? What did you do with her?"

Blanche/Sheryl frowned. "Your mom is on her own path. And I've given her her space because that's important to her, important for her growth as an individual."

"The lymphid with the golf course said you took her."

"Took her? No. I did check in with her, though. I was curious about her journey. That was it. Then we went our separate ways. I care about your mom. She's very special to me."

"As is my whole family, I'm guessing. I see how you treat people who are special to you." I caught movement in the corner of my eye and looked out the window. Three people, featureless in the low light, walked around the back of the building. A moment later, from either side of the street, two fast-moving crowds spilled into the parking lot, merging into one.

Caroline sprang to her feet, shouted, and pointed at the door, but Warren was already on his way. In two more strides, he reached it and flipped the lock.

The crowd was eerily silent as it pooled around the building. I heard only their footsteps, no conversation. The individual faces looked confused, and their eyes darted around as if they were looking for something they'd lost. They appeared to have no interest in the locked door.

The green potion I'd sprayed outside before coming in was called Bitch in Heat. The book hadn't indicated if that was the common name or the one Lou had given it. When exposed to air, it attracted every barren human within half a mile. Side-effects included disorientation, inability to focus, and sexual arousal. According to the book, barrens were drawn to the scent of the potion, even though they were unconscious of that scent. The people outside would look back on this episode as a waking nightmare. They wouldn't understand why it had happened and would be afraid of it happening again. Many would seek psychiatric treatment.

I looked at their poor, confused faces. They'd just been shopping for groceries, Christmas trees, or sitting in their houses, eating dinner, watching TV, and now they were here, and they didn't know why. I felt sorry for them. But I was in dire need. My family was in mortal danger, and this was the only power I had at the moment capable of helping them.

"Did you do this?" Blanche/Sheryl said.

"No," I said, hoping I sounded innocent. "It's pizza night here. People love my sister's pizza."

Warren, still standing by the door, said, "They're not here for the pizza. Someone search him. Now!" For once, he wasn't smiling.

Before anyone could reach me, I drew the orange bottle from my coat pocket, pointed it at Blanche/Sheryl, and pressed the button on the lid. She coughed and covered her mouth as the cloud of poison expanded around her head. The closest Zaditorian lifted Blanche/Sheryl like she was a new bride and carried her toward the kitchen. The other one followed.

"The backdoor!" Warren yelled as he ran across the dining room. Caroline jumped to her feet.

Then the screaming began.

By itself, the orange potion was inert, but when used in tandem with Bitch in Heat, it provided a target for the crowd, a focal point for its simmering energy. It created what the book called a "Worship Mob," something like Beatlemania.

The people outside trembled with excitement. They screamed and pointed at Blanche/Sheryl, and pressed their palms into their cheeks. Some even cried. The front door rattled as they pushed and pulled on it. The back door flew open with a bang before Warren or Caroline could reach it, and the Worship Mob flooded the bakery.

In seconds, they filled every corner, packed together shoulder to shoulder. I was pressed against the front windows. I couldn't find May or Em through the scrum of frantic faces so I climbed onto a table next to me. Warren and Caroline had gotten trapped against the display case on their way to secure the backdoor. Even in these dire circumstances, part of me worried about the cost to my sister's business if that glass broke.

The Zaditorians had been separated from Blanche/Sheryl, pushed to opposite corners of the dining area. Blanche/Sheryl was in the center of the room, alone, trying to fight off the mob of worshippers. They pressed against her, petting her, tugging at her clothes, sobbing in her face. Some of the people closest to her kissed her.

Over the cries of fevered joy, I heard my name and turned. My sister held Em in her arms just a few yards away by the front door. They were being jostled but not trampled.

I expected tape-worm arms to shoot out of the shoulders of the Zaditorians any moment. But they didn't. They were looking at Blanche/Sheryl, who gave them some sort of hand signal.

A sphere of translucent yellow light appeared, reaching from floor to ceiling, cutting me off from my family. The Zaditorians were on opposite ends of it, their arms outstretched like twin Atlases, the front halves of their bodies shining with a blinding light that fed the sphere.

The worshipers inside the sphere became translucent. Little sparkling blue worms swam through their bodies. Now their haranguing attentions passed through Blanche/Sheryl, who was solid. She stood freely, arms crossed and chin raised, staring up at me like a disappointed coach.

Em and May were on the outside the bubble, on the edge. Their bodies were unchanged but their clothes were translucent and full of sparkling worms, the same as the insides of the ghost-like worshipers.

Warren and Caroline, also inside the bubble, also solid, walked toward May and Em, slowly passing through the mob as if it were made of honey.

I dove off the table into the bubble and on top of the mob. I sunk slowly through it to the floor, then plowed ahead toward May and Em, hoping to reach them before Warren and Caroline. As I pushed through the ghost-like people, my calves and thighs burning with the exertion, I felt a tingling warmth inside me.

Then the yellow light quavered, and the glowing Zaditorian on my left flickered as the mob jostled him. A few threw their whole weight onto his outstretched arms, which fell to his sides. He lost his shine. And the bubble disappeared while part of me was passing through a rapidly materializing man. I was propelled forward, as if by magnetic force, and landed at May's feet. Over the shrieking worshipers, she said, "Charlie! Come on!"

Em had opened the front door and was hopping up and down, waving us on. May helped me up, and we surged through the crowd. Outside, the mob was sparse. Most had gone around to the back. The yellow bubble reappeared inside the bakery, and I heard Blanche/Sheryl call out to me: "If you want to know where your mom is, go ask that wanda girlfriend of yours." Her voice was not so composed now.

Caroline and Warren were almost to the door now, trudging through the translucent mob.

Stopping at her car, May said, "My keys are inside!"

"This way," I shouted.

And we ran out of the parking lot, down the street. Em kicked her legs high, fast for her age, but not fast enough for my comfort. I hefted her up into my arms and sprinted. A long line of cars was parked in the street, still running, abandoned by the poor people I'd drugged. When we piled into the truck, Caroline and Warren were a block away, running under a streetlight.

The tires peeled out in the mud as I drove us around the parked cars, almost tipping us over into a drainage ditch. "Are you guys okay?" I said, my eyes darting back and forth from the road to their hands, necks, and faces. "Did they bite you? Did the tape worms come out of their arms?"

"We didn't see any tape worms," May said. "No one bit us or anything. But they put these little black bubbles on our feet that kept us from running. But those disappeared when they made that big yellow bubble."

"I think we just got extremely lucky. But we'll have to ask Lou about those black bubbles, if there are any side effects. Don't forget. How did they find you, anyway?"

"They just showed up at the bakery."

"You went back to the bakery!?"

"I needed to check on a few things."

"You promised to wait. Oh my God. Don't go back there again? Please."

"For how long?"

"I don't know. This lady Blanche is insane. She wants to infect the whole world with her cackle—basically turn everyone into her. And for some reason, she needs my rekulak to do it."

Em chimed in, "Is that the giant centipede thing that was in my dream?"

"Yes."

"There's a fox in my dreams now. She talks to me."

In the past, I might have responded with something patronizing like, "That's really cool," or, "Is it a nice fox?" But now I knew better. Em's dreams weren't dreams at all, but whorls. She'd seen the rekulak in them before I'd even been infected by it. Now she was seeing a talking fox. So with all sincerity, I asked, "Is it a nice fox?"

CHAPTER 6

SHERYL IN HER FLEECE robe and cushioned chair, the quilt with the same pattern as the shower curtain, "The Price is Right" playing on the TV, and my towering rekulak all faded away, and I was back in the room of mirrors, sitting across from Em, with the shower-curtain Omen Totem draped over the table between us. Em held a pencil and notepad.

"Nathan George," I said, and she wrote it down.

Lou would not have approved of what I was doing, but he wasn't here. Morning had come and gone. He hadn't called, and he wasn't answering his phone. If he didn't come back—if Kaliah didn't come back—my family and I would be on our own. I needed to prepare for that.

I'd researched the Friends of Blanche Duluth on the internet but had found nothing, no record of the cult, no record of the memoirs Blanche had mentioned, and no record of the death of Blanche and her followers during the 1964 Christmas Flood that Hugo had told me about.

Before all this, I'd done a lot of research on the flood for my tour. In my introductory speech, I would quote an article from the *Times-Standard*, a local newspaper: "The '64 flood was caused by a deadly combination of weather events that dumped massive amounts of snow in the mountains, followed by warm rains that melted the snow and inundated local watersheds in a matter of hours. [. . .] The flood cut a huge swath of destruction across the North Coast, killing 29, causing millions in damage and cutting off entire communities from the outside world for months."

Accompanying the article were black and white photographs of the destruction and aftermath: washed-away houses, trees, and bridges, families on boats motoring through flooded streets. I'd included them in my pamphlet.

But what did all of it have to do with my family—now—forty-nine years later?

I needed to know more about this cult. That was why I kept going back into the shower curtain whorl. Even if I corrupted it, some information was better than none.

I'd entered it three times since lunch, and each time I'd withstood the pain a little longer, seen a little more. With Em taking notes, I'd retrieved three more names from the Humboldt Historical Society's donation ledger, along with two phone numbers and one address. I'd left four corruptions behind that should have been wreaking havoc on the accuracy of the memories, but they just sat on the floor or wandered down the hall and kept to themselves. I never noticed any changes in the loop.

"I'm bored," Em said in an accusatory tone, and glared at me.

"You are?" I couldn't remember her ever saying that to me before. "I was beginning to think you never got bored and were unique among children."

"I *am* unique among children," she said, defensive. "When can I go back to school?"

"Soon, I hope. I'm working on it."

She twirled the pencil with her fingers, then rubbed the eraser on the back of her hand, where I noticed for the first time an ugly red burn. I reached over the table and grabbed her wrist. "Stop that," I said, horrified. "What are you doing?"

"Nothing," she said.

"Look at your hand. Why did you do that?"

She looked down and pouted. "I don't know. For fun."

"For fun?"

I let go of her wrist and mentally took a step back. She had been traumatized by the recent events and changes in her life. She had a disease of nightmares. She had been held captive. And she had been taken from her school, her home. She didn't need my anger and disappointment.

I stepped around the table, kneeled, and asked her for a hug. She looked confused, and I doubted my instincts, but she consented, and I held her and told her I was sorry. "It's okay Uncle Charlie," she said.

I leaned back and desperately searched my mind for something comforting to say until I came out with this: "When I was your age, I broke my arm riding my bike. I told your mom I was never going to ride a bike again. But she wasn't having it. She made me ride my bike to school the next morning with a cast on. She told me, *Pain can be a good teacher, and it can be a bad teacher.*"

Em crinkled her brow.

"Do you understand?" I said.

She nodded, but I could tell she didn't. I tried another approach: "Sometimes when we try to avoid pain, we do something that causes us more pain."

Her brow was still crinkled, and I was about to elaborate more when the door at the top of the stairs opened and my sister called down, "Charlie, come up here. I need your help. Hurry."

Not knowing if she needed help taking out the garbage or if there was a Zaditorian on the front lawn, I told Em to stay put, and I ran up the stairs. The front door was open. I went through it and found May in the driveway helping Lou out of his truck. He was alone. He moved slowly and winced when he stepped down. A crescent moon of dried blood ran from a gash above his left eye down to his chin. He had another gash on the arm he held over his ribs. I rushed to his side, got my shoulders under his good arm, and supported his weight as he limped into the house. Slowly, May and I lowered him onto the couch. As he put his foot up, his pant leg peeled back, revealing a purple, swollen ankle.

May fetched some gauze and alcohol from the bathroom and began cleaning his wounds.

I asked him what had happened, but he just shook his head.

"Is Kaliah still in prison?" I said.

He nodded.

"Can't you talk?"

He shook his head. With his hand, he made the letters, L-

I-C-E, then pointed to his mouth and looked at me with eyebrows raised expectantly.

He had been poisoned as well as beaten.

I went to the garage, retrieved a bottle of otalith tincture, and brought it to Lou. He took a swig of the medicine, then leaned back and closed his eyes. May put a pack of frozen peas on his ankle, but he didn't flinch. He was already asleep.

CHAPTER 7

WITH THE BAKERY UNSAFE to return to, my sister—never one to sit around—manufactured chores for herself. She randomly cleaned Lou's already spotless house, and she'd even taken the liberty of rearranging furniture. She'd been here only two days and already had several ongoing culinary projects in various stages of completion: fermenting and pickling green tomatoes, infusing olive oil with garlic, growing alfalfa sprouts on the windowsill, baking pumpernickel bagels, making apple butter and apple pie filling from the apples going to waste on Lou's apple trees, in addition to preparing all the meals.

Lou woke up in the morning in a good mood, despite his injuries. He limped around the house, groaning and complimenting my sister on the new furniture layout and the smells coming from the kitchen. After listening to my account of the harrowing escape from the bakery, he gave me a "Not bad, Doughboy" and told me the Zaditorians were infamous for having aided the Nemaloki in the Zaditorian Wars twenty-four thousand years ago, which inspired a set of questions from me he waved away with his hand, saying he was too tired to answer them. He also dismissed my questions about Kaliah and how he'd gotten hurt with, "Kaliah's alive. We'll talk later." Then he took my sister up on her invitation to help boil pumpernickel bagels.

I was glad Kaliah was alive, but I'd expected her to be. As long as Kayak Brad had her, he'd keep her alive to keep on abusing her, stuffing his corruptions into all of her whorls until she didn't know who she was anymore.

I missed Kaliah. I'd only known her a few days, but I missed her. Traveling through her whorls gave me an unnatural sense of her heart, her character. I missed just being around her. When I remembered what Lou had said about her being in love with me, I felt something flutter in my stomach.

As I watched TV with Em in the living room, taking a short break from training, I couldn't help but hear all the flirting and giggling going on in the kitchen. To hear my sister so carefree, so ready to laugh, made me happy, but I doubted if Lou was worthy of her. Three ex-wives!

I sat on the couch, stewing in these conflicting emotions and enduring the giggling for most of my break until I couldn't wait for breakfast any longer. Today I was going to rescue my family's most precious heirloom, our sourdough starter. I couldn't put it off any longer. According to the prisoner I'd helped in Arampom, it was a totem that held the key to defeating Blanche and her Friends. I only hoped

Naomi hadn't thrown it away already.

I didn't want to tell May or Lou about my plans because they would only try to stop me. So I lied to them both. I told them I was going out to pick up some groceries. May gave me a list of things she needed, and Lou made me promise to be careful and avoid stores I usually frequented. After sneaking a bottle of otalith tincture into my pocket in case of an emergency metaphor infection, I borrowed the can of pepper spray May kept in her purse, hopped in Lou's truck, and drove thirty minutes south to Eureka, where there was an army surplus store that sold doomsday supplies.

They were having a Christmas sale, and I was able to get the biohazard suit I wanted at ten percent off. Still, the purchase took a big chunk out of my withering bank account. Suits like this one, I'd learned from reading Lou's book, could withstand up to an hour of continued exposure to airborne cackle. With it on, I would be immune, at least temporarily, to Naomi's magical metaphors. I could get in the apartment, grab the starter, and get out. No problem.

With the help of the instruction booklet that came in the box, I put on the suit and the breathing apparatus in the parking lot. I ignored the looks of the patrons coming and going, and I politely laughed at the two zombie-apocalypse jokes I heard. When I was confident in the job I'd done, I drove back up north to McKinleyville, to the apartment I'd once practically lived in with Naomi.

When I saw her Prius was in the parking lot, my heart quickened. I could've stayed in the car and waited for her to leave, but I wanted to see her, to meet the person behind the mask. I wanted to know if I'd truly loved her, if I still loved her, or if our entire relationship had been a manipulation.

I checked the suit once more to make sure it was airtight before climbing the outer stairs on the face of the apartment building. The suit was clammy where it touched my skin, and the sound of my breath was augmented by the apparatus.

The nosiest neighbor I'd ever known was in his usual spot by the window. He'd heard me coming and was peeking through the blinds. I had no doubt he knew exactly how long I'd been gone, no doubt he'd gossiped about my absence to the other neighbors and pestered Naomi for an explanation.

"Hi Bill," I said, and waved pleasantly.

He pulled up the blinds to get a better look. Watching confusion, recognition, then fear dance across his face gave me a satisfaction that was cathartic in a small way. Constantly keeping track of my comings and goings finally had a consequence for Bill. Now he could sit there and ponder whether or not his home was ground zero for some new and deadly disease outbreak, or if I'd lost my mind and was about to go on some kind of anthrax rampage. I knew he'd call the police because he called them almost every week for something, and they'd send a car as they always did, but the car would just roll right by because they knew the call had come from him.

So, in a somewhat lighter mood, I knocked on Naomi's door. She opened it and smiled when she saw what I was wearing. "You think you're smart, don't you?"

I showed her my sister's pepper spray. "Don't try anything."

She put up her hands. "I won't. I promise." Then she stepped aside. "Come in. I was hoping I'd get to see you. You haven't returned my calls."

All of the furniture was gone. The walls were bare. Boxes

labeled with black markers were stacked by the door, and cleaning supplies were scattered throughout the living room. A man I didn't recognize made squeegee sounds with a newspaper as he wiped a window and ignored my presence.

As I looked around, I felt loss. This was once a loving home, even if it had all been a sham, even if it had only been for a couple of months. "You messed with my head," I said, the words coming out more forlorn than I'd hoped.

Her face expressed . . . pity? Sorrow? Regret? "Not the whole time," she said. "You would've fallen in love with me eventually. I just didn't want to wait. Is that a crime?"

"It's a crime against me."

She came toward me with outstretched arms, and I hopped backward and held up my pepper spray. Her arms dropped to her sides, and her face contorted as she looked into my eyes and struggled to hold back tears. "I'm sorry," she said, her voice cracking.

I pointed to the man cleaning the windows. "Is he . . . ?"

"A mummer?" she said, regaining some composure. "Yes, but so much more. He's one of my lovers."

I shuddered looking at him. That could've been me, pieced-together scraps of a self inside a mummer's body—an abomination.

"Wandas live a very long time," Naomi said. "We have many lovers. This is a way of preserving them, their memory, of lessening our grief. It's natural."

I snorted and shook my head. "If by natural you mean a praying mantis eating the head of their mate mid-coitus, then yes, this is natural. Don't you see that? I thought we were going to spend the rest of our lives together, and you tried to eat my head."

Naomi's stance widened, and her face became indignant. "I tried to save you. I would have loved nothing more than for you to remain in your body until you were an old man, but you were in danger, and still are. The Friends of Blanche Duluth are after you, and you don't understand how dire that is. We can still do this, Charlie. You can spend many lives with me."

"What does Blanche want from me?"

"I only know that she wants *you*, and that she's a very powerful mobiak who refuses to die. She blackmailed me, but that is over now. I cut off my arm for you, to betray her, and I will live with that. Come with me. You will be safe. I promise."

"How do I know you're not still working for Blanche? How do I know anything?" Without turning my back on her or the abomination cleaning windows, I went to the kitchen and opened the fridge. The shelves were empty and clean. I hung my head.

"Relax, Charlie," Naomi said, leaning against the kitchen threshold. "Your sourdough's alive. I've been feeding it."

"Where is it?"

"I'm not telling, but if you do something for me, I will give it to you."

"What?"

She stacked her hands over her heart. "Bring my Bruce and Pam back to me."

"I can't. They're in Arampom."

"In the mummer prison camps? How did that happen? They were just trying to help you."

"I don't know."

"Well figure it out, sweetheart. Bring me Bruce and Pam

or your precious sourdough dies." She pulled out two vials of clear liquid from her pocket and placed them in my gloved hand. "If they're not themselves, gives them this. It will bring them back. They'll know where to find me."

Her hand lingered in mine. She said nothing, but her eyes, sad and imploring, said she wanted me back. And I wanted her in a way too, even without the influence of her cackle, or at least I wanted a memory of her. But I would be a fool to trust her again.

The man who'd been cleaning windows came into the kitchen and shattered the moment. "Love-Nugget," he said. "Someone's coming." Then he sneered at me, his face painted with jealousy and disgust, and I knew then that everyone in Naomi's harem looked at each other the same way.

The front doorknob jiggled. Then there was a loud knock. Naomi went to the peephole, and I went to the front window.

A scrawny woman with dirty blonde hair and pale blue eyes stood outside the door. She had deep creases in her face and the start of sagging cheeks. A stranger might have thought she was approaching sixty, but I knew she was forty-five. Her clothes were much nicer than the ones she'd worn the last time I'd seen her. Her hair was combed now too, and it had a healthy shine. She was clean—no drugs—and had been for at least a few months.

I stepped toward Naomi and her man, pointed the pepper spray in their direction, and said, "Let my mom in."

CHAPTER 8

MY MOM STEPPED THROUGH the open door, and when I moved to hug her, the confusion on her face turned to fear, and she stepped back and showed me her palms. Thinking she didn't recognize me in my getup, I said, "It's me, Charlie. Your son."

"Collisions are dangerous," she said. "Be courteous and follow the rules of the road."

"What?"

"Traffic fines are doubled in construction zones. The Highway Patrol is monitoring the situation. A slide has taken out a portion of the highway, and the detour is treacherous due to a lack of guard rails and frequent elk crossings."

Horrified, I turned to Naomi. "You trapped her in a metaphor?"

She shook her head. "No. This has nothing to do with me."

"Don't lie to me. It's obvious she thinks Life is a Highway, and we both know that's your favorite song."

"That's not my favorite song."

"You love Tom Cochrane."

"I love him ironically," Naomi said. "And if you followed me on social media you'd know that. Your mother is manipulating you. She's evil. You don't know her."

"I don't know my own mother? Are you kidding me?" I pointed the pepper spray at Naomi again, and she rolled her eyes and put her hands up. "Fix her," I said.

"I can't. Nothing's wrong with her. She's faking."

"She's faking this?"

Naomi put her hands down. "Yes! This isn't how my cackle spells work. Listen to me, Charlie. You need to know this. It could save your life. Say your mom was infected by my cackle and really thought life was a highway, and I'm not saying she does, but if she did, and I set up the spell so you could activate it with your voice, you would be able to manipulate her. To do that, you'd have to establish the spell before each command. For example, you would say, 'Life is a highway, drive with caution.' And that would trigger her to behave in a certain way.

My mom got on her hands and knees and crawled out of the apartment. I shook my head at Naomi, my face pinched with disgust. "She's not faking."

"Yes, she is." Naomi leaned close, and I flinched. She looked down the porch at my mom, then whispered so that I could barely hear. "I put a spell like the one your mom is faking on Warren. He's my sleeper cell, my insurance plan in case I wasn't able to save you. Look to him in a tight spot and it could save your life. When the storm comes, the ducks will have to share the duck pond with the seagulls. That's the metaphor. Remember it."

"That psychopath is your sleeper cell? The guy who forced me to eat a cheese danish at gunpoint?"

"Shhh. I made the spell so you can activate it with your voice. I did that for you. I love you."

Why was she telling me this? Was this part of another manipulation? As I turned and went after my mom, who had almost crawled to the top of the stairs, Naomi called after me, "Remember our picnic in Sequoia Park."

Picnic? I wished I could forget that and every other good memory we shared. She was trying to get in my head even through this suit.

When I reached my mom, she muttered something about pulling over to the side of the road, then sat cross-legged at the top of the stairs.

I needed to get her the otalith tincture I'd brought along in case of an emergency, but that was in the truck, and I didn't want to leave her here alone so close to Naomi. I thought back on when I'd been under Naomi's spell, and how I'd responded to different stimuli. I'd seen reality in terms of the metaphors she'd burned inside my head. Her mummers, Bruce and Pam, had been able to steer me in different directions with those metaphors.

I gave it a try.

If life was a highway, then were people cars or drivers? Or were cars the bodies and drivers the brains? I was pretty sure Naomi was the landslide my mom had mentioned earlier, but who or what were the guard rails and the elk?

"Life is a highway," I said to my mother. "I'm a tow truck. You're broke down, and I'm taking you to the shop."

My mom looked at me for the first time and stood up. I grabbed her hand. This time she didn't pull away or say anything. "I'm a tow truck," I said. "Life is a highway. I'm towing you to the yard. You're in disrepair. I'll have you fixed up in no time. Life is a highway." I led her past my peeping neighbor, down the stairs, and across the street to Lou's truck. When I told my mom to get in, she just stood there looking at me like I was speaking a foreign language. I opened the passenger-side door and tried to gesture my meaning, but she remained confused. If people were cars, then what were actual cars? Did they exist in her world?

I rummaged around the backseat, pulled out the bottle of otalith tincture, and held it in front of her. "Life is a highway," I said. "You're low on oil. You need this. Life is a highway."

Recognition sparked in her eyes, and to my relief, she took the bottle from me and gulped down the potion in seconds. Afterward, she stood in silence as I watched her face, waiting for the otalith cackle to do its job.

More than once, I blinked away tears and swallowed a sob. Regardless of her faults, she was my mom, and seeing her in pain, on drugs, not herself, always hurt, always made me feel alone and exposed like a child lost in a crowd.

A few minutes passed before she looked up at me. "My sweet little boy," she said, and I hugged her, and she petted my back and told me everything was going to be okay. "But we should go before the rest of Naomi's harem shows up."

I nodded and let go, and we both got in the car, and as we pulled onto the road, I took off the hood to my suit.

My mom sat with perfect posture, as she always did when she wasn't using. A slight smile was stamped on her face.

"What's going on?" I said. "How did this happen?"

"I was looking for you," she said, "and the next thing I know I'm in highway land. I'm lucky you came around. Look at you in your suit. My little hero."

I smiled.

"Is Naomi your girlfriend?"

"Was."

"Did you have sex with her?"

"What?"

"That's a yes," she said. "Wandas are notoriously great in bed. Was it amazing? I'm jealous."

"I'm not talking about this with you."

"Why? I'm your mother. You can tell me anything. We don't have secrets."

"You serious? You kept entire races of people a secret from me. Entire subcultures. I didn't even know what cackle was until a few days ago. Turns out it's everywhere."

My mom crossed her arms, her slight smile gone. "Everything I did was to protect you, all of you. You don't know what I went through before you came along, what I had to do to escape. There was no way I was going to put my children through that same pain. That's why I'm here now, to protect you, as I always have, as I always will. The Memoirist is after you, and I'm the only one who can save you."

"How long has Blanche been your bond?"

"Don't say her name out loud." My mom pointed ahead. "Take a left up here."

I put on the blinker and was about to repeat my question, minus the name Blanche, when my mom said, "I joined the Friends of the Memoirist when I was pregnant with you. I was desperate to find something to keep the seasons at bay besides heroin. The Memoirist said she could help, and she did for a while, but then when you got older, she tried to take you from me, so I grabbed you and your sisters, and we ran and hid. I had to start taking heroin again but I had no choice. I'm sorry. You know that."

"What do they want from me?"

"I'll show you when we get to my truck," she said. "If it hasn't been towed already. I've been trapped in that damn metaphor the last two days."

I followed my mom's directions to her truck, which needed new tires and, knowing her, an oil change and several lights replaced. It was an old red Ford diesel, with a rusty cab-over camper shell. She'd parked it at the vista point overlooking Clam Beach and the mouth of the Mad River. While she retrieved her hidden key, I took in the view.

The ocean was rough and the sky overcast. A group of Harbor seals—grey sausages from where I stood high on the bluff—lounged on the bank of the river among the driftwood, their barking carried by the wind. The air was wet and salty and cold.

When my mom found the key, she called me over, and I followed her into the camper, where we sat on a bench seat opposite a sink and mini-fridge. An unmade bed was over the cab. The smell of dirty laundry, slept-in sheets, and mildew brought me back to my childhood.

My mom told me to hold out my hand, and I did, almost reflexively. She'd always said the same thing when I was a kid and she had a surprise for me like candy or pastries. But this time her surprise was very different. In two fluid movements, she pulled a knife out of her pocket, flipped the blade from the handle, and sliced open my palm. I flinched and jumped back. The pain was sharp, stinging, and full of voices. I watched the skin split apart. The cut was deep. Scared and confused, I kept an eye on my mom while looking for something to wrap my hand in before the bleeding began.

"Calm down," she said. "Look at your hand. Shhh, shhh. Look at your hand. It's okay."

I searched her eyes. Had she finally gone completely crazy? Was this one of her drug-induced manic episodes? Was this part of the metaphor spell? Did she think there were demons inside me? Or did she think there was water in my oil?

"Look at your hand," she said again.

I found a dirty shirt on the floor, but as I went to wrap my hand, blue scrill foamed over my wound. The pain was gone, replaced by a tingling sensation. The rekulak saliva dissipated in seconds, leaving my palm healed and without a scar. I let the shirt drop to the floor and sat down, staring at my palm, marveling at what had just happened.

"That's why the Memoirist is after you," my mom said, scooting close and wrapping an arm around my waist. "She wants your rekulak. She wants its power."

"My rekulak heals me?" I said, still in shock.

"To a point," she said. "But don't go jumping off any buildings."

"How did you know?"

She put a hand on my cheek. "I knew you were a sojourner since you were a baby. Warren smelled it on you."

"Warren? That sociopath?"

"Yes, him. The Friends have been waiting for you to come of age ever since, planning on how to get you infected. I knew they succeeded because I'm still connected to the

Memoirist. To become one of the Friends, I took a diluted form of her cackle. She knows what I do, and I know what she does, so don't tell me anything about where you're hiding or how you're getting otalith cackle."

"I don't understand. Is she listening right now?"

My mom shook her head. "It doesn't work like that, but eventually she'll know the basics of this conversation. She'll know I'm plotting against her, but she's known that for years." My mom leaned forward, snatched an envelope from the counter, and dropped it in my lap. "I've been searching for another sojourner to train you for years, and I finally found one. You have to start right away. Today if you can. Their address is in the envelope. Just don't open it in front of me. I can't know where they live, but they know you're coming."

I stuffed the envelope in my pocket and glanced at my hand again, half expecting to see gushing blood. "I can't start today. I'm busy with other training. My bond's in prison. I have to help her."

"Why?" my mom said with venom in her voice. "I've heard of your shanika. Kaliah Sinclair. Did you know she's had three shakas die on her? She's a black widow. She doesn't care about you. You have to worry about your family now. You're the man of the house. Protect your family." She gathered my hands in hers and looked into my eyes. "I know about Em. With this training, you can cure her. You can free me and you from our shanikas. We can live in peace. Together. As a family."

"I can cure Em?"

"Yes. You can cure all of us with this training. We can live a normal life together. No drugs. No mobiaks. Just us."

She hugged me, and I hugged her back, stunned. Kaliah never told me my rekulak could heal me, could heal Em. She also never told me there were two other dead shakas in her past besides Diane.

My mom let go first and said Blanche would find us if we stayed together any longer. After we exchanged numbers, I told her I would leave money at the shop in town for her to get new tires and a tune-up. She called me her sweet little boy, and we said goodbye.

CHAPTER 9

I CLOSED THE FRONT door with my foot and greeted Em, but she ignored me, got up, and left the room. I carried the groceries to the kitchen and set them on the counter. My sister was washing dishes.

"Is Em mad at me?" I said.

"You didn't take her with you," May said over her shoulder.

"She didn't say anything."

My sister shut off the water and turned around, wiping her hands on a dishtowel. "You didn't ask."

"I'll apologize. I got her candy." Then I pointed to the back of my hand. "Have you seen . . . ?"

"Yes. And I'll handle it. Don't worry about it."

"Did you talk to her?"

"I said don't worry about it." She slapped the towel over

her shoulder. "Lou wants to talk to you. He's in the basement."

"Saying don't worry about it doesn't make me not worry about it," I said, and left the room.

Lou was in downward-facing dog, wearing jeans and a T-shirt when I descended the stairs. After glancing up at me through his eyebrows, he pushed off the floor and unfolded into a standing position with surprising ease and grace for a man his age.

"Your ankle feeling better?" I said.

"Eh," he said. "No pain, no gain. Turns out I'm a little rusty. I'm going to need your help after all. You get a second chance. You think you can follow instructions this time?"

I thought of how many times I'd entered the Omen Totem while he was away, but he didn't need to know about that, so I nodded to him. The more I learned, the better equipped I would be to protect my family.

"Good," he said. "This backwood prison has more security than Buffalo. It's ridiculous. One road in, one road out. But I got a plan. You're going to be my inside guy. We get you in full season, have you wander to the Lodge, okay? They take you to this prison, and then you let me in from the inside. But for this to work I'm gonna have to teach you a little trick that not many people can do, okay?" He moved both his hands in circles, like he was waxing a car on either side of him. "You see all these mirrors? These are here for a reason, okay? Mirrors are used to control mobiaks in full season. You have all this cackle bouncing around in your head and you don't know who you are, but there's a part of you that recognizes your reflection, and you just can't let it go."

"I've seen it before," I said.

Lou exaggerated a frown and nodded. "Good. You know what I'm talking about then. We need to get you not to do that. Because that's how they're going to get you to prison, and that's how they're going to keep you there. That's standard operating procedure." He stepped over to the shelf of Kaliah's totems and took down the crystal candy dish and the stuffed fox. "You need a guide, one voice in the cackle louder than the rest. Okay? Now I don't know what's on the other side of these totems, but I know you're about to feel more pain than you've ever felt in your life. You think you can handle that? I need to know now."

"What kind of pain?"

"Hard to describe. It's not permanent, though, so you don't have the fear that comes with mutilation torture. It's not the worst but it's definitely not the best either. Takes about a week to build up the tolerance to get a guide. On average."

"Okay," I said, nodding, trying to mentally prepare myself and not knowing how. "Tell me what to do."

He shook the candy dish and the fox. "These two totems belong to a specific ancestor in Kaliah's line and appear in at least one whorl together, according to your girl. You need to graft to these totems at the same time inside one of their whorls. You get it?"

"No."

"You will. Now, this is gonna cause so much pain that the cackle you have inside you that's from Kaliah will get permanently imprinted with the ancestor of these totems. And when you mix that with your own cackle . . . presto, this ancestor become alive like Frankenstein, sentient, but only while you're in season. It's called forging the Ghost. Now Kaliah told me this ancestor's her great-grandaunt, Zelda Sinclair. Supposedly a famous taxidermist and thief. But I never heard of her."

Lou brought out the stash of bloom and frowned at how much was missing but said nothing. I sat down at the table, the totems in front of me, and caught the bottle he sent sliding toward me.

He said, "Most people think the only way to break a graft and come back from a whorl without leaving a corruption behind is to ride the Ghost. But forging the Ghost, or the pain from trying to, those can both bring you back. Just don't get lost in the ancestor's life story and lose your purpose, and you'll be fine. You don't want to get in the habit of leaving corruptions behind. Corruptions are bad, okay? Any questions?"

"Why are they bad?"

"First off, they muck up whorls, so that's no good. Second, you leave too many behind and you lose your mind."

I lost my breath. By my count, I had left ten corruptions in whorls already. "How many is too many?"

"Depends on the person. A couple hundred usually before your family starts noticing a change. Couple thousand after that before you're a different person."

I remembered the fighting whorl I'd entered. How many corruptions of Brad were in there? A hundred at least. Maybe that was why I didn't like him why he was such an evil dude. Maybe he'd been a stand-up guy before that.

"You got two totems," Lou said. "Graft to one first— doesn't matter which. Once you're inside its whorl you find the totem you grafted to and the other totem and you graft to them both while you're in the whorl. So if you're in the candy dish whorl you find the candy dish and the fox and graft to them both at the same time. Capeesh?

"I think so."

"It's a different kind of pain than riding the Ghost, but if you stick with it, you'll be fine. It's just gonna hurt like a son of a bitch."

I could barely handle the voices that shot through me when I stubbed my toe. Now I was going to feel worse pain?

Lou put his hands on the table. "Relax. You're not getting out of this trouble without taking risks, and this is going to be the least risky thing you do before this is all over."

I thought of Em. I thought of May. I thought of my mom. I thought of Kaliah imprisoned in Arampom. And for them, I dropped bloom and began muttering my Pictionary poems to a stuffed fox.

CHAPTER 10

A WORKSHOP MATERIALIZED AROUND me with dead creatures hanging from the walls in various poses: a hawk on its perch, an owl mid-swoop, a martin on its hind legs, a squirrel upside down on a branch. Against the far wall, a mountain lion and a black bear stood facing each other. I sat at a workbench, a yellow light shining from above my head and strange tools strewn out in front of me beside yarn, wire, small bleached bones, glass eyes, a steel stand, and a fox pelt.

I was in a Skill Whorl, which meant there was likely a spiky disc called a Quick in my heel, and if I tapped my foot, I could easily find the thread of pain this whorl was built on without the use of Foundation Gestures. But I wasn't here to learn how to stuff a fox, and by the lack of corruptions in the room, I gathered Kaliah's family wasn't interested in the skill either.

Diverging from the loop, I stood and searched for the candy dish. Right away, Zelda's identity began seeping in, accompanied by feelings of security, acceptance, love, all tempered by the pain of the Quick as I walked around the room, pain that lessened more and more the farther I got from the workbench. I resisted Zelda's identity by focusing on my task, but a few drops still made their way through.

She'd been an only child with doting parents. I saw memories of her with friends. She liked to stand out, to shock, to be spontaneous. She loved the news, loved politics. She was a suffragist, even though the other mobiak women ridiculed her for being one. Mobiak women had all the power they wanted. They didn't need the vote, but if they decided they did, they wouldn't march in the streets like fools. They'd just take it with poison. Zelda knew that, but she wanted to support the human women, the barrens. She wanted them to have power too.

I searched the whole room for the candy dish, in drawers and boxes, behind and under furniture. It wasn't here. I tried to open the door but it was jammed. I tugged hard, and it came free, swinging open fast, sending me stumbling backward. Roiling blue mold was all that was behind the door. The whorl did not extend beyond this room, not during this stay anyway. Opening the door was a big mistake. Zelda's memories flooded my mind, and my rekulak shot out of the pool of moldy scrill, crashed through the threshold, and sprayed me. Then the graft broke. The whorl dissipated. And I was back in Lou's basement.

"I thought I told you not to leave a corruption," Lou said, scraping scrill from my arm into a jar.

"The candy dish wasn't there." I felt sick knowing I'd left

another piece of myself behind. I didn't need Lou scolding me about it. I felt like me. I felt normal. But if I wasn't me anymore, would I even know?

Lou must have read my face because he said, "I've left seventy-seven corruptions behind. I left the last one about a year ago. Wasn't paying attention. It happens. You'll be fine. You got plenty in the tank." He patted my shoulder, then limped over to the chair against the wall and sat in it. With a twirl of his hand, he gestured for me to continue.

I pictured the unfortunate shakas Kaliah and I had found babbling to mirrors in a seedy cabin in the woods. Losing a few small pieces of myself was a small price to pay to become immune to that fate.

I dropped bloom and grafted to the other totem, the candy dish. This time I found myself in a living room, sitting on a couch, filing my nails. Beside the couch was a hospital bed in a slightly inclined position. An old woman with thin, white hair and thin, sagging, spotted skin sat in the bed, semi-upright, drinking out of a mug with a straw. Between us was an end table. On the end table were opened envelopes, a small bunch of green grapes sprawled over a white paper towel, and a crystal candy dish full of colorful, striped hard candy.

A small army of children sat in front of us, staring at the old woman and the candy dish, like supplicants at an alter, or dogs begging from their master. The far wall was extended to make room for them all. In the midst and above the sitting army of children, on a stand, was a TV playing a soap opera. Besides the sounds from the show, the room was quiet. The room smelled of toast and furniture polish.

On the other side of the couch, I saw the stuffed fox on a bookshelf against the wall. I went to it, veering off the path of the whorl, ignoring as best I could the tendrils of Zelda growing in my mind. I felt a stabbing in my chest as I reached for the fox, and my skin became hot all over, like I was approaching an inferno. My face pinched. I began to cry. Grief and hopelessness overwhelmed me. But I didn't give up. I grabbed the fox, held it, felt the scratchy fur in my hands, repeating the same Pictionary poems I'd used in the real world. But the pain only got worse and worse, growing like a crescendo, until I couldn't take any more. I tossed the fox to the ground and retreated into Zelda's memories, basking in her narrative. My rekulak burst through the floor, sending children flying, and sprayed me. The graft severed, and I returned to reality.

Lou saw the scrill on my skin, shook his head. "Again?"

Frustrated, wasting no time, I reentered the candy dish whorl. The corruption I'd left behind sat beside me on the couch, muttering the Pictionary poems I'd been using when I failed to graft to the fox. I snapped my fingers at him, and he turned to me with a blank look, continuing to recite the passwords.

Seeing a shell of myself like that was uncanny, but it gave me an idea.

I scooted toward the candy dish, and as I did, all one hundred or so of the children sitting on the floor, in unison, turned their heads toward me. I saw hate in their eyes. Confused and frightened, but determined to follow my plan, I grabbed hold of the candy dish and began grafting. As the fiery pain consumed me, as Zelda's memories offered a warm and welcoming escape, the children attacked, climbing over each other to get to me. They punched kicked, bit, scratched, and tore at my body. I howled uncontrollably, making sounds

I'll never forget, sounds that still haunt me. But I held on to the candy dish tight, hoping I could find the strength to keep grafting, resisting the tiny, prying hands as I was being crushed under the weight of the mob.

Then the weight lessened and lessened again. A child disappeared in front of me, then another and another until I could see the ceiling again. Mangled wounds all over my body squirted or poured blood. I was broken. More children came forward, but as they came in contact with my blood they disappeared. I knew they weren't real children, but the scene was so disturbing, so horrifying, I gave up. I threw the candy dish into the mob. The old woman cursed as the children fought over it, as I surrendered to Zelda's memories once more.

Back in the basement, Lou said, "Okay, that's enough for one day."

"No," I said, not wanting to prolong the torture any longer than I had to, not wanting to dread returning to these whorls day after day for a week. "One more time." I began grafting to the candy dish before he could respond. I entered the whorl again.

My corruption on the couch to my right was reciting the passwords for the fox. My new corruption on the left was reciting the passwords for the candy dish. I went to the bookcase, getting better and better at resisting Zelda's narrative, and I tossed the fox at my first corruption like it was a hot potato. It landed in his lap. "Pick it up," I said, and he did, still reciting the passwords.

I then sliced open my hand with the nail file and strolled down the rows of sitting children, pressing a bloody thumb to their foreheads, as if blessing them with holy water, and they disappeared one by one in my wake. I didn't understand why my blood had this effect on them, but I remembered the Brad corruptions from the fighting whorl I'd entered, and how they'd been afraid to get too close to me, and I wondered if there was a connection. The children here had the opposite reaction to me. After making a whole row disappear, they lined up in front of me, polite and organized, and took turns taking my blood until all but three, who must have been the original players in the whorl, disappeared. I permitted myself a nice thought: I had set them free.

The old woman in the hospital bed set down her tea and watched as I gave the candy dish to my second corruption, sat down between him and the first one, and rested a hand on each of their shoulders. The pain was nothing compared to holding the totems directly. I grafted to the pain itself, and the three of us sat there muttering gibberish passwords until I was back in the basement.

Seeing no scrill on my skin, Lou raised his eyebrows and said, "That's what I'm talking about, Doughboy. Now we're cooking."

I leaned back in my chair and took a deep breath. "It's done. I did it."

Lou tucked in his chin. "What do you mean?"

"I did what you asked. It's done."

"You grafted to both totems at once?"

"Yep."

Lou laughed. "The quickest I ever heard of someone forging the Ghost is three days. Trust me, you didn't do it."

"Trust me, Lou. I did it."

He stared at me a few moments, then said, "Okay, we'll see." He pointed to the desk in the corner. "There's a lock picking kit in there, okay?" He wiggled his hips as he sat up straighter, exuding attitude. "I'm going to douse you with enough bloom to put you in season, then I'm going to lock the basement door from the outside, okay? If you get past these mirrors and pick that lock like a master thief should be able to do, then I'll believe you forged the Ghost and Zelda Sinclair is your guide, okay?"

Lou doused me with three times the bloom I'd been using to enter whorls, and I felt throbbing behind my eyes and tingling deep inside my brain. Then the voices rushed in, and before I blacked out, I smiled, because I heard Zelda's voice as clear as a bell, louder than the rest.

When I came to, I was sitting on the couch in the living room, Lou standing over me with his arms crossed. "How did you do it?" he said.

"I like Zelda," Em said, sitting next to me, smiling. "She's cool."

I recoiled at the thought of someone occupying my body while I wasn't there, but if I had to go into season, I'd rather Zelda was in charge than some nameless, mad throng of Kaliah's ancestors.

"How'd you do it?" Lou said. "Tell me everything."

I recounted to him my exploits in the candy dish whorl, excluding some of the more unpleasant parts about the children, and when I finished, he looked disgusted. He pointed at me and said, "You used your corruptions to take the pain for you? Like whipping boys? That's a weaselly shortcut. Now it's going to be that much harder for you to learn how to ride the Ghost. You have to take the pain at some point, Doughboy. You can't run from it forever." Then he stomped off before I could express my own indignation.

CHAPTER 11

THE ADDRESS IN THE envelope my mom had given me came with a name: Lonnie Cartwright. He lived in Willow Creek, a small mountain community thirty-five miles east of Lou's place. People on the coast went there in the summer to get away from the fog and swim in the Trinity River. When I was a kid, my sisters would take me there sometimes with their boyfriends.

The drive over was beautiful but treacherous. The road was windy, and snow was piled up on either side. Crushed brick spattered against the wheel wells as I drove. On one of the summits, gusts of winds slapped against the side of the truck, forcing me to hold the wheel fast. Through and over the trees that lined the road, I caught views of snow-covered foothills and deep ravines.

During the forty-five-minute drive, I sorted out my plan

for the coming days. I would learn all I could from Lou, and I would also train with this Lonnie guy. I couldn't rely on Lou or Kaliah to stop the Friends of Blanche Duluth. Kaliah was imprisoned in Arampom, and Lou was acting out of a mysterious debt he owed her and might bail as soon as the debt was paid. If Lou and I managed to rescue Kaliah, she would help, but I doubted her ability now. Three of her shakas were dead, and she'd failed to anticipate this most recent plot against her.

The rekulak was my best option. I'd seen its power when it healed my own body. If I could master that power, I wouldn't need Kaliah's or Lou's help ever again, or anyone else's.

The highway ran through the middle of Willow Creek—a grocery store, a bar, two gas stations, two restaurants, and a few shops. I followed my phone's navigation north of town, over a Trinity River swollen to the banks, into a neighborhood with modest houses packed together on small lots, bordering an icy and desolate golf course.

I parked in front of a beige, one-story, stucco house surrounded by large pine trees. The curtains were drawn, and the snow on the front walk hadn't been shoveled in some time. It crunched beneath my feet as I took careful, deliberate, and sometimes sinking steps to the door. The air was dry and cold.

I was apprehensive, not knowing what to expect from this new training. Everything seemed to be about pain for these mobiaks. Would the training involve being cut? Being dressed in leather and whipped? Or would I be subjected to some strange agony I couldn't even imagine?

I rang the bell. Inside, a dog barked, and there was a

honking noise, like a chair being pushed out from a table. I heard heavy footsteps, then a raspy, man's voice, "Who is it?"

"Charlie Allison," I said. "I'm looking for Lonnie Cartwright." The dog barked some more, but I received no other response. "Hello?" I waited a few moments and was about to knock again when a piece of paper was slid under the door.

"Come back bearing gifts," the man said. "Then we'll talk."

A grocery list was written on the paper in nightmarish handwriting: hot dogs, peanut butter, chili, rum, daiquiri-mix, mac n cheese, chips . . . . "Is this part of the training?" I said, being a smartass. When he didn't respond, I walked back to the truck, shaking my head.

This type of guy felt familiar to me, like a flashback of my childhood. My mom was a magnet for flakes and assholes. Or maybe I was just being sensitive. After all, I didn't know the details of my mom's arrangement with him. Maybe this was part of his payment.

I drove back through town to the small country store where everything was marked up at least ten percent. I bought all the items on the list, came back, and rang the bell again, cradling a grocery bag in each arm.

Over the barking dog, Lonnie shouted, "Shut up Shirley." Then, to me, "Come in."

Using a knee to help balance one of the bags, I turned the knob, then pushed the door open with my shoulder. An off-white Cocker spaniel greeted me with a wagging backside, and Lonnie beckoned me to the kitchen with a wave of his hand. I set the grocery bags on an olive-green countertop as he fed ice into a blender.

He was tall and lanky, in his sixties, with white, slicked-back hair, a white mustache and goatee, square glasses over gray-blue eyes, and a few missing teeth. Sharp cheekbones stretched the otherwise loose skin on his gaunt face, and faded tattoos covered his arms. He wore a white T-shirt and leather vest, jeans, an eagle belt buckle, and a chain attached to his wallet.

A Harley, partially dismembered, took the place of a table in the dining room. Parts lay on faded, yellow newspaper on the floor next to a ratchet and sockets. The walls were beige and the carpet was orange and spotted with stains. Sickly yellow nicotine stains were on the ceiling above the lazy boy recliner in the living room. The house smelled of cigarettes, unwashed dog, and something sweet and putrid I couldn't place until I saw the dog rubbing its head, in a fluid and practiced motion, along a black, uninterrupted stain lining the bottom of the couch.

"Your dog has an ear infection," I said.

"I know," Lonnie said. "There's only one vet out here, and she's an idiot." He spread his arms out. "I'm in the middle of nowhere. Purgatory. I'm used to civilization. I'm from Sacramento. And my shanika put me out here in purgatory, next to this damn golf course. I hate golf. Bunch of idiots yelling four all day. Golf balls hitting my roof. Can't wait to get my Harley running. Can't wait to see their faces when they hear my straight pipes cracking like thunder. What? What'd you say? Brahhp! Brahhp!"

I got the feeling Lonnie didn't entertain many guests.

"Look at that," he said, pointing out the window. "That tree on the right. It's blocking the satellite. I don't get any of the nudie channels, man, all because my neighbor won't cut that damn tree down. Says he needs the shade for the summer. But look at all those trees. He's got plenty of shade. He's lucky I got two strikes, that's all I can say."

Lonnie poured some rum and daiquiri-mix into the blender and slammed down the puree button, filling the room with the sound of crushing ice. After a minute, he poured himself a thick, blue daiquiri, said, "Follow me," and led me down a hall to a dark room, where a small lamp illuminated a typewriter and two stacks of paper on a desk in the corner.

"You know how to type?" Lonnie said, the bottom third of his mustache now blue.

"Yes," I said.

When I was a kid, my mom worked from home transcribing audio from businesses, private law firms, universities. She taught me the skill so I could help her out when she was too busy or too high. I transcribed depositions, conference calls, lectures. I became good at spelling words I didn't know the meaning of. I impressed a teacher once by telling her to stop being facetious. She put me in a gifted class, where I parroted a lot more big words and was quickly exposed as a fraud and kicked out.

"I've got the last user agreement that came with the iTunes update there," Lonnie said, pointing to the papers on the desk. "I want you to make a copy of it."

"Is this a joke?"

"No."

"I was told you could train me to heal cackle diseases with my rekulak. Is that true?"

"What do you know about Rekulaks?" he said.

"Nothing really. That's why I'm here."

He sighed. "If you want something from a Rekulak, you

have to learn how to speak its language—one of its languages anyway."

"Rekulaks speak in iTunes user agreements?"

Lonnie rolled his eyes, leaned against the threshold, and took a long sip of his daiquiri before answering: "No, man. Rekulaks are extra-dimensional beings that live simultaneously in the past, present, and future. Their language is a little more complicated than user agreements. They eat choices. Wrap your head around that. Choices are symbols in the language they use to tell themselves stories about themselves. It's the language of their identity. Imagine if you ate broccoli and it changed your sense of humor. Imagine if you ate a cheeseburger and it made you attracted to men. You'd be damn careful what you ate, wouldn't you? The power of a sojourner is in taking these choices, these symbols back, for yourself. But before you can do that, you have to learn how to take away the symbols, make a gap in your rekulak's identity. You have to learn how to empty your mind of choices. Meditation works best, but it takes time to master and it's dangerous for beginners because they can't control how the rekulak fills the gap. Typing boring crap is the fastest, safest way I've found."

"What do you mean by fill the gap?" I said. "Fill it with what?"

"Start typing. You'll see."

"How long?"

"Depends. A couple hours your first time. Maybe more."

"Any advice?"

"Nope. Just get in there, get it done. You'll know when you did it." He patted my shoulder, then left me alone.

The typewriter didn't look ancient, but it didn't look new

either. It was boxy, plastic, and grey, from the seventies or eighties, I guessed. I'd never used one quite like it before. But in very little time, I had the basics down and was pounding away like the pro I used to be. I planned to leave after two hours of work, whether something happened or not. I couldn't be gone too long. I'd told Lou and my sister that I wanted to go on a hike alone to clear my mind. I felt bad for lying, but I didn't completely trust Lou—I didn't completely trust anyone after Hugo's betrayal—and I hadn't been able to talk with my sister alone yet.

The first two pages of the user agreement actually held my attention somewhat. For example, I learned Apple had the right to track location through iTunes. But after transcribing five pages, my mind wandered. What was supposed to happen? Was my rekulak going to materialize in the real world? Was I a snake charmer and this typewriter my flute? By page seven, I was in the flow, on a mission to get this over with as soon as possible. Then, on the tenth page, it happened. I smelled menthol and strawberries. And when I stopped typing, writhing worms of blue mold swirled over the ink freshly stamped on the page. Then they disappeared, leaving behind new words, words I had never typed.

With my mouth hanging open, I pulled the page out and read a formal letter to a health insurance company asking for something called an out-of-network exemption to be applied to a kidney surgery performed three hundred miles from the nearest in-network provider. My name was at the bottom of the page.

Lonnie was in his lazy boy, smoking, watching cable news when I came into the living room.

"I think I did it," I said.

He spun around in his chair and threw up his hands. "Hey, that was fast." His eyes were glassy, and the wrinkles around them told me he was smiling under his blue mustache. He stood, swayed a little, then walked a crooked line toward me. "Let's see."

I handed him the letter. "It was covered in the blue stuff, then the words changed."

"Scrill," he said, looking over the letter. "Looks like you did it. You got a genuine homunculus diary here. Not bad, kid."

"What's a homunculus diary? It looks like some letter to an insurance company to me."

He shook his head. "We live in the fourth stomach of Arawok. He only has seven stomachs, but he has an infinite number of bodies, which means we have an infinite number of bodies. When you take away your choices from a rekulak, you put a hole in its identity, and it fills it with whatever comes easiest. Kind of how our eyes work when things move too fast. In this case, your rekulak pulled in something from a version of you that apparently has kidney troubles, a version of you that was typing in the same place at the same time in a stomach with a timeline somewhat like ours, or close enough." He slapped me on the back. "Got it?"

I was struggling with what question to ask first when my phone rang. May was on the other end. Her voice was frantic, on the verge of cracking: "I can't find Em, Charlie. I lost her. I lost her."

CHAPTER 12

I DROVE MUCH FASTER on the way back to the coast, roaring up hills and out of turns, throttling the steering wheel, clenching my jaw, and trying not to spin out on worst-case scenarios. In just over thirty minutes, I arrived in Arcata, a small college town a few miles south of McKinleyville. The sky was dark by then, and the street lights were on. May had been grocery shopping here to avoid being seen by the Friends of Blanche at her usual store. I found her walking on a sidewalk near the downtown plaza with Lou. I honked, parked, ran to them, and hugged my sister. Her face was red.

"I hope the hike went well," Lou said.

I couldn't tell if he was being facetious, so I ignored him and turned to my sister. "What happened?"

"We were in the store," May said. "I told her to get some

apples and she didn't come back. We'd been fighting. I thought maybe she went back to the truck but she wasn't there."

"Did you call the police?"

"Can't risk it," Lou said. "These Friends are definitely in the police."

"Who cares?" I said, losing my temper. "This might have nothing to do with them. Some man could have taken her. Some human man. Even if it was one of the Friends, we still need to know." I turned to May. "Call the cops right now. I'm going to the store. Maybe she went back."

I strode up the hill in the direction my sister pointed. I was so afraid for Em the world seemed to lose dimension, like everything was flat, expanding, or compressing as I moved. I searched the parking lot, the entire store, down every aisle, in the men's and women's bathrooms. I asked a clerk if he'd seen a little girl, but I didn't know what Em was wearing. I texted my sister. She texted back, "**White jeans, yellow shirt, blue jacket**." I asked more clerks, the manager. No one had seen anything. I went back outside. Maybe she was hiding. But why would she hide? My sister said they were fighting. About what? Did it matter? I looked around for hiding spots just in case. I called her name. People stared, concerned, appalled. I didn't care.

Then a name on a flyer tacked to the corkboard by the automatic sliding doors caught my eye: Nathan George. That was one of the names from the donation ledger in one of the shower curtain whorls. I inspected closer. Nathan George was performing poetry inspired by the 1964 Flood tonight at The Bean Grinder.

Had Em seen this, remembered the name? I'd told her to

write it in her notebook. Would she go to the performance? Would she do that? Was this a part of her acting out, her preteen rebellion, her need to assert some kind of control over her life? Was she trying to be useful, proactive?

I called my sister, some hope now warring with terror: "I think I know where she is." As I ran down the hill, dodging the moseying young college students clogging the sidewalks, oblivious to my family's private crisis, I breathlessly explained the Omen Totem, how Em had assisted me with it, and the flyer I'd just seen at the grocery store. My head never stopped moving, looking for Em, just in case my hunch was wrong. Could the flyer be a coincidence? No. No way.

I caught up with May and Lou on the other side of the plaza. May's movements were stiff, her jaw set, lips taut. "Don't you ever involve my daughter in this craziness again," she said, pointing at me, pushing the words out with a low growl.

"She was bored," I said. "She wanted to help. She doesn't have a choice but to be involved. None of us do."

"Never again, Charlie. You understand? If it's so important you come to me first."

We approached The Bean Grinder, a stucco building on the corner of a four-way intersection.

"Blanche might be in here," I said. "Lou, do you have your spray bottles?"

"Of course," Lou said with a huff.

He was mad at me too, but what right did he have?

May charged into the coffee shop, and Lou and I followed. Standing just inside the doors, we scanned the room. The lights were off except for a few above a small, rug-covered stage where a young man with a trimmed beard and bleach-blond hair sat on a stool, reciting poetry into a microphone. On a table beside us were two stacks of programs entitled, "The Flood and You: Our Quest for World Peace." The place was packed with people. They sat at tables, sipping from mugs, their upturned faces painted by the yellow stage light. They all had bleach-blond hair that almost glowed in the dark. They were quiet. Only the poet spoke:

> *. . . The rain falls*
> *Mama says my hair is too blond, like Papa's*
> *Mama says Papa's hair turns blonder in the sun,*
> *like mine*
> *Papa is a bad man*
> *Does my blond hair make me bad, like Papa?*
> *Mama's hair is brown, like hot cocoa with lots of milk*
> *Brown like the river*
> *I can't tell the difference*
> *And the rain keeps falling . . .*

My sister let out a small whimper, then walked forward with purpose. As I went after her, weaving around tables and chairs, I saw her destination: a small child sitting alone in the darkest corner of the room, an open program obstructing the face. The room was so dark I didn't recognize the clothes until I was a few yards away. May began to cry, and she crouched down and hugged Em. I smiled, partly out of relief, and partly because of the look on Em's face. She knew how much trouble she was in. Neither of us had ever seen her mom cry like that. I felt the muscles in my stomach relax, muscles that had been seized for the whole ride to the coast, and I began to breathe freely. I suspected I would be hungry soon.

Then all the lights in the place turned on at once. The poet stopped talking, and he, the two baristas behind the counter, and the entire audience turned and stared at me and said in unison, "*Hello Charlie.*"

The muscles in my stomach re-seized, and my scalp lit up with goosebumps.

"It's Blanche," Em said. "She's part of them."

"That's impossible," Lou said. "These are all humans. They can't be vesseled."

"Whatever," Em said. "It's Blanche, I'm telling you."

"We have to get out of here," I said, although I didn't know how. Twenty Friends were between us and the only doors.

Lou was already reaching into his coat pocket. He pulled out a bottle full of purple liquid, sprayed it in the air, and said in a booming voice with his shoulders back, "What is the best toaster oven money can buy?"

I hadn't expected that, but I'd learned not to question Lou's expertise in the strange and mysterious ways of cackle. I trusted something would happen to facilitate our escape: the audience would run away screaming, become suddenly engrossed in conversation, or maybe just all fall asleep. When they reacted by standing up and taking a step toward us, I was surprised.

"Whatever you're doing isn't working, Lou," I said.

"What is the best toaster oven money can buy?" he repeated.

The audience didn't appear to be affected. I looked around for some avenue of escape. Our only options were to make a run for it through the crowd or flee into the unisex bathroom to the right.

"In the bathroom," I said. "Hurry." I opened the door, waited for May, Em, and Lou to rush through, then I jumped inside and flipped the deadbolt.

"What now?" May said.

"I don't know," I said, looking around. "I thought there'd be a window in here."

The doorknob jiggled as someone tried it from the other side. Then there was a loud thud. They were trying to break the door down. It looked solid to me. We were safe for the moment.

"What's the best toaster oven money can buy?" Lou shouted at the wall.

"Give it a rest, Lou," I said.

He hung his head. "I don't know why it's not working. It always works."

"Well, it's not this time. What else do you have?"

"This is it. I've got more in the truck, but . . . . . I don't know why its' not working."

"Maybe there's something we can use in here," Em said, holding up the program she had in her hand. "They were having like a class before you guys got here. They went over all the stuff in this booklet. They seemed really afraid of this." She flipped through the program and showed me two pages occupied by eight different, colorful patterns that were nearly exact replications of the eight patterns on the shower curtain, the Omen Totem currently in Lou's basement. Each pattern was labeled. I learned the names of the patterns later. The pink polka dots had three labels: Emadine, the Void, Instant Death. Plaid was labeled Optivar, the First Stomach. Paisley was Elestat, the Second Stomach. Damask was Zaditor, the

Third Stomach. Argyle was Crolom, the Fourth Stomach. Houndstooth was Pazeo, the Fifth Stomach. Greek key was Alocril the Sixth Stomach. And herringbone was Xalatan, the Seventh Stomach.

"What is this?" I said.

"They talked about it like it was a map," Em said, and pointed to the polka dots. "They talked about Emadine a lot. They seemed to be afraid of it."

"Have you heard of this?" I said to Lou.

"I've heard of the Seven Stomachs, of course. But I don't know anything about these patterns."

"Isn't Zaditor an allergy drug, like eye drops?" May said. "And I'm pretty sure Xalatan is for glaucoma. And Optivar is definitely an allergy eye drop."

"These other worlds are named after eye drops?" I said.

"That's ridiculous," Lou said. "The eye drops are named after the seven worlds."

"And that's not ridiculous?"

Lou shrugged. "You don't think mobiaks work in the pharmaceutical industry? They gotta name those drugs something. Why not after the seven stomachs?"

I was having trouble believing that an old shower curtain could be a map to the Seven Stomachs and something called the Void. I didn't see how a bunch of patterns could be the key to travel between magical worlds, but that didn't matter at the moment. We were trapped, and we needed to escape before more of Blanche's Friends showed up. But how?

"If these people are afraid of pink polka dots," I said, "then maybe that's what we should give them. May, you have pink makeup in your purse, right?"

"Yes?" she said.

"Good. Okay, what if we paint pink polka dots on those toilet seat covers over there, and then slide them under the— no, we put them on like clothes and walk out of here? If those creeps are afraid of pink polka dots, then maybe they won't touch us."

Lou threw up his hands and said, "Sweet Mary and Joseph. This is a farce."

"The pink polka dots aren't the farce here," I said. "Your toaster oven is the farce."

Lou wagged a finger at me. "My poisons are based in reality. They take magnificent skill to make. They work. You've seen them work. They saved your life more than once. This crap about pink polka dots is absurd. You're losing it."

"Stop," May said, and took a Leatherman tool out of her purse and handed it to me. "You take apart that toilet seat." Then she pointed at Lou. "You take the toilet lid. I got a can of pepper spray in my purse. I'm going to spray everyone behind that door. If anyone's still a threat after that, you guys come in and hit them over the head. Lou, if I get spray-back in my eyes, you guide me out of here. You guys got it?"

Lou nodded, smiling, looking at my sister with unabashed admiration.

"Yes," I said, a little embarrassed by my plan now. "But why do I get the toilet seat?"

"You know why?" she said.

Grumbling to myself, I cleaned the toilet seat as best I could before removing it. May gave Em a scarf, and Em wrapped it around her mouth, nose, and eyes, and claimed she could see just fine. Lou and I positioned ourselves behind May, our weapons ready. May stood at the door, her purse over her shoulder, pepper spray in one hand, and her daughter's hand in the other, waiting for a break in the thuds. I was shaking, breathing heavy, hoping the others didn't notice, hoping May would open the door soon because the waiting was torture.

Then without warning, she swung the door open and sprayed. The room filled with the smell of engine oil, and the sounds of coughing, sputtering, suffering people. The first row of Friends went down, and May sprayed the next. They went down too, and May stepped aside and let me and Lou go out first.

We kicked a path through my sister's victims as they grasped blindly for our legs. Two women and the poet were still standing. They came at us, and I swung the toilet seat like an ax, hitting one of the women on the shoulder. She screamed, and she and the poet kept their distance after that, hopping around, looking for an opening. May came up from behind and sprayed them too. Then I heard Em cry out, and I turned to see a man on his knees, eyes closed, snot running down his chin, clutching Em's leg as she hopped on one foot, struggling to break free. Rage flared in me, and I brought the toilet seat down on the man's ear, hard, and he howled and let go.

We ran, all of us. Lou held open the doors and tossed his now broken toilet lid aside, and we were out in the streets, free. No one was chasing us. But that didn't mean more Friends weren't on the way. Ignoring the looks from passersby, I kept the toilet seat in hand until May and Em were safe in Lou's truck.

CHAPTER 13

I SAT CROSS-LEGGED BY a campfire. The samurai sword rested in my lap, and the night breeze wafted smoke in my eyes. I had just moved out of the smoke's previous path, trying to maintain focus before the start of the next loop. This whorl didn't have many corruptions, so the time between the start and end of the loop was short. Still, with each loop, my ability to mimic the ancestor's movements and tolerate the pain degraded, like a top wobbling toward the end of its spin. I had left two corruptions behind already. They stood across the fire, watching me.

According to Lou, an experienced shaka could ride the Ghost on the first or second loop, but beginners like me usually needed seven or eight, so maintaining my focus in the corrupted space between loops was key. I had to ignore my narrative, the ancestor's narrative, and any other narrative that crept into my brain. "Describe what you see without bias," was the tip Lou had given me. So I ignored the shells of myself across from me, and I studied the smoke, the fire, the coals.

Then the first rancher stepped into the firelight, the back half of him still dipped in shadow, the desire plain in his eyes. He didn't say a word. The loop had started again.

I was a woman, young, judging by my hands, and living some time in the 1800s, judging by my clothes and the narrative I'd already slipped into twice. I was traveling by foot over the Bald Hills to visit . . . . No, I had to stop indulging in that, forget all of it, and lose myself in the movements of the ancestor.

I stood and made the foundation gesture for fear, and I followed the pain as I unsheathed my sword and said, "Leave me be and I'll be on my way." Two rifle barrels floated forward on either side of the rancher, and before I could see the men carrying them, I turned and sprinted into the darkness through the tall grass of an open field, leaving my pants wet with dew. When my eyes adjusted, I crouched under the grass and doubled back with stealth and grace. I heard grass slapping and snapping against the men's thighs as they looked for me. I heard them separate. One spewed nasty taunts into the night. I found him first, a gunman, and I slashed his hamstring. He cried out as he fell, and again after I sliced open his forehead and the blood cascaded down his brow and into his eyes. I heard the crack of a rifle as the second gunman took his shot and missed. I ran, then crouched and doubled back to the now wailing injured man, and I waited. The second gunman came. He wasn't expecting me. As I stood, emerging from the grass, I lopped his arm off below the elbow. Blood splattered the grass, and I ran straight for the first rancher.

I was starting to wobble now, like the top, like a drunk. Involuntarily, I was shrinking away from the intensifying pain. The loop was almost over. If I could just reach the end, I could try again. I needed to mirror the movements of the ancestor to entangle my cackle with this Skill Whorl and all the other Skill Whorls in Kaliah's line that housed memories of samurai sword mastery. Once entangled, the graft would dissolve, and I would return to the normal world riding the Ghost, wielding my newly entangled cackle—the aggregate of samurai skills collected over generations—until the bloom wore off.

Memory Whorls worked the same way, but instead of returning with skills, shakas returned with a perfect recollection and an intense case of déjà vu.

The rancher ran from me, ran from the screams of his companions, but I couldn't keep up. Shaking with pain, I dropped the sword, fell to the ground, and escaped into the ancestor's narrative. Before the graft failed completely, my rekulak burst from the corruption I'd made and covered me in blue scrill. As the whorl dissolved, I wondered why my rekulak insisted on doing that every time. Was it re-infecting me? Was it marking its property? Or was it upset over me leaving a corruption, and this was its retaliation?

Back in Lou's basement, Lou used a rubber spatula to scrape the drying scrill off my arm into a large glass jar. "You'll get there," he said. "Your mind just doesn't know how much pain it can take, but it'll learn."

I'd been training almost nonstop since I got here, eating hot peppers and trading off between taking the trout test, practicing tai chi, yoga, martial arts, and foundation gestures and expressions. I lifted weights. And I tried to ride the Ghost.

Growing up, I wasn't that into sports. I'd wrestled a few years in high school, but I hadn't been that great. And I hadn't played any sports since, so I was surprised by how my body was responding to exercise. I was losing the little fat I had and gaining muscle. Even sitting down I could feel the new energy in my muscles just waiting to be called on. It felt good.

After we'd gotten home from the poetry reading, Lou and I had studied the program. Most of it was comprised of facts about the 1964 Christmas Flood, but the last section, the one with my shower curtain patterns, had instructions on how to form portals in a Nexus Whorl. It called the patterns seeds in the language of the Gods and claimed these seeds required only thought to grow.

These Blanche-infected humans were learning some method of traveling between worlds—something only rekulaks and sojourners could do, or, at least, that was the commonly held belief. That would explain why Blanche needed me. But why did she want these people to go to the other worlds? Was she amassing an army, an invasion force? And why did she need to train them if they were infected by her cackle? Wouldn't they just know what she knew?

Blanche had told me that God's vomit reflex took longer to detect her in a human host than in a mobiak one. Maybe that meant she couldn't completely take over the minds of her hosts without being immediately expelled. I recalled the flood-obsessed tourists who'd booked seats on my bus and waited in that long line to purchase a flood-themed calendar.

They were all infected by Blanche on some level. No sane, autonomous person would behave that way otherwise.

After Lou finished collecting my scrill and left, I went at the heavy bag, practicing my kicks. Ten minutes into the workout, my sister came down the stairs carrying a loaf of bread and a dish of butter on a wood chopping block.

"What's this?" I said, wiping away the sweat already caught in my eyebrows.

"I feel bad we lost the starter," she said, sawing into the loaf. Steam escaped from the gash. "I know how much you loved it. I should have kept my own. Anyway, I started a culture after you told me. It isn't the same but it's sourdough."

I watched the butter melt as she spread it over a slice. My mouth watered—nothing like fresh bread. She handed the slice to me, and I hugged her. "Thank you, May."

"I'm mad at you," she said. "But I still love you."

I let go, leaned against the table, and took a bite. The flavor wasn't the same, but the bread was still delicious. May cut and buttered a slice for herself, and we chewed in silence for a moment, then she swallowed and said, "What do you think of Lou?"

"What do you mean?"

"You know what I mean."

"I think he's been divorced three times."

"I know," May said, holding her slice of bread like a microphone. "But do you think . . . ? Do you think he's . . . ?"

"What May? What's going on?"

"Do you think he's, you know . . . mean?"

My sister had been with three abusive men in her life, and all three had appeared wonderful at first before they turned. I knew she was afraid of that happening again. I knew she didn't trust her judgment in men and was probably warring with herself over whether or not finding a life partner was worth the risk, whether or not she was selfish for even considering bringing another man into Em's life, another potential monster.

"I don't know," I said. "How do you tell? I used to think I had some sense of it, but then Robert . . . completely threw me off. I don't know. I like Lou. He said he'd protect you and Em if anything ever happened to me. I think he means it."

May scoffed. "You men all think you can protect the people you love from the world, but you don't realize your most important job is to protect those people from yourself."

"His ex-wives would know," I said, not trying to be snarky at all. "I could ask them."

"No."

"Why not? You always check references when you hire someone, and this is way more important than that."

May set her half-finished slice of bread down. "I keep thinking of those assholes Mom dated when we were kids. Maybe that's why, you know, like she cursed me."

"No. It's not your fault the world's full of assholes."

"Yeah," she said, but she didn't sound like she believed me

"I saw Mom."

May locked her eyes onto mine. "What? When?"

"A couple days ago. Sorry, I've been meaning to tell you. She's clean."

"That's good. Did she say why she didn't tell us what we were, about all of this?"

"She wanted to protect us."

May scoffed again.

"I know," I said. "But she's trying to help now. She says I can cure Em with my rekulak."

"That parasite thing you got?"

"Yeah. It has the power to heal. I've seen it. That's why the Friends are after me. They want it. But Mom says if I learn how to use it, I can cure Em. I can protect us. She put me in touch with an expert. Lonnie. He's been training me. We can have our lives back."

"What does Lou say about this?"

"I didn't tell him, and I'm not going to. He has his own agenda. You know he threatened to stop helping me just because I disobeyed him. No. We keep this between us. Family. Besides, he doesn't know anything about rekulaks. He can't help us there. Em shouldn't have to drink lice juice for the rest of her life. She should be in school with her friends, not here, hiding and bored."

May sighed. "You need to know something. Lou didn't want to tell you because he wanted you to focus on your training, but your friend Kaliah is being tortured in prison. Lou learned when he was trying to break her out. He didn't tell me the specifics, but it sounds like it's some kind of psychological torture." May put a hand on my back. "I'm sorry."

"Thank you for telling me, but I already knew."

CHAPTER 14

THE SNOWBANKS LINING THE curvy two-lane highway to Lonnie's house had grown taller. Fresh snow floated down in large flakes. Trucks passed with attached snowplows scraping and rumbling against the concrete, feeding the growing snowbanks with chunky brown and white slush.

Earlier, I'd confronted Lou about Kaliah's torture. I wanted details. Whether I was looking for inspiration to push through my training or I wanted to torture myself thinking of her pain, I didn't know. But he told me, after pushing out an exasperated sigh, that he hadn't witnessed it, but he'd smelled it on her. She was enduring Doegerot, a particularly sadistic form of mobiak torture that involved methodically corrupting her personal whorls—whorls produced in her lifetime—and thereby transmuting the core of her being. If the torture continued, and we didn't rescue her soon, she would cease to be Kaliah, and become a perverse and rare piece of living art, one that had been sculpted by her torturer. The damage would be permanent, according to Lou. Not even otalith cackle would be able to repair it. But Kaliah had said that same thing about Em, and she had been wrong about that. If my Rekulak could cure Em, maybe it could also cure a too-far-gone Kaliah.

When I reached Lonnie's, he sent me back out with a grocery list nearly identical to the last one, except this time he opted for pina coladas over daiquiris. The blender was already full of ice when I came in with the groceries and set them on the counter. As Lonnie rummaged through the bags, Shirley, the cocker spaniel, reared up and pawed at me, and I knelt and rubbed her stinking ears, which made her eyelids sag with pleasure.

The tools and Harley parts in the dining room had not moved since I was here last.

After Lonnie blended and poured his first pina colada, I washed my hands and gave him a bottle of ear drops I'd picked up from the vet. He accepted it with a cold grunt, like maybe he thought I was judging him over the condition of his dog, but I didn't care. I was judging him.

"Do you know anything about Doegerot torture?" I said.

"What about it?" Lonnie said.

"Is there a cure?"

"Not that I've heard. He put the ear drops in his pocket.

"There's nothing a rekulak can do?"

Lonnie stuck out his bottom lip and shook his head. "Not that I've heard." Then he walked out of the room and down the hall. After a few moments, he returned with a hardcover book and slapped it down on the counter. "You ever hear of Help Me Rhonda? Not the song. The syndicated advice columnist."

"No."

"Well, you're about to become familiar. This is a collection of some of her columns over the years." He flipped the book open with the hand not holding the pina colada, tore out a random page from the middle, and handed it to me. "I want you to pretend like you're an advice columnist and go type out a response to one of those letters. You can peek at what Rhonda wrote but don't copy her. Do your own work. Think it through."

"Okay?" I'd thought he was leading up to something about Doegerot torture, but apparently, he'd moved on without telling me. "Is this part of the training?"

Lonnie gave me an exaggerated nod, like a horse. "Zen koans are traditional, but I think these work better. Hell, I've used critical thinking questions at the end of textbooks before, but it's better to use a dilemma, and Rhonda's always good for one of those."

"This will help me learn how to cure Ghost Heart?"

Lonnie nodded again. "You have to walk before you can run. Go on. All will be clear soon."

I took the torn page to the backroom, loaded paper into the typewriter, and read one of the letters:

Dear Rhonda: I am a breeder of schnauzers. One of my dogs (Diedra is her name) has won best in her class twice and best in show once. I have been very protective of her chastity, as I don't want her to be bred for another two years and I want to find her the perfect mate. So imagine my surprise and consternation when I one day found her pregnant.

Long story short, my grandma had been pestering me to mate her golden retriever with my Diedra to make a golden schnauzer (the dog of her dreams). After expressly forbidding the coupling over and over (I don't do designer breeds) she and my mother arranged a romantic rendezvous behind my back when they were supposed to be taking Diedra on a walk.

I'm so angry and hurt and embarrassed. I've had to drop out of two dog shows. I don't know what to tell my friends. Worst of all, my mother and grandma don't act very sorry, like *I* was being the selfish one. I don't know what to do. When the puppies come, should I even give my grandma one?

Help me Rhonda.

—Bred for Disaster

I was outraged that someone's mom and grandma would do something like this, and I was mildly disturbed by Rhonda's response. She advised giving Grandma a twisted kind of choice: Grandma could have her golden retriever, or she could have the golden schnauzer puppy, but she couldn't have both. Who was this Rhonda lady, and how had she become syndicated?

My advice was considerably more sober: If Grandma wanted a golden schnauzer, Grandma and Mom had to pay for and attend family counseling.

While I typed, no scrill or homunculus diaries appeared. When I finished and presented my work to Lonnie, he crumpled up the paper without reading it, threw it in the trash, and handed me a standard yellow pencil.

I pointed a palm at the trash. "Are you just messing with me now? Why did you have me do that?"

"We needed to establish a choice," Lonnie said. "Now we start mutilating that choice. Like I told you last time, your choices are symbols in your rekulak's language of self. We're trying to reclaim one of those symbols, and you do that by mutilating a choice until you grow on it like a cancer. Then it's yours. That pencil is going to help you do that. You're going to turn it into a Homunculus Totem. Go back into the room and read the letter again, only this time your answer should be one of the many uses there are for a pencil. Example: say the question is, should I tell my cousin his breath stinks? You answer by saying, this pencil writes. Then you do it again. Should I tell my cousin his breath stinks?"

Lonnie raised his eyebrows and pina colada at me, and I responded, "This pencil draws."

"Good," he said. "Now you do that over and over for about an hour and then you got something. Type out the letter and the response. Never repeat an answer. It gets hard. You have to be creative with the things you can use a pencil for. But that's how you make a Homunculus Totem."

"What's that?"

He patted my back and smiled. "I'll show you when you're done. And you'll know when you're done."

I walked down the hall with the pencil, shut the door on the blaring TV noises coming from the living room, and got to work. I typed the letter, followed by a use for the pencil, typed the letter, followed by a use for the pencil . . . . When the puppies come, should I even give my grandma one? This pencil erases . . . should I even give my Grandma one? This pencil picks teeth, picks noses, picks guitar. This pencil plays drums. This pencil helps start fires. This pencil stabs . . . . I quickly ran out of the obvious uses for a pencil and had to get a little more creative: This pencil resets modems to factory defaults. This pencil paints impressionistic dot paintings. This pencil replaces the plastic man missing from a parachute toy. After ten minutes I began dissecting the pencil in my mind: This pencil catches fish, the metal part holding the eraser can be used as the lure, and the wood as the bob. This pencil can be sawed into rounds, which can be hollowed and used as beads. This pencil can be hollowed and used as a snorkel. This pencil can be shaved into confetti. After thirty minutes I was listing the pencil's sexual potential. After forty minutes, I was desperate, reaching for anything no matter how thin: This pencil is a previously agreed-upon signal that the cops are coming during a bank robbery . . . .

Then, finally, after typing, "This pencil can help demonstrate how the pyramids were built," I smelled menthol and strawberries and something else, something like ammonia, and the pencil erupted with tiny, yellow—not blue—hairy, wriggling worms that together made an undulating mold, but only for a moment, and then the mold was gone, leaving the pencil unchanged as far as I could tell.

I was proud of myself and glad I didn't have to think of any more uses for a pencil. I was a lot better at this rekulak stuff than I was at riding the Ghost. I brought the pencil to the living room and shouted over the TV, "Something happened."

Lonnie swiveled around in his chair, a bag of chips in his lap, and Shirley trotted around, sat in his new line of sight, and resumed her begging. With his mouth full, Lonnie said, "What happened?"

I held up the pencil. "Some weird yellow stuff I've never—"

"Ha!" Lonnie said, tossing the bag of chips onto the carpet as he stood. Chips scattered everywhere, and Shirley darted back and forth, sucking them up. "You're a natural."As he wiped greasy hands on his jeans, he looked around the room as if searching for something and sent me back to the room to grab the typewriter and user agreement.

When I returned, he'd placed a TV tray table and a folding chair between the Harley and the kitchen counter, in front of the sliding glass door. He told me to set the typewriter and agreement on the table, then pointed out a specific tree in his neighbor's yard and triple-checked that I was looking at the right one.

"Now," he said, after shutting one eye and lighting a cigarette, "I want you to make a gap in your choices like you did the other day, and as soon as you smell your rekulak coming, stop typing and read the Help-Me-Rhonda letter out loud for the first time, and at the end, answer it with these exact words: This pencil knocks down that tree. And when you do it, make sure you're thinking of the right pencil and the right tree."

"Okay, so let me get this straight. I'm making a gap in my choices, and I'm going to fill that gap with the choice I reclaimed with this pencil, or whatever, and this choice is to knock down that tree?"

Lonnie shrugged. "Basically. I want all my channels. And this is how you're going to repay me for training you."

Apparently, the groceries I kept buying him weren't enough payment for him. "Is this tree actually going to fall down?"

"If you do it right. But even then, maybe not. You're

conducting the Homunculus. That has a lot of limitations. Think of it this way: you tricked a god and stole one of its symbols. If you want to use that symbol, you have to do it without the god noticing. Imagine all of your choices make up a huge mirror that this god, your rekulak, uses to look at itself. If you replace a small piece of this mirror with a small piece from a different mirror, a different universe, like knocking down a tree or breaking into an ATM, your rekulak's probably not going to notice. But if you replace a big chunk of the mirror with something like murder or a volcanic eruption, your rekulak's going to see that and stop it. Conducting the Homunculus only works for small things, or some big, if you're clever about it. And it basically follows the rules of entropy and time, which means that any destruction you cause will be permanent and anything you create will be temporary. If that tree goes down, it stays down. But if you say instead, 'This pencil makes daisies in the lawn,' the daisies will come, but they'll be invisible, and they'll only stay for twenty or thirty seconds, maybe a minute at the most, but they'll be there."

"What?" I cocked my head. "How will they be there if they're invisible."

"The effects of them will be there. There'll be little spots in the lawn where they are, and you'll be able to feel them, but light won't reflect off of them. I don't know why. Things get weird when you leak one universe into another."

The tree Lonnie had pointed out was a large pine. Depending on how it fell, it could crush the neighbor's house. I decided to add a few words to Lonnie's script, then sat down at the tray table and started typing. I lost myself in the legalese for only an hour this time before I smelled my rekulak. A pang of anxiety shot through my stomach. This is it. I read the letter: "Dear Rhonda: I am a breeder of schnauzers . . . . When the puppies come, should I even give my grandma one? Help me Rhonda. –Bred For Disaster." I held up the pencil. "This pencil knocks down that tree over that fence." And I looked at the fence between the neighbor's yard and the golf course.

Blue scrill enshrouded and dripped from the pencil in my hand as I heard a cracking noise. Then the pencil disappeared, and the tree began to fall toward the golf course. Branches snapped off the surrounding trees as the pine fell, its descent slowed by the roots still entangled with the earth and sod. The tree landed almost gently on the fence, breaking a handful of boards.

Lonnie threw his hands up and cheered like his team had just won the super bowl on a last-second play. He high-fived me three times, then shook his arms and shouted, "I am become couch potato, the watcher of nudie channels, baby!" and slapped his thigh, tossed back his head, and croaked out a machinegun laugh.

I sat there with my mouth open big enough o catch flies. With a typewriter and a pencil, I'd tricked my rekulak into knocking down a tree.

After the astonishment wore off a bit, I was struck by how sad this man's life was to be so happy over a few more channels to watch. He went to the living room, grabbed his remote, and began accessing his newly acquired riches, grunting now and then with satisfaction.

He'd left the ear drops on the counter, unopened. I used what was left of the potato chips to entice and subdue Shirley while I administered her medicine. She didn't struggle too much. Lonnie didn't even notice what I was doing.

Before I left, and without taking his eyes off the screen, he told me I was ready to cure Ghost Heart. He said to bring the person who needed to be cured next time. I stood by the door, frozen, staring at him with my eyes welling up. "Thank you," I said.

He waved his hand.

CHAPTER 15

I WATCHED THE BURBLING creek on the TV and counted the trout that swam by while out-of-frame birds sang, while my hand screamed with pain from inside a tub of ice water. There was a small white glare reflecting off the backs of some of the trout as they passed, so I counted them, thinking I'd finally figured this test out. When the video ended, I removed my hand from the ice water, shook it, stuffed it in my armpit, and said, "Five rainbow, twelve cutthroat."

Lou stopped practicing acoustic guitar from his seat against the wall, looked up, and shook his head.

"Then twelve rainbow," I said, "and five cutthroat."

"Nope. Try again."

I jumped out of my chair. "How am I supposed to know how many damn trout there are? They're all either underwater or flapping wildly through the air." I paced back and forth with my hands on my hips. I was tired of counting fish, tired of plunging my hand into ice water, tired of failing to ride the Ghost, tired of the pain. Why was the rekulak training so much easier? I could knock down a tree with a pencil. Lou couldn't do that.

Tonight was the night we attempted to rescue Kaliah, whether I was ready or not. Lou had a mysterious inside man who was going to separate Kaliah from Kayak Brad for a small window of time. It was our best opportunity, and there was no telling if we would ever get another like it. Lou had admitted to me, in a roundabout way, that Brad was the one who'd thwarted the first rescue attempt.

Lou looked bored with my little outburst, so I decided I shouldn't be the only angry person in the room and said, "Why are you helping me anyways? This is a lot of work. You must really owe Kaliah. What did she do for you? You never told me."

"That's because it's none of your business."

"I think it is though. If you're going to come on to my sister every chance you get, I think I should know a little more about you."

"You do, do you?"

"I wonder what your ex-wives would have to say about you."

Lou raised his eyebrows. "You want to talk to my ex-wives, be my guest, and good luck." His eyebrows dropped. "But if you keep talking to me in this disrespectful manner, in my own house, I'll break this guitar over your head." He didn't move or raise his voice, but his whole demeanor stiffened.

"So you're a violent man," I said.

"Sometimes." He shrugged four or five times in quick succession, like he was having trouble shaking off a clingy shawl. "But I can respect where you're coming from. I'll tell you this, if your sister will have me, I'll treat her like a queen. I'll worship the ground she walks on. I promise you that."

I'd heard that one before—twice, actually—blusters from blustering men who wanted to put my sister in a display case.

Lou stood up. "We good, Doughboy?"

"Sure."

He walked away with his guitar. I was starting not to like Lou so much.

Before he reached the bottom of the basement stairs, a loud buzzer sounded, followed by another, and another, and another.

"What's that?" I said.

"The gate alarm!" Lou said, and ran up the stairs.

My knee hit the table as I jumped to my feet, spilling the ice water. I snatched my bloom from the desk and the samurai sword from the shelf and ran after Lou. Upstairs, May came out of the kitchen. "What's going on?"

"Someone's at the gate," I said. "Where's Em?"

"In her room."

As I ran to get Em, I tried to comfort myself by thinking this could be a false alarm, a family of deer could have tripped the sensors. We were in the country after all. I'd seen deer around before, along with skunks, possums, raccoons, a fox, and even a bear.

When I opened the door to Em's room, she was on the floor, crouched over a half-finished collage, surrounded by stray clippings. A glue stick rested next to a book of the complete works of Pieter Bruegel, which she must have taken from Lou's library. The collage, so far, was dark and a little disturbing, and unlike any I'd seen her make in the past. She looked up at me.

"Come downstairs," I said. "We might have to leave in a hurry."

Without a word, she stood and dropped her scissors. I watched the expression on her face go flat, and my heart sank. She had become resigned to this life, to the running, hiding, fighting, to the fear and instability. She had been so bubbly and full of life before. I mourned that child. Would she ever bounce back? It had only been a few days. Was the damage permanent? The wound on the back of her hand seemed to answer my questions.

I told her I was sorry, and she said in a flat tone that unnerved me, "I know. It's okay."

We found Lou and May in the living room. Lou zipped up a backpack, threw it over his shoulder, and grabbed a mini cooler with his free hand. "We have to go now."

"Is it the Friends?" I said.

"The same ones from the bakery," May said. "I recognized them on the monitor."

"You got Em's tincture?" I said.

"Yes," he said. "And we don't have time to grab anything else. Let's go."

Lou led us to the garage, where we all piled into one of his four-door trucks with the extended cab, Em and I in the backseat, Lou behind the wheel, and May beside him. The garage door, screeching and creaking, opened onto Lou's expansive front lawn. Rain fell in streams, overflowing Lou's gutters, and slapping against the circular gravel driveway. I leaned forward and said, "Are they out there?"

May said, "Yes."

Lou held up a little rock sculpture of an owl and said, "Don't worry about them. One of my ancestors fought in the Zaditorian Wars." He turned to May. "Can you harmonize?"

"Like singing?" she said. "No."

"Okay, never mind. There's a radar gun in the glove compartment. If the Zaditorians make any bubbles, point it at them. Radar collapses their bubbles. Too bad we didn't have any of those twenty-four thousand years ago." He nudged May and laughed as if she had anywhere near a frame of reference for his joke.

Although Lou sounded confident, I was still worried. I looked over at Em. Her eyes were big, and her mouth was ajar. "We'll be okay," I said, trying to sound confident. "We won't let those guys get us again."

"Back in Jersey," Lou said, "the winter break of my junior year, I snuck out with my buddies to meet some girls and go ice skating at night. Real romantic . . . ."

I was dumbstruck. What was he doing? We didn't have time for one of his stories. But then I saw him rubbing the little owl sculpture and realized that telling anecdotes about his formative years "back in Jersey" wasn't just a pastime for Lou or even a compulsion, it was his grafting technique. The owl was a totem, probably a facsimile of something that existed twenty-four thousand years ago, and he was grafting to it.

As he continued with the anecdote, he drove us through the sheet of rain spilling from the gutter. The engine roared, and we accelerated into the lawn, bypassing the driveway for a straight route to our escape, tearing up sod and sending it flying over and around us.

". . . Jimmy thought it was an owl pellet but no one told him it . . . ."

The windshield wipers streaked back and forth, clearing the mud and rain for brief moments, dissecting the world into frames. Then one of the frames was illuminated with yellow light, and the truck passed through me, leaving me behind, all of us, outside, encased in a globe of light, falling in slow motion. The air was elastic, like bread dough, but the rain, like the truck, had passed through unaffected, soaking my clothes in seconds.

In my periphery, I could see one of the Zaditorians holding out his arms as he had in the bakery the first time I'd been a victim of this trick. The truck, driverless and passenger-less, out of the bubble and no longer a ghost of itself, slammed into a tree across the driveway as all of us managed to get our feet under us before landing.

A strange sound came from Lou and grew and grew until I recognized it for Tuvan throat singing, or something like it. As far as I could tell, Lou had grafted to the owl totem in time and was now riding the Ghost of a twenty-four-thousand-year-old, inter-dimensional warrior. The singing became more rhythmic—rumbling, other-worldly notes, but no words that I could decipher. He sustained one note for several bars. As it reverberated around me, the globe of light vanished and the air lost its viscosity. We were free.

The Zaditorians stood prostrate, frozen, waves of transparency pulsing through them. Ahead, Warren and Caroline, the Marshals of the Mendocino Lodge, sprinted through the entrance of the driveway toward us. Lou stopped singing a moment to say, "Get to the truck."

Without hesitation, May, Em, and I ran through the

squishy lawn, across the driveway. The hood of the truck was smashed but there was no smoke. I hopped in the driver seat. The seatbelt alarm dinged as I turned the ignition. The truck started!

While Em and May climbed in, I glanced Lou's way. He was holding his own against two opponents, the three of them together performing an elaborate dance of punches and kicks.

The tires lost traction—but only for a moment—as I backed away from the tree. I threw it in drive, rolled up to the melee, and managed to clip Warren's hip with the front bumper, sending him to the ground hard. Lou used the opening to kick Caroline in the chest before diving into the bed of the truck. As I sped off, he yelled through the back window, "The gate is blocked! Take a right!"

I turned down the single-lane gravel road that had no outlet and drove as fast as I dared around the blind turns. Lou knocked on the back window, May opened it, and he slithered through the small opening with a diverse array of grunts.

"What now?" I said.

"There's a way out ahead," he said between loud gulps of air. "Keep driving."

We were all soaked, and I had to turn up the defrost to keep the windshield from fogging. Trees and underbrush lined the road. We passed the occasional driveway to other multi-acre plots. Though we were close to the ocean on this hill, snow had fallen once already, and patches of it remained in the shadows that went untouched by the low winter sun.

A mile or so down the road, Lou told me to slow down and turn into a small opening in the trees and underbrush. I yanked the wheel. Branches cracked and scraped against the truck as we bounced along what may have once been a road but was no longer. I had to keep a firm grip on the wheel. After twenty yards, we came to a small grassy meadow. Despite the four-wheel-drive, the truck spun out a few times in the sod before we reached a muddy driveway on the other side, which led to a paved street I recognized. We were on the south end of McKinleyville, by the reservation near Dow's Prairie. I'd lived in McKinleyville my whole life, but I'd never known there was this back way into Fieldbrook.

No one was on our tail. We'd escaped again. But any relief I felt was tempered with the knowledge that the Friends would just keep coming. Relentless. They would find me and my family wherever we went. I had to end this somehow.

"What do we do now?" I said.

"We go ahead with the plan," Lou said. "We get your girl out of Arampom, then . . . I don't know. I got some buddies back east I could call. I'm all wrapped up in this thing now too, so . . . I'll take care of it. These guys don't fool around. The hicks out here won't know what hit 'em. Trust me."

Lou had us drop him off in Arcata, the small college town a few miles south, so he could check on his son, make sure the Friends hadn't found his new apartment. He didn't want our help. "This is family stuff," he said.

"So you're just leaving us?" I said.

"You'll be fine. Act like you been here before. Get some dry clothes and meet me at the mall in an hour. We'll go to Arampom from there."

He and my sister hugged before he walked off through the rain.

While driving to the nearest store to buy some dry clothes for all of us, my mom called.

CHAPTER 16

WHEN MAY HAD TURNED eighteen, she'd filled out all the paperwork and jumped through all the hoops to become my legal guardian and free me from foster care. I remembered the day she'd picked me up, how happy I'd been. She was pregnant with Em and showing. The father was absent at the time, but he'd come back. I was just becoming a teenager, and she was trying to grow out of being one. We fought plenty, but we always made up, and she never gave up on me. I did well in school and stayed away from drugs, but I was a needy kid, and May worked, took classes at the community college, had to take care of a baby, and sometimes the father of that baby.

I'd been selfish and resentful sometimes.

When May had earned her associate's degree, she'd made a reservation at her favorite restaurant. Em's father didn't show up, and neither did I. I went to see a girl. And May celebrated her special day with two-year-old Em.

I cringed inside whenever I conjured the memory. I wasn't there for her then, but I was going to be there for her now.

"What can't wait?" May said after I got off the phone with Mom.

I'd pulled over sometime during the conversation. The sky was loosing hail, and the countless tiny impacts made a kind of loud static in my ears. "That was Mom," I said, raising my voice over the ice rocks banging against the metal roof. "The Friends went after Lonnie, that guy I told you about. Mom helped him escape, but he's leaving the area tonight, so we have to cure Em now."

That meant we'd miss Kaliah's window for escape that Lou had worked to create. But if I didn't take this opportunity now, Em could have Ghost Heart for the rest of her life.

May shook her head, looked out the window, and sighed. "I don't know this Lonnie guy and I'm supposed to trust him with my daughter? This isn't right. I don't like this."

"Mom trusts him."

"Mom's an addict, Charlie."

"Who's Lonnie?" Em said.

"He's someone who's going to help cure you so you don't have to take that terrible medicine anymore," I said.

"I don't mind," Em said.

"I know, but we may not always be able to get that medicine." Then to May, I said, "You didn't see Mom this time. She's clean, and she knows how serious this is. Here." I grabbed the samurai sword from the floorboard and unsheathed it an inch. "Let me show you what Mom showed me." I pressed my thumb against the naked part of the blade.

"What are you doing?!" May said.

I hissed, pulled my thumb back, and displayed the already trickling blood for my sister. In moments, the scrill gathered over the blood and dissipated, leaving the skin smooth and unmarked.

"Wow," Em said.

May opened her mouth but didn't say anything.

"This is what a rekulak can do," I said. "My training's been going great. I really think I can do this. I can cure Em."

"Did you see that, Mom?" Em said. "That was crazy. Do it again."

"No, Em," I said. "It's not fun. It hurts."

"You're like a superhero. This is crazy."

"You can't tell anyone about this. Not your friends or anyone."

"Oh my *God*. Who am I going to tell? I sit in a house all day and don't talk to anyone."

"Life's going to be back to normal soon. I promise."

May was solemn when she finally spoke. "Okay. Let's do it. Do you want me to tell Lou?"

"Sure," I said.

Then the guilt clamped onto my brain. Tonight was maybe the only opportunity to free Kaliah from her torturous confinement. She needed my help, and I was turning my back on her. I told myself that Em needed me more, that Lou could rescue Kaliah on his own, that I could help later if he failed, but still the guilt wouldn't let go. That was the price of the choice. I imagined my rekulak was gorging himself on this one.

Mom and Lonnie were held up at the Mad River Inn on the northern edge of Arcata, just off the highway, across from a shopping center. Fallen hail carpeted the ground and crunched beneath our feet as we walked through the parking lot between cloud bursts. We'd bought dry clothes at a thrift store and changed in the truck, but still, I was cold, and I could tell May and Em were too by how high they held their shoulders.

Em didn't have a relationship with her grandmothers. She'd met my mom twice since she was five. And she was too young when she met her dad's mom to remember. Though I didn't have a grandma growing up either—one was dead and the other was attached to an unknown father—I'd tried, based on what I'd heard from friends and seen in movies, to fill in that role for Em, to give her the grandma experience, spoiling her, lavishing her with treats and gifts on birthdays, holidays, and random occasions. So when we passed a vending machine in the lobby of the inn, and Em proclaimed in that kingly way that children do, "I'm hungry," I naturally bought her peanut M&Ms. And when May gave me a look, I naturally said, "What? They have protein in them."

We found the elevator around the corner from the lobby bar, which was half-full of loud men watching football. Mom's room was on the third floor, the top floor. Em insisted on pressing the button. Even though she was eleven now, she still got a little excited about elevators. There weren't many in Humboldt County.

As we walked down the hallway, searching for the right room number, I had a little hop in my step, despite the guilt I felt over Kaliah. I was finally taking some control over our situation. Once Em was healed, I would get my hands on a typewriter and manufacture an arsenal of Homunculus Totems. If Blanche or Warren, or any other Friends came after me and my family again, I'd destroy them with a thousand tiny cuts, a thousand unnoticeable cracks in my rekulak's mirror. My enemies would start waking up with minor ailments and major inconveniences: a rash and car trouble, vertigo and a dispute over property lines. I'd attack their bank accounts, their credit scores, their vital records, and expose them to identity theft. I'd bury their cult in bad luck and make sure they knew I was responsible. They'd learn to fear me.

Mom answered the door and hugged each of us as we went in. She'd rented a suite with a small kitchen and living space. Hanging on the wall was a painting of a cottage with flowering trees and shrubs in the front yard. It reminded me of the painting we'd had when I was a kid before my mom was declared unfit by the state.

Mom was nervous. I could tell by her smile and all the extra breath that came out when she talked. She commented on May's weight, and May nodded and managed a tight-lipped smile that didn't reach her eyes. Em offered her grandma an M&M, and Mom accepted it with a gleeful chortle.

"Where's Lonnie?" I said.

"In the adjoining room," Mom said. "I'll get him in a minute. I just want to talk to my kids alone first."

I wondered where Lonnie and Mom had gotten the money for two adjoining suites in the Mad River Inn, which wasn't a shabby place for the area, but I didn't ask. She told us to sit on the couch, and we did, and she sat in one of the chairs, on the edge, elbows on knees, hands pressed together, pointing downward as if she were praying to the floor. Her legs vibrated, and I realized she wasn't nervous at all. She was excited, giddy.

"I know you don't think I was a good mother," she said, "but . . . . Are you familiar with the mobiak concept of grace?"

"I am," I said.

May shook her head.

"Basically," Mom said, giving herself the wrap-it-up signal, "it's the belief that the more perspectives you have, the closer you'll be to the truth, the closer you'll be to grace." Her words poured out at a high clip. "And it ties into Arawok and the seven stomachs and how we may or may not be digestive enzymes, and on and on. But that's the problem about perspectives, darlings. Everyone has one. It's like that parable about the blind men trying to figure out what an elephant is. One man describes a tail, one describes a trunk, another describes an ear, and they're all right, but they don't have the whole picture. Now imagine the whole world is blind, which isn't far off, and some people believe the tail guy, and others believe the ear guy, and they form factions and go to war, and so on. You get my point. All of these perspectives don't help us get to the truth, they keep us from it. You see? But that's all about to end. Because of you, my beautiful children, and my beautiful granddaughter. My job as your mother wasn't to be your best friend. My job was to raise you to make a better world. I know you don't believe me now, but everything I did, I did to prepare you to save the world. And now here we are. Now you're going to show us all what that damn elephant looks like."

"Ohhh-*kay*," May said, standing up and pointing at Mom.

"I've heard enough. I can't believe I thought I could trust you. You're just as crazy as ever. We're leaving. Come on, Em."

While May took Em's hand, Mom stood and strode to the adjoining room's door and knocked.

I understood why May was upset. Mom's manic episodes had pocked our childhood. I remembered Mom keeping me up on school nights with her diatribes. At the time, it had made me feel important, special, like an adult. I'd tried following her logic, but it was like a twig floating in a river, vanishing in rapids and waterfalls, only to pop up again two hundred yards downstream.

To me, and I considered myself an expert, Mom wasn't having an episode, and even if she was, I didn't want to leave without seeing Lonnie. He'd shown me what a rekulak could do. This could be our only chance to cure Em, and I didn't want to waste it.

"May," I said. "Just wait."

I wonder sometimes now if I hadn't tried to stop her, would she have been able to get away?

She turned and looked at me, dumbfounded, like she couldn't believe I still wanted to go through with this. Then the door to the adjoining room opened. Shirley, the cocker spaniel, came through first, wagging her tail, then Lonnie, in his leather vest, holding some fancy green drink with a straw and a miniature umbrella in it.

When Warren walked through the door, wearing his perpetual smirk, a little sack of panic ruptured inside my stomach, sending tingling shockwaves to my ears and fingertips.

CHAPTER 17

I SHOUTED TO MAY, "Run!" Then I dove at Warren's knees. He hopped to one side, avoiding the brunt of my attack. From the floor, I latched onto one of his legs and pulled until he fell, cursing. He twisted his leg free and wriggled around to my back. While May and Em escaped into the hallway, he wrapped an arm around my neck and his legs around my legs. His clothes were still wet from fighting Lou in the rain. He whispered in my ear, "Silly duck. I told you a storm was coming. Tranquil pond begone. The seagulls are here with their oceanly ways."

Again with the duck pond crap. Had Naomi told me the truth about poisoning him? Would he help me if I asked him? As incredible as that sounded, the guy did appear to be under the influence of one of Naomi's metaphor spells.

I wanted to tell him that he was a swan and the king of

the duck pond, that I was one of his subjects, and he had to protect me from the invading seagulls, but I couldn't make a sound. I couldn't even breathe. He'd sunk his forearm under my chin, against my throat. I watched from the floor, helpless, like a turtle on its back, as square-shouldered Caroline pushed my sister back into the room. One side of May's face was red. The Zaditorians entered next, the bearded one carrying Em, followed by Sheryl/Blanche, who still had bleach-blond hair.

The bald Zaditorian crouched beside me and pried one of my hands loose from Warren's forearm and cupped it in his. My hand felt cold, then what looked like black air seeped through his fingers, and he let go, leaving an inky black bubble around my hand. I tried to bring my hand back to the arm that was still choking me, but my hand was stuck in midair, stuck within the bubble, no matter how hard I pulled. Warren released me from his chokehold, but my hand remained imprisoned. As I coughed and wheezed, sucking air as fast as I could, Blanche/Sheryl said, "Leave now. Everyone," and Warren, Caroline, Lonnie, with Shirley in tow, left the room before I had enough air to talk, to try out my theory on the duck pond metaphor. Mom stayed.

I sat up but could do little more than that with my hand trapped where it was. The bald Zaditorian finished installing a black bubble around my sister's hand as Blanche/Sheryl crouched in front of me, smiling. "Hello, Charlie," she said.

The bearded Zaditorian held Em a few feet away from May, but he did not imprison one of Em's hands. Em looked angry, not scared, which surprised me. Mom stood behind Blanche, looking down on me with pride in her eyes like I'd just graduated preschool. "Why?" I said to her.

"Everything I've done is to make you the hero you are about to become," she said.

"Everything?" I said, not trying to hide the disdain I felt for her right then. "So the heroin addiction, the child abuse, that was all part of the plan, huh?"

"You had to be damaged psychologically for reasons you won't understand now."

I was speechless as I tried to wrap my head around her absurd claim. The trauma I'd experienced as a child had been by design? Was that possible? A thought occurred to me: she had taught me how to type so I could do her job while she got high, and typing had been strangely integral to my rekulak training. Could she have known? Had that been her plan? No, that was crazy.

"I feel terrible about what we've done to you," Blanche/Sheryl said. "And I feel sick when I think about what happens next. And I know you probably don't believe that, but I care deeply for you. We're family. I'm your grandmother, Charlie. I practically raised you. My empathy is real. When you hurt, I hurt."

"It's true," Mom said. "She was regurgitated before you were born, but I saved her blood and totem and used them to bring her back. She saw you grow up, both of you. I'm sorry but this was the only way."

How could I believe a word my mom said? Her lies had led me here. She was either a collaborator or a full-blown member of a group that had poisoned her own granddaughter. "The only way for what?" I said. "Say everything you say is true. You were or pretended to be, a heroin addict in order to ruin my childhood? Why? To what end?"

"You should go now, Sweetie," Blanche/Sheryl said to my mom. "Call when everyone reaches a safe distance."

I looked to my sister. When I saw she was calm, I felt a little flutter of hope. Maybe she knew something I didn't. Maybe she had texted Lou and told him where we would be.

"Bye my children," Mom said, and went to the door. Before she left, she looked back at me, and I looked away. I didn't know if I should hate her or pity her, if she was evil or insane. I didn't know what was real.

Blanche/Sheryl snapped her fingers, and the bald Zaditorian pulled out a phone and began filming me and Blanche/Sheryl, as he had at the bakery.

"I have traveled the seven stomachs and conquered death to be here today," Blanche/Sheryl said, standing and adopting an oratorical tone. "I have toiled—so long I have toiled—to build an arc that will hold every soul in every stomach, not to save them from God's wrath, but to carry them to God's door. Today, we begin filling that arc. Today is a glorious day."

She waved at the Zaditorian, and he put his phone away. Looking down at me, she said, in a more conversational tone, "I need you to understand something, Charlie. I'm not evil. My position in this world, or any other, is precarious. Arawok sees me as a disease, a threat. If I inhabit a body too long, Arawok finds me and expels me. The second I inhabit more than one mobiak body, Arawok finds me and expels me. You have never been vomited into the void, but trust me when I say it is frightening. I am tired of being frightened.

"I need to inhabit Em's body. But don't be alarmed. She will have it back as long as you do what I ask. There is a catch, though. Remember the first time we met, when you aroused a mob, and you ran away before I had the chance to explain myself? Because you did that, I was unable to put Em through the Untethering, as I did for you when I put you away in that dark tank full of water. Remember? And now the flood is almost here, and there's no time to Untether your sister from Em, which means, when I inhabit Em's body, I will also inhabit her mother's. I never wanted to kill May. She's my own granddaughter for Harold's sake, but you forced my hand, and the Zaditorians can only shield one of us at a time from Arawok's vomit reflex. And I can't bring any more Zaditorians into this stomach until you do what I ask. And you can't do what I ask until I have Em's body. It's a sort of gift-of-the-magi deal. I'm so sorry. The guilt you're going to feel for rescuing them that night is going to be tremendous. Just know that I will feel that guilt vicariously. When you hurt, I hurt."

"What is she talking about, Charlie?" May said.

I didn't know if Blanche was trying to scare us, or if she was truly going to kill my sister, but we were at her mercy, and I was desperate. I started yelling, "Help! Help!" as loud as I could, and yanked on the black bubble as hard as I could, but the bubble didn't budge.

Blanche/Sheryl had a pained look on her face while I yelled. She took a phone out of her purse, looked at it, then nodded at the bald Zaditorian, who pulled a syringe full of dark liquid from his coat and walked over to Em. "Charlie!" May shouted. I yanked on my bubble. I kicked it. May started yelling for help with me. Em squirmed, but the bearded Zaditorian held her firmly by her shoulders. May reached for a table, grabbed a lamp, and threw it at the bald Zaditorian. It bounced off his shoulder and shattered on the floor, but that didn't stop him from plunging the syringe into Em's arm. Em yelped.

The bearded Zaditorian released her, but she just stood there, silent. She didn't try to run. And her eyes were vacant as the Zaditorians backed away from her on either side, spreading their arms. A transparent green bubble eight feet in diameter appeared around Em, glowing, coloring the whole room in green light.

Blue, foamy scrill exuded from my skin and circulated in on itself, shades of it spinning and darting like shadows in a tide pool. I could see it above my eyes, on the verge of falling, but always flowing back in.

May dropped to her knees. "Em, are you okay?" she said. "What's happening, Charlie?" Her head bowed. A pained expression was on her face. "Help me," she said. "I can't see. Help me. Charlie. It hurts." She let out a deep, throaty groan, then her body went limp and hung from the bubble, like bait on a hook.

"No!" I cried out. "May! May! No no no no no."

Blanche/Sheryl fell to the floor next, landing with a thud, like a puppet whose strings had been cut. Scrill continued to churn on the surface of my skin. My clothes were sodden with it.

The green bubble disappeared.

Em's eyes were no longer vacant . . . and they were no longer hers. She arranged her eyebrows to convey the maximum amount of empathy and stepped toward me, stopping in front of Sheryl's lifeless body. "I know you just lost your sister," Blanche/Em said with Em's voice. "But you can still save your niece."

I glanced at my sister hanging from the black bubble and

jerked my head away. She was just hanging there. Gone. "Let her down," I said, fighting back the imminent wave of sobs. I yelled, "Let her down!"

The bearded Zaditorian went to her and put his hands on her black bubble. I turned away. I couldn't watch her drop. I couldn't hear it either. I put one ear against the black bubble and covered the other ear with my free hand. And I wept.

When the convulsive sobs grew further apart, a faded aquamarine Tupperware bowl—my faded green Tupperware bowl—was placed on the floor in front of me. The Tupperware lid was removed, revealing the sourdough starter that had been in my family for generations.

CHAPTER 18

BLANCHE/EM CUPPED HER HANDS in front of her chest. "Look at all that scrill! Your rekulak's trying to protect you from my cackle. This is why I needed Em's body. She's the only one who can produce enough of my cackle to get through to you. Your rekulak will block most of it, but there will be enough inside you for you to enter the whorl of the sourdough starter. There's a typewriter inside, on the desk, along with a mortgage contract. I want you to type out that mortgage contract, just like Lonnie taught you. And that's it. Once you're done, Em can have her body back."

"Where is she now?" I couldn't look at my niece's face knowing she wasn't the one in control of it.

"She's in here. She's fine. Just waiting on you."

"Is May dead?" I already knew the answer, but I

desperately wanted to be mistaken.

"Yes, unfortunately. But you can still save Em. Don't forget that. It's real easy. I give you bloom. You graft to the totem, do some typing. All done. Easy as pie."

I held out my hand for the bloom while keeping my eyes down and fixed on the sourdough starter. One of the Zaditorian's feet shuffled into view. I felt something cold and wet drop onto my palm, then a surge of pain and voices all over my body, voices talking nonsense, Zelda's the loudest among them.

I felt stupid grafting, saying my stupid Pictionary poems—Pillow Case Concussion, Mattress Fort Collapse . . . . But I said them for Em's sake, and the graft took, and I found myself sitting in a large room with a vaulted ceiling and a wall of bay windows that looked out onto a turbulent ocean and a sky thick with dark clouds. A door opened behind me, and the sound of footsteps mingled with the crackling fire to my right. Not far from the fireplace was a typewriter on an ornate and imposing antique desk.

I sat in a leather chair, wearing a pink polka dot dress, a new aquamarine Tupperware on my lap, open and full of sourdough starter. The smell of yeast and fermenting flour mixed with the smell of leather from the chair.

May had always doubted I could smell the difference between our family's sourdough starter and others. She'd always threatened to put me to the test but never had, as if she were afraid of bursting my bubble.

A young man stepped into my eye line. He wore a leather vest and jeans and Lonnie's belt buckle. I studied the face and recognized the eyes. This was Lonnie as a young man. He still had baby fat in his cheeks.

"What's that for?" he said, pointing to the starter.

I ignored the question and set the starter on an end table next to a plate that held a knife and fork and a cheese danish. And I remembered the words of the prisoner from Arampom, "The secret to defeating the Memoirist lies beyond the cheese danish in the whorl of the sourdough starter." And here it was. But what had the prisoner meant by *beyond?* Did I have to ride this whorl, endure its pain past a certain point? Did I have to leave this room? Or did I have to wait for a server to come and take the cheese danish away? Or did I have to eat it?

Whatever the vague instructions meant, that wasn't what I was here for. If I typed the mortgage contract, as Blanche had asked, she would let Em have her body back. So that was what I was going to do.

I left the cheese danish and the sourdough starter, and I went to sit at the typewriter. I felt the pain of the whorl slip away. This was not the path.

"What are you doing?" Lonnie said.

"Leave," I said.

"You called me here."

"Leave."

Lonnie left without another word.

Usually, when I veered off course in a whorl, avoiding the pain, I would be inundated with the ancestor's life stories. But that wasn't happening.

In her first body, Blanche was an oshara, like Em, the rarest kind of mobiak. Maybe they had the power to create whorls where their stories were hidden from visitors.

May was dead.

I started to cry again. I felt ashamed but didn't try to stop.

May was dead because of me. I'd convinced her to trust Mom. I'd brought her to the inn. I'd made all the wrong choices. Would she still be alive now if I hadn't rescued her that night at the bakery? Was Blanche telling the truth about that? What was real? Mom claimed her heroin abuse had been an act, part of some elaborate plan to manipulate me. She claimed Blanche was my grandmother. How could I believe anything she said? She'd sacrificed her daughter. For what? For Blanche? For some cult? For some notion of saving the world?

She was the worst kind of monster. She had a cause.

As I began transcribing the mortgage contract on the desk, I heard Zelda's voice in my head: *Stop typing. You have a choice.*

I was used to hearing voices in my head by then, but Zelda's was so clear and sharp and unexpected, it startled me. "How did you get in my head?" I said out loud.

Rather a stupid question. You put me here.

"You can just talk whenever you want?"

That sounded vaguely fascist. But no, only when your cackle is up. For now, anyway.

"For now?"

I'm sorry about your sister and niece. You need to know that Em is gone too.

"I don't know that."

Nothing can survive Blanche's cackle, except a Sojourner.

"I have to try." I was on the verge of more tears. I refused to believe Em was gone too.

This whorl is Blanche's link to Zaditor. It's full of their magic. I can smell it. She's used it to manipulate the whorl. There are only two ways out: do what she wants, or ride the Ghost. If you do what she wants, it will mean the end of reality as we know it, in this world and all worlds. You have to ride the Ghost out of here.

"How does typing a mortgage contract end reality?"

Don't lie to yourself, Charlie. You're not just typing, are you? You're summoning your rekulak. If you leave a corruption of that behind in here, your rekulak will be trapped in this whorl—one of its fingers anyway—watching you type loop after loop. Rekulaks exist outside and inside of Time and Space. They can go wherever and whenever they want. By trapping a finger in Blanche's whorl, you will make Blanche immune to Arawok's vomit reflex. And the disease that she has become will spread everywhere, change everything.

I couldn't believe that. If I believed that, then Em was dead. But Em was still alive. And she needed my help. I started typing again.

Stop, Charlie! Listen to me. Do you think it's a coincidence that a cheese danish is sitting on the table over there? Here? Now? I know your pain, Charlie. You created me with it. Blanche and your mother manipulated you. They made the cheese danish the symbol of your pain, your weakness, because it existed here before your birth, in this whorl. To you, the cheese danish might as well be the Great Wall of China. Your pain was built to keep you from going beyond a certain point in this whorl. They're using your weakness, a weakness they created, to hide their own, whatever that is. You have to overcome.

As farfetched as Zelda's assertions sounded, they made sense. The cheese danish had been at the center of my childhood trauma. And now it was here in the worst moment of my life. And the prisoner had told me it would be here. This wasn't a coincidence. Maybe Blanche was trying to hide something from me beyond it. I couldn't trust her. I knew that.

Zelda was right. Em was gone too. After Blanche had

been done with Sheryl's body, it had fallen to the floor, lifeless, a spent balloon. Sheryl had not returned to it. Em would not return to hers. I couldn't think of what that meant. I kept it an abstract concept in my mind, because if I touched it, if I attached any kind of thought to it, I wouldn't be able to function. Em was a cupboard of fire to me now. Opening a drawer would only make the fire spread, and I wouldn't be able to breathe.

I got up and went back to the leather chair, a soundtrack of encouraging words from Zelda playing in my head, and I placed the sourdough starter back in my lap. While I waited for the loop to restart, I went through my foundation gestures, searching for the pain. By the time young Lonnie came back into the room, I'd found it in tapping the quick Blanche had inserted into her heel to imprint this whorl.

"Why are you tapping the quick?" Lonnie said.

"Partly a backup plan," I said, following the pain, "in case you fail me. And partly because I want to preserve the look on your face for my future selves."

"What look? What are you talking about?"

"How did you do it? Some Sojourner trick?"

"How did I do what?" Lonnie crossed his arms over his chest, widened his stance, and rocked from side to side.

"We searched that whole tomb. We found the totem, but no book." I frowned. "Odd. So odd. We even searched you. Remember? Where did you hide it? Did you go back for it later?"

"I can't hide something that doesn't exist."

"Denial is such a powerful tool if you have the gall for it. People want to believe people. I'm sure it has been useful for you your whole life." I sighed and shook my head. "We found the book. Has anyone ever told you you look like a rat?"

Lonnie's face twitched, and I smiled and reached for the cheese danish on the table. The moment my fingertips touched it, I felt intense pain throughout my whole body, like my blood had turned to acid. I screamed, jumped back, tumbled over the arm of the chair, and hit the floor, where I writhed and whimpered. I'd worked hard to build up my pain tolerance, but I was not prepared for this. I was helpless, exposed. I would have done anything to ease the pain. If just touching the danish did this, there was no way I could go any further in this whorl, no way I was riding this Ghost.

As soon as I thought of the typewriter, the pain lessened. I crawled toward it like it was an oasis in a desert. The pain lessened. I climbed the chair and pushed my fingers into the keys. The pain lessened. Zelda protested loudly in my head, but I focused on the contract, focused on the typing. Her voice faded with the pain, faded with my thoughts, and I was lost in the oblivion of now.

Then I smelled menthol and strawberries. A pool of blue mold appeared on the floor. My rekulak's head emerged, but nothing more. The graft broke, the room dissolved, and I was back in the suite at the Mad River Inn.

There was a black bubble on my other hand now. The Zaditorians crouched on either side of me and helped me stand by lifting the bubbles that I couldn't budge.

"I can already feel it, Charlie," Blanche said. "You did so well. Thank you."

"Now give Em her body back," I said.

Blanche patted me on the shoulder, then turned and walked out of the suite. I yelled after her, but she didn't come back. The Zaditorians lifted me by the black bubbles, and I looked at May's body one last time as they carried me out. I stifled tears. I knew she was gone, that the body on the floor was no longer her, but I felt like I was leaving her, like she would be lonely here without her family.

The Zaditorians dragged me down the hall to the elevator. I yelled for Blanche, yelled for help. No one came. When the Zaditorians carried me past the lobby bar, I saw why. The TV was still playing football, but the men had stopped talking, their bodies slumped over the bar or laying on the floor. I called to them. They didn't move. They had been regurgitated along with my sister.

CHAPTER 19

THE ZADITORIANS PUT ME in the backseat of a car, and one sat on either side of me, holding my bubble-hands. A woman I never saw before was in the driver's seat. I saw her check me out through the rearview mirror, but she didn't speak. I didn't ask where we were going. I didn't care. May and Em were dead because I was too stupid and weak to save them. I thought about suicide, and it kept me from crying.

We drove almost an hour south, past the population center of the county, to where giant redwoods lined the highway so thick and so tall in places they left only a narrow strip of sky visible overhead. We turned east off the highway, then south, then east again onto a narrow and windy road that followed a tributary of the Eel River, the same road Kaliah and I had taken to Arampom. It cut through the side of the mountains. It had no guardrails. There was a steep drop to the muddy and tumultuous waters below, running high and fast with the winter rains. Fallen rocks were strewn across the road in places. I stopped thinking about suicide and committed myself to revenge.

May and Em were dead.

The grief came in waves, as if it knew I could only take so much at a time. My throat ached as I stifled sobs.

We caught up to a line of slow-moving cars. Around one of the bends, I could see a sporty little Honda at the head of the line. I estimated twenty cars were stuck behind it. But no one honked. As we drove, more cars lined up behind us.

The trees were more sparse here, and smaller—second- and third-growth firs and pines. The road climbed away from the river a few miles before descending into a small round valley, where dozens of identical white houses had been built in neat little rows with neat little yards, around a small school with a football field. The river skirted around the southern edge of the valley and cut across the eastern third. On the other side was a mill and what looked like a town center, with a handful of larger commercial buildings. Between the town and the surrounding mountains were pastures and farmland.

Arampom.

When we hit the valley floor, the road straightened out, and we traveled for a mile, past grazing sheep and cows, before the whole line of cars stopped. Two hundred yards ahead and fifty yards in the air, there was something new: a cloud of flying birds, perpendicular to the road and stretched out on either side as far as I could see. Their cries mixed like shards of glass and metal in a blender. Under the cloud was the line of one-room concrete buildings, spaced a hundred yards apart. But now their construction was finished, and there was a person inside each one, or at least in the ones I could see in.

We inched forward slowly. Bird carcasses littered the ground between guard buildings, forming a morbid and grotesque moat. In the moat and in the air above the moat, I identified ravens, buzzards, hawks, owls, quail, sparrows . . . .

A woman standing in the road, eating an apple, was stopping and inspecting each car before letting them pass. When our turn came, my driver powered down the window, and the woman poked her head inside, looked at me, smiled, and said, "Welcome, Charlie. No need to lift the gate for you. Just roll on through." I'd never seen her before. She went back to her post in the road and waved us forward. As we passed her, fresh scrill surfaced on my skin and swirled for the next forty yards, then went stagnant.

We drove to the school. The parking lot was full. People were filing into the gymnasium. We found a spot across the street, and the Zaditorians awkwardly ushered me out of the car, holding my bubbles. Dry scrill sloughed off me.

As we crossed the street, walking toward the gymnasium, I spotted Kaliah standing in a cluster of five people, chatting. Her hair was held up in pins, and she wore a purple Victorian-style dress, like she'd just performed, or was about to perform, in a play of manners set in the late 19th century.

Despite my grief, I was happy and excited to see her, which made me feel guilty. "Kaliah!" I said.

She turned. Recognition flared in her eyes, then sorrow, then nothing. She turned away. "Kaliah!" I called again, but she ignored me. As the Zaditorians escorted me past her, I called her over and over but succeeded only in getting the attention of those she was with. Kayak Brad was among them. He smiled at me.

I'd known Kaliah was being tortured, being chiseled into a living sculpture. But seeing it firsthand was different. Kayak Brad's smile sparked hatred and rage in me that felt powerful and good compared to my grief. I gave in to the feelings and lost control, violently throwing my body around like a wild animal in a trap. I cursed Brad and promised retribution. But his smile only broadened.

I was dragged by the black bubbles for a bit before I calmed and put my feet back under me. People were staring. I was the only one around with bubbles around my hands. I was the only one throwing a fit. I composed myself. I'd never felt so alone.

The gymnasium had a decent number of people inside, their combined chatter sounding hollow in such a large space. The potent smell of treated hardwood floor reminded me of high school football rallies. But the general mood here, judging by faces and body language, reminded me more of a funeral.

I was led to the center of the basketball court and sat in one of four metal folding chairs arranged behind a microphone on a stand, facing the bleachers. The Zaditorians stood behind me. They'd rested my bubbles on the tops of my thighs. I watched people finding their seats. I saw Hugo Sinclair, Kaliah's brother, and when he saw me, I slowly looked away. *Traitor.*

Kaliah came and sat in the chair farthest from me, and Brad and his bond, Meadow filled the seats between. Kaliah would not look at me. I didn't bother to call her name again. I avoided looking at Brad. He would get what he deserved, as soon as I got these bubbles off my hands and found a typewriter.

When the audience settled in and was silent, my childhood therapist, Nancy, who was also Brad's mom and the Prime Nabob, walked to the microphone, wearing a Christmas sweater, and spoke: "Welcome mobiaks of the Humboldt and Mendocino Lodges. I'm afraid that you've all been lured here under false pretenses, under the notion that there was an imminent war with Zaditor on the horizon. And for that, I apologize, but that was the best option available to us at the time."

A murmur rippled through the crowd, but the Prime Nabob continued: "This is a historic day. Some of you may know of Blanche Duluth, and others may not. A little background: Blanche was born an oshara, a very rare breed as all of you know, in Boonville. An intelligent child, she spoke her first word at the age of one, when she pointed to a glass of ice water and remarked, 'Entropy.' Her intelligence was rivaled only by her emotional capacity. She was especially sensitive to the suffering of others, and at the age of five, she made a vow to end all suffering forever. Now, eighty years later, thanks to her tireless efforts, we are on the precipice of realizing Blanche's dream.

"She discovered early on that if she could unite every living thing in every stomach, not only would we live in harmony, but we would rise up to be a God, together. The obvious vehicle for such an ambitious endeavor was nemaloki cackle, but, as many of you know, when the cackle of a mobiak is tainted by the cackle of a nemaloki, Arawok will regurgitate that cackle. However, earlier today—" The Prime Nabob pointed a hand toward me. "—Blanche's grandson,

Charlie Allison, a young Sojourner, was able to make Blanche immune to Arawok's vomit reflex, a truly historic feat, freeing Blanche's cackle to spread throughout the seven stomachs.

"Unfortunately, for those of you gathered here today, your suffering will continue. You will not be united with Blanche, along with this stomach and the rest, because she has bestowed upon each of you a great burden and a great honor, and that is to chronicle and critique—yes I said critique—Blanche Duluth's glorious rise. And for that purpose, your perspectives must remain independent."

I saw what looked like resignation on some of the faces in the crowd, Hugo's among them, like everything the Prime Nabob said was old news. But on the majority of faces, I saw shock and bewilderment. I tried to avoid eye contact. They would blame me for whatever came next.

"The mummers have been relocated to the monastery, freeing the housing for you all," the Prime Nabob went on, motioning to a group of people standing around boxes stacked near one corner of the bleachers. The people began opening the boxes. "Each of you will be placed in a house with roommates and given an assignment according to your strengths. To get you started, you will all be receiving a copy of Blanche Duluth's latest memoir, *Teatime with Arawok: My Humble Journey to Omnipotence.*"

The group pulled books out of the boxes and walked up and down the bleacher aisles, passing them out. "For your own safety and independence," the Prime Nabob said, "you will not be permitted to leave this valley. Some of you may be wondering what you saw when you drove in today. That is the Wall of Blanche. In those little houses are the previous Mummer Wardens who are now infected by Blanche and are spreading her cackle up and out, surrounding this town day and night. I assure you if you try to cross the wall, you will be united with Blanche. For those of you who cannot handle your new responsibilities, this option is always open to you.

"My son, Brad is the new Mummer Warden, and I have the utmost confidence in his ability to control the growing mummer population. His shanika, Meadow, is in charge of the tributes. You will be having one-on-ones with her shortly. As for keeping order in the town of Arampom, Blanche has brought in Zaditorians from our sister stomach. They're standing by the door there, and behind Charlie here. They haven't walked the earth in many many millennia. Let's give them a warm welcome, shall we?"

The Prime Nabob began clapping, but only the people who were handing out the books joined her.

The crowd, which had kept it together to that point, erupted with guffaws and inarticulate cries of protest. A young woman sitting next to Hugo in the front row stood up and began singing a soulful song in a language I'd never heard before. She was tall and thin, with a buzz cut. Hugo reached out and grabbed her wrist, but she yanked it free and stepped forward, singing and holding up a little statue of an owl similar to the one Lou had grafted to earlier in the day, which seemed so long ago now. Determination showed in her eyes.

"Oh Rhonaya," the Prime Nabob said in the tone of a disappointed mother. "Someone please stop her."

The Zaditorians by the door started to run toward Rhonaya, but they were too late. She was already riding the Ghost, her voice shifting to the unique throat singing I'd heard from Lou. The Zaditorians fell to their knees, covering their ears, all except my Zaditorian guardians, Baldy and

Beardo. They walked forward with bright yellow bubbles around their heads. Black, spider-like creatures crawled partially out of the bubbles and rested their legs on the Zaditorians' shoulders. The Zaditorians each formed a large green bubble around one of their hands, and out of these shot milky-white flippers five times the diameter of their arms. The flippers came to a point with a yellow claw, and on either side of that were two flat thumbs, also pointed with yellow claws. The Zaditorians swiped at Rhonaya with the flippers, but she flipped, twisted, and ducked out of the way. Her throat-singing adopted a faster rhythm and took large leaps in pitch. Just as the color of the bubbles began to fade, one of the flippers wrapped around Rhonaya's waist and lifted her into the air. She cried out briefly before her body went limp. I couldn't tell if she was dead or unconscious. The crowd gasped.

After she was carried away, the other Zaditorian, Baldy, retracted his creepy flipper and spider head, dispersed his bubbles, and resumed his place behind me.

The Prime Nabob made a few closing remarks, but I couldn't focus enough to listen, and I don't think anyone else could either.

When the talking stopped, Baldy grabbed me by the bubbles and led me back to the car. The sun had set, and the sky was nearly dark. We drove to a little white house on a street full of little white houses. There were no cars on the street and no neighbors moving in. They were all lingering at the gymnasium, prolonging the inevitable.

Baldy took me in the house—which was modestly furnished—dispersed my bubbles, and left, but not before leaving a copy of Blanche's latest memoir on the coffee table.

As I wiggled my newly freed fingers, I contemplated suicide again. I went to the kitchen, found a knife, and held it to my wrist. One slice and I could end all of this. I could free my rekulak, and Blanche would no longer be immune to Arawok's vomit reflex. Sure, everyone she'd infected since this afternoon would be regurgitated with her, just like my sister and those poor people at the inn were, but at least the infection would stop spreading. One slice and I could save the world.

Killing yourself won't free Craig, Zelda said inside my head. *Your rekulak, I mean. I hope you don't mind, I named him after my first kiss. And if you want to free him, you have to go back to the sourdough starter whorl. Killing yourself will just trap him there forever.*

"How did you get in my head?" I said out loud. "I haven't taken any bloom?"

I'm a little more independent now.

"What does that mean?"

Open the door.

"What?"

Open the front door and I'll show you.

I tossed the knife on the counter, went to the front door, and opened it to find a small gray and white fox sitting on the porch, looking up at me. *Hello,* Zelda said.

CHAPTER 20

ZELDA WALKED DIRECTLY TO the kitchen, her little claws tapping on the linoleum. *Anything to eat?* she said.

"I don't know." My mouth hung open. "How . . . ? Is this normal?"

No, but you're a Sojourner. Nothing's normal with you. When you fouled up in that whorl, I got trapped in there with Craig. We had a moment. I don't know how to explain it, but he offered me an out. The details were pretty murky because I don't exactly speak Craig, but I took the chance and ended up here.

"Just now?"

A few hours ago.

Watching Zelda sniff around the kitchen, I felt an intense pang of guilt. I had created her. She was a sentient tapestry of whorls stitched together by my pain, and now she was in a fox's body, a freak. She didn't ask for this.

Zelda's laughter echoed through my mind. *I'm not Frankenstein's monster, Charlie, and I'm not having an existential crisis. You didn't create me. You created a vessel through which I can choose to express myself. So whatever you do, don't waste your time feeling sorry for me. The afterlife is a crazy place. You can't even imagine. You become an amalgam thing. This here, me being a fox, is just one aspect of me, and it's an aspect that's starving. I tried catching a mouse earlier, but it was way too hard.*

The refrigerator and cupboards were stocked with food. Sitting patiently on the floor, Zelda made me list everything I found, then requested what seemed like half of it. I talked her down to five courses—mashed potatoes, sardines, pickles, chocolate milk, and a quesadilla made with corn tortillas. While I boiled the potatoes, I realized I was hungry too and made a bean taco for myself. I put Zelda's food in five separate dishes, per her instructions, and set them on the floor, and we ate together. I couldn't help smiling at the feelings of joy coming from her, and the awkward way she ate pickles. She complained about how little chocolate milk I'd given her and acted offended when I told her chocolate was bad for dogs and most likely foxes too.

"I don't really understand what happened in that hotel room," I said, "what happened in that whorl."

I know. A piece of sardine fell out of her mouth onto the floor while she chewed. *It's a lot to take in all at once. When nemaloki cackle is combined with the cackle of an oshara like Blanche, whose cackle is constantly spreading, that cackle becomes a disease that can infect anybody. It's a disease of the mind, of personality. It turns people, anyone, into Blanche, basically. It gives her control of them. Arawok, or God, or Nature, or whatever you want to call it, has a natural defense against this. It vomits the infection into the void. Or however you want to describe it. The point is, it gets rid of it. Zelda* moved on to the quesadilla, trying to flip the whole thing into her mouth at once. *Now here's where you come in. There are seven stomachs, or worlds, right? Seven worlds and the void. And one of the only things that can travel through these worlds is a rekulak. Now forgive me but we have to use the stomach metaphor for this next part. It's going to be gross but it's the easiest way to picture this. Imagine your rekulak is an infinitely long string passing through all seven stomachs, extending out from the anus and the mouth for infinity. When you left a corruption of yourself summoning your rekulak inside of Blanche's whorl, you attached her to the string, changed its nature. As long as your corruption is typing inside her whorl, Blanche will be part of the string. And it won't matter how much Arawok tries to regurgitate her, more string will just keep coming up from the anus for eternity, and she will have access to all of the stomachs, and there is nothing Nature or Arawok can do about it. She's infecting this stomach, this world now. And she'll move onto the next one and the next one soon enough.*

"Okay. But why did my sister have to die?"

She wanted Em's body, an oshara's body to help her spread her disease. But more importantly, she needed the vast amount of cackle an oshara can produce to get through your rekulak's defenses so you could even enter her whorl in the first place. But mobiak cackle is always tethered to their mothers until they go through an untethering ceremony, which is what you went through in that deprivation tank when this all began. So when Blanche took over Em's body, she also took over May's, which caused May to be regurgitated into the void. Em was spared this fate because the Zaditorians were hiding her from Arawok's detection.

My head was swimming. On top of this, Blanche had used the Nabobs of the Lodge, like Nancy and Brad, to convince everyone who might have been able to stop her that there was an impending war with Zaditor, and Arampom was the safest place to wage that war. Every mobiak at the Lodge, every potential threat to her plan, had marched into their prison voluntarily.

After our meal, Zelda had me draw a bath, then jumped in before the tub was full. The water turned brown. I poured some soap in while the faucet ran, and bubbles stacked up around her little fox face. She closed her eyes halfway. *Ahhhh.*

I shut off the water, sat against the opposite wall, and gave her a few minutes of silence before saying, "I don't think I can do it. I don't think I can go back to that cheese danish whorl."

You have to. The fate of reality depends on it.

"The pain was too much."

It won't be next time. I'll help you. You get in, use your blood to free the corruption you left behind, like you did in my candy-dish whorl, then ride the Ghost out of there. Bob's your uncle, Craig will be freed and the world will be saved.

"But we don't have the totem. And we don't have Blanche's cackle."

We have the Wall of Blanche, don't we? I should say that's enough cackle to get past Craig's defenses. And I have a plan for the totem— two, actually, in case one goes wrong. We make the totem. There's no flour in this house but I'm sure I can find some somewhere. It takes what, five days for a sourdough starter to be viable? It won't be the same as your family's, but it might work. In the meantime, we plan our escape. If the new starter doesn't work, Naomi has a piece of the original, right? All she wants in exchange are Bruce and Pam. Well, Lou brought Bruce and Pam here, so they must be somewhere around. We can bring them to her.

"How do you know about all that?"

I know everything about you, Charlie. Up to the point I became a fox, at least. I lose you now if you are far away and not in pain.

She knew everything? The thought made me recoil. Sensing my discomfort, Zelda said, *I judge without condemnation, Charlie, and I love you unconditionally.*

Then I felt her love, genuine, warm, and beautiful. Tears welled in my eyes. I'd never needed a friend more than I did now, and I was surprised to find that I loved her too, this strange little fox in the bubbles that was so much more than that. I was so grateful I didn't question my feelings. I gave into them.

Bubbles floated into the air as Zelda leapt out of the tub. She shook her whole body, covering me in heavy drops of water, then rolled over and wiggled her butt on the rug before springing back up and shaking again.

"Hey!" I said.

The sooner we get this sourdough starter started the better. You get some rest. I'm going to go find some flour to steal.

"How?"

I'm a master thief, remember?

"But you don't have hands."

A challenge! Delight was in her eyes as she pranced out of the bathroom.

After opening the bathtub drain, I went out to the living room, where I found Zelda gone and the front door open. She'd opened it somehow, as if to show me she didn't need hands. The night air had already chilled the room. As I closed the door, I worried about her going out in the cold still wet from her bath, then realized foxes were built to withstand worse.

Feeling a sense of loss at her absence, I busied myself with the dishes but didn't make much progress before I heard a bang behind me over the running water and turned to see

Kayak Brad entering through the door I'd just closed. He wore a tight-fitting T-shirt, no jacket—despite the cold—and a flat-brimmed hat. He carried a staff. Kaliah came in behind him, still wearing that ridiculous Victorian dress.

Before I could even curse at Brad, he was taking long, swift strides toward me, devouring the distance between us. I didn't care if he had a stick. I would never run from this man. I threw two wet plates at him. He dodged one, and the other bounced off his shoulder before he reached the kitchen. I managed to duck his first swing, but he brought the staff back around low, sweeping my feet from under me. My back landed flush against the linoleum, knocking the wind from my lungs. Brad stood over me, and, like he was sweeping the floor, landed three quick strikes to my face. They didn't rattle my brain, but they stung badly. I lifted my hands to shield myself and felt blood leaking out of me. Voices blossomed from the pain, Zelda's the loudest of all: *What's wrong? What happened? I'm coming! Hold on.*

"Brah," Brad said. "You can't be starin' at my girl like that. She ain't yours anymore. I catch you doin' it again, your gonna get some more kisses from Gidget here. Only next time they won't be little pecks. She'll give you the tongue, and trust me, you don't want the tongue."

I took my hands away from my face to see Kaliah crouched over me, her skirt touching my stomach. "St-st-stay awah-wuh-wuh-way from me you disguh-uhs-sss-ting pig."

I'd never heard Kaliah stutter before. As she leaned closer, I felt her hand slip behind my back. Then she spit in my face. Brad laughed, and they both left without another word, without closing the door behind them.

When I sat up, I found a piece of paper on the floor

where Kaliah's hand had been. On it was a note in her handwriting:

"After orientation, go to the room by the ficus plant."

CHAPTER 21

THE LEFT SIDE OF my face was completely healed when I woke up in the morning. Though Craig had closed the cuts with his saliva last night, the area was still sore when I went to bed. Now it felt as if nothing had ever happened.

Zelda, who'd gotten back late the night before after failing to fulfill her promises to both find flour and *bite Brad's face off*, had slept at my feet and gotten up only after the bacon had been sizzling for a few minutes. She insisted on having pancakes with her bacon and eggs, but with only cornmeal in the house, the pancakes came out flat and rubbery. She enjoyed them anyway, as vessels for maple syrup.

In the middle of her third helping, the landline phone attached to the wall next to the refrigerator rang, and I picked up. A man on the other end skipped introductions and said, "Your orientation is scheduled for 10 AM. Check-in is at the school library. If you are not checked in fifteen minutes before your appointment, an escort will be sent to find you."

I used the hour before I had to leave to clean the kitchen and take a shower. I found some men's clothes in one of the dressers. They were a little baggy on me but clean.

Before I left, Zelda described a ficus plant to me one more time, then trotted off to resume her search for flour.

A light snow was falling outside. I didn't have an umbrella, but the heavy coat I'd grabbed from the front closet was enough to keep me dry and warm.

I held three main assumptions about Kaliah's note: 1) the room by the ficus had to be somewhere in the school because that was where orientation was, and I couldn't imagine Kaliah making me search the entire town for a ficus; 2) Kaliah was probably not there, otherwise she would have written "meet me in the room" instead of "go to the room"; 3) some part of Kaliah remained *Kaliah*. There was still hope to save her.

I was happy Kaliah wasn't fully gone, wasn't fully a creation of Brad's twisted, Victorian-obsessed imagination, but I was also horrified, because that meant Kaliah was conscious of her captivity, of her torture, of the slow death of her identity.

My hatred for Brad and Blanche and all the Friends burned brighter and brighter every day.

I walked three blocks past white houses with new snow gathering in the lawns to the school, where I asked a woman for directions to the library. She looked at me like I'd just exposed myself, then turned and walked away. Being called out by the Prime Nabob at the assembly for helping Blanche achieve her dreams had not made me a popular man in Arampom it seemed.

I wandered the hallways, with their steel-pipe columns and peach, stucco walls, until I came to double-doors, propped open, and saw bookshelves inside. Warm air wafted into the hall, carrying the smell of dust and old books. People stood in line in front of the check-out desk. I took my place at the back of the line. The few people that made eye contact with me quickly looked away. My curt nods were ignored. I was a pariah.

So be it. I had Zelda on my side, and soon Kaliah. The three of us could defeat the Friends on our own, or so I told myself, trying to inject myself with a little courage.

Be posigetiful.

Truthfully, I was terrified of reentering the cheese danish whorl. Even if I got my hands on a sourdough totem that worked, I didn't know if I could endure that type of pain.

I scanned the library. It was small—a handful of tables with chairs, six tall bookshelves in addition to the bookshelves lining the walls. I spotted indoor plants, a fern first, then a palm, then, in the far corner, the telltale waxy leaves of a ficus in a pot by a door. I thought about going in the room right then, but the note said "after orientation," so I stayed put.

I overheard whispered conversations between the others in line, mostly about their new living situations. One person spoke of the Friends forcing Mummer Wardens out of retirement to build the Wall of Blanche.

When I reached the front of the line, the woman behind the desk was curt with me, said I was late, and they had already sent out my escort to find me. Out of habit, I almost apologized, but caught myself and righteously remained silent. She gave me directions to my orientation room, and I followed them to an open, red steel door. The classroom inside had thirty or so empty school desks and a variety of flags from Hispanic countries hanging on the wall, along with posters of Mexico City, a Dia de los Muertos celebration, Frida Kahlo, and random Spanish phrases buffeted by polarized exclamation marks. A few piñatas hung from the ceiling.

Brad's bond, Meadow sat on top of the teacher's desk, her sandals dangling a foot above the checkered floor. She wore a gray wool cardigan with oversized wooden buttons and a thick collar. She had flowing auburn hair, round spectacles, and the patient and patronizing smile of a seasoned kindergarten teacher. She opened her arms in greeting and said, "Welcome, Mr. Allison. Please take a seat. My name is Meadow."

Ignoring her outstretched hand—which was difficult for me, with my background in the hospitality industry—I sat at a desk in the front row and rested my crossed arms on it while Meadow smiled down on me.

"It is an honor to give orientation to Blanche's grandson," she said.

"Where are all the children that used to come here?"

"The children are on Christmas break and have been relocated to the more populated areas of the county, where they will be of better use to the cause. There are children still in town, but they are mummer children, and they are with their parents in the new monastery."

"What new monastery?"

Meadow tilted her head. "I'm sorry I forgot you weren't born into a Lodge. Arampom had a monastery in another town north of here where mobiaks who violated the laws of cackle were sentenced to rigorous lessons. Those who ran the monastery had children who attended school. Mummers who were predatory toward mobiaks also populated this town, and they were made harmless, of course, by the Mummer Wardens. Arashanikas each one, who took shifts providing the personalities of their ancestors to the mummers, which kept them happy and docile, living out lives of long-dead mobiaks. But none of that is necessary in this new town where the mobiak and mummer prisoners were relocated. Because of Blanche, there is no need for cackle laws anymore. Because of Blanche, dangerous mummers will no longer be coddled, and monasteries all over the world will soon be converted to holding barracks to keep their greedy little bourgeois mummer minds from soiling Blanche's dream." At the end of her little speech, Meadow's otherwise pleasant and smooth delivery turned halting and vitriolic, leaving tiny drops of spittle caught in the fibers of her wool collar, like dew in a spiderweb.

I needed to know more about the holding barracks where Bruce and Pam were being held. If the plan to make a sourdough totem didn't work, I would have to break them out somehow. "Are the mummers locked up?" I said. "Are we safe?"

"Oh don't you worry about that," Meadow said with such condescension I worried my questions had been transparent. "Brad is doing a phenomenal job with the mummer problem. Now . . . ." Meadow grabbed a file from a stack next to her and held it out to me, but it was too far to reach. She shook it as if she expected me to get up and take it from her. I didn't move. She sighed, slid off her desk, and dropped the file in front of me, then shimmied back on top of her desk with a grunt—a petty victory, but a victory all the same.

"Those are instructions from Blanche on how you can best succeed here in Arampom," Meadow said, her patronizing smile back in place. "You are to run your own bakery, in honor of your late sister, May. A building has already been picked out for you and furnished with all the supplies you need. Blanche expects you to channel your rage and grief into your baking. For example, if you harbor any revenge fantasies, she would like to see them reflected thematically in your menu. However, she does hope that, with time, you will come to understand her actions, and that your views about her will continue to evolve, and that you will honor these evolutions with an ever-evolving menu."

"Don't ever say my sister's name again," I said through clenched teeth, and threw the file across the room.

"I didn't mean to be insensitive. I realize this is a difficult situation for you. And Blanche does too, you know? She does not lack self-awareness. She understands that dedicating an entire town to chronicling and critiquing her greatness is a self-indulgence, but she has done and will do so much for the universe, that we believe this is the least we can do to honor her. And make no mistake she knows how dangerous you are to her plans, her legacy. She decided not to kill you, not just because your rekulak's reaction would be unpredictable, but because you are her grandson and she values family. But if you do not cooperate with us, there are ways we can punish you." That last part she said wearing a mask of sympathy over her face.

"You people murdered my family," I said, keeping all emotion out of my voice, "and turned my bond into a zombie. What more could you possibly do?"

Meadow exaggerated a sigh and looked up at the ceiling. "If this town isn't celebrating the grand opening of your bakery in three days, we will peel the skin from your forearm like it was a banana. An extremely painful procedure. But you will heal quickly, I'm told. And we will continue to skin you alive until the bakery is open, per Blanche's instructions, of course."

I knew the Friends were capable of anything, but the threat of physical torture took me by surprise. I expected more cackle-based methods from them. But I wasn't afraid, mostly because they were giving me exactly what I wanted. A bakery would have flour. I could suffer one more indignity for that, for the opportunity to defeat this smug and twisted cult.

"By the way, before you get too excited, this is a gluten-free town," Meadow said, as if reading my mind. "So your bakery must be gluten-free as well. As I said, we know you are dangerous, and we aren't stupid. In preparation for your arrival, we expelled all the gluten from this town, as well as the typewriters and keyboards. You will not be entering Blanche's whorl again. You will not be summoning your rekulak, as I have been assured the meditation method takes years to master. You will be baking delicious, gluten-free treats that honor the greatness of Blanche Duluth."

CHAPTER 22

AGLUTEN-FREE TOWN. I was truly in a living hell. There was no way to make a passable totem with cornflour. I had no choice now. I had to find Bruce and Pam and escape. They would lead me to Naomi, to the sourdough totem.

I hoped whatever was inside the ficus room would help, because I had no clue how to get the others past the Wall of Blanche. I had no intention of creating a gluten-free menu in honor of the person who murdered my sister and niece. And I didn't want to find out what being skinned alive felt like.

I marched to the library, where a dozen or so people were still lined up at the check-out desk, and I pretended to peruse the books on the shelf nearest the room by the ficus plant until I was satisfied no one was watching, then I delicately opened the door and slipped inside. A dying fluorescent bulb on the ceiling provided enough light for me to see I was in a storage closet—shelves full of office and cleaning supplies—and Hugo Sinclair was standing at the back of the closet in a black robe. His large nose cast a shadow over his mouth.

"What do you want?" I said.

"I want you to be of help for once," Hugo said in his alarmingly deep voice. "As the shaka of the Sinclair line you have been pathetic, but now you have an opportunity at a smidgeon of redemption."

"I've been pathetic?" I tried to keep my voice down. "You betrayed me and your own sister."

"I saved my sister." His eyes were flat, as if he were tolerating an ignorant child. "She was about to be poisoned. If I hadn't protected her, she would be insane now. As for you . . . I don't know you. Your existence threatens the nature of reality. It's not personal. The world is just a safer place with you dead. I'd try to kill you again, but the damage is already done. It would be pointless."

"It may not be personal to you, but I take it very personally."

He swatted the air. "Kaliah didn't send you here to argue with me about things you don't understand. We are running out of time. In three, maybe four days, there is going to be a flood like we haven't seen in fifty years. That will be our opportunity to strike, when this whole town is inundated."

"How do you know that? Are you a weatherman?"

"I listen to the radio. It has been snowing in the mountains for weeks, the rivers are already overflowing, and in a few days, a tropical storm will land on our shores. That means warm rain. That means the snow is going to melt. That means a flood is coming—a big one. That means we have three days to figure out how to stop the Friends. Thanks to you, our efforts will be too late for some. We can only hope to limit the damage. Best-case scenario: thousands of people die. Worst case scenario: reality, as we know it, ends."

He was right. I hadn't realized it before, but he was right. The best-case scenario, stopping Blanche, meant the death of thousands of people. They would die the same way my sister had. I'd been so focused on revenge, on fixing my mistake, I'd failed to realize what that would mean. Blanche was infecting the whole county and beyond with her cackle right now. The moment I freed Craig from the Sourdough Whorl, everyone Blanche had infected would be regurgitated. They would die just like May. How many? How many people had she infected? How many people would she infect before I could escape this gluten-free hell?

I stopped breathing. Blood rushed to my face, and the skin around it felt tight. My arms and hands tingled and felt light. My gut felt like a sinking stone.

What's wrong? Zelda said.

Go away, I said.

"Let's start with how this happened?" Hugo said as I forced myself to start breathing again. "How did Blanche trap your rekulak?"

I gave Hugo the bones of the story, and when I was done, he said, "If we get you back in that whorl, can you undo what you did?"

"Yes," I said with more confidence than I felt. I couldn't shake the idea of all those people dying because of my weakness. "The Prime Nabob said they were going to infect all seven stomachs. If I free my rekulak, will all those people be regurgitated too?"

Hugo nodded. "Yes, but I wouldn't worry about their blood being on your hands. Each stomach has stalwart defenses against invasion from another. Blanche would need an army for her infection to get a foothold."

I remembered the program Em had shown me from the coffee shop where all those Blanche-infected people were enjoying spoken-word poetry inspired by the '64 flood, and I had another terrifying realization. "The flood is a totem."

"What?" Hugo said.

"You once told me when Arawok regurgitates someone, it creates a Nexus Whorl. Well, Blanche was regurgitated during the '64 flood, so it makes sense that another flood could act as a totem for the Nexus Whorl created in '64. The conditions you described are eerily similar to the ones back then."

Hugo raised his eyebrows. "Even if that's true, Blanche would need an army, as I said."

"She has an army." I grabbed pen and paper from one of the shelves, drew the patterns from the shower curtain Omen Totem, labeled them with the stomach names they were given on the program, and showed the drawing to Hugo. "This is a map to the stomachs, right?"

"It is roughly similar to ones I have seen in ancient texts."

"I found a map like this inside a program being handed out at a spoken-word show commemorating the '64 flood. All the people there were infected by Blanche. People. Barrens. She can last longer in them before being regurgitated. She told me herself. The Humboldt Historical Society, with Brad at the helm, by the way, a man who apparently wears many hats, is funding events all over the county, showcasing original art inspired by the '64 flood in honor of its forty-ninth anniversary: movies, documentaries, plays, paintings, sculptures, poetry, fiction, memoir, all culminating in a huge celebration in Rio Dell, where she died. Why celebrate a forty-ninth anniversary when the fiftieth is right around the corner? Makes no sense. But now the answer is clear. They knew this flood was coming. I don't know how, but they did. And they've been preparing an army of locals, teaching them art, teaching them how to graft and how to navigate between stomachs. When the flood comes, this army is going to waltz right into the Nexus Whorl and go to whatever stomach they want."

Hugo looked down at the floor like he'd just discovered a stain in his carpet and was trying to identify its origin. "I thought we had more time . . . . We need to find this sourdough totem of yours before the flood comes. But first, we need to free my sister. We can't get past the Wall of Blanche without her, and she is almost completely under Brad's control. As her shaka, you are the only one who can save her now."

"How did you let it get this far? How could you just stand by and watch Brad do this to her?"

Anger showed on Hugo's face. "I did not have the power to intervene. I noticed when this Lou character came to town to aide my sister you were not with him. You, who had the power to intervene. So let us not speak of the past no more, shall we." Hugo sniffed, then continued before I could offer a defense. "Brad towed Kaliah's mobile totem library all the way out here to administer the Doegerot to her. There are four totems inside from Kaliah's personal life that do not belong to our ancestors: a paintbrush, a handsaw, an agate, and a beer bottle from the old west. You need to enter the whorls from these totems and clear them of all the corruptions Brad has so carefully positioned in them. There are a few ways to do this, but as a Sojourner, all you must do is touch the corruptions with your blood. Once you've cleared those four whorls, Kaliah will be able to do the rest."

I nodded, remembering the candy-dish whorl in which I'd freed all those children in the same way. "Where is the library?"

"Across the river, outside the monastery. It is an aqua blue trailer, very difficult to miss." Hugo pulled a small bottle out of his robe pocket and handed it to me. "For you. Bloom. Steal the totems. Free my sister. I will do the rest."

"How will you deal with the Zaditorians?"

"Don't worry about my end. I have a radar gun that Lou gave me. And many here are willing to fight, including Rhonaya, the finest warrior I know. You just worry about my sister. I can deal with the Zaditorians. But without Kaliah, we're not getting past the wall."

"Do you know where I can get a typewriter?"

Hugo let a laugh escape, short and concise. "Ahhh, the second mystery."

"Excuse me?"

"Two weeks ago, the Zaditorians scoured the entire town, confiscating computers, laptops, typewriters—such as they found—and everything with gluten in it. I understand the gluten now, but why the typewriters?"

I considered telling him, but for some reason—spite, most likely—I decided to let him wonder. "A Sojourner secret," I said, immediately feeling ridiculous for uttering the phrase.

Hugo nodded as if he respected my choice. "Fair enough.

Try the house at the corner of 4th and D. Cassandra lives there. From what I hear, she's running a black market of sorts. But be careful. She is an unsavory woman. We once considered making her the otalith of our lodge, but wisely chose to seek another."

"There's an otalith here?"

"That is what I said. Brought here against—"

Charlie! Zelda burst into my mind again. I could feel the excitement and urgency in her voice. *I was wrong. Em's alive!*

CHAPTER 23

SNOW CRUNCHED UNDER MY feet, and my nostrils and lungs burned with icy air as I gingerly ran over the bridge, careful not to slip and fall. The Eel River flowed high and swift beneath me. I cackled like a madman. I was full of joy, delirious with relief. Em was alive.

A ten-foot fence with razor wire at the top surrounded the monastery, which had been converted from an old sawmill. Two women I assumed were Zaditorians guarded the gate. Half of the once paved lumberyard was now a labyrinth of raised beds growing trees and shrubs. Snow-covered benches were scattered here and there along the path, like an offseason botanical garden. The other half of the yard was filled with a series of small, igloo-like glass structures connected by clear tubes, the purpose of which I couldn't even guess. The driveway was lined by abstract sculptures made from old forklift parts. At the end was a long, purple building with three stories of windows on the front face and a tower and peaked roof over the entrance. A line of people filed from four parked buses into the open front doors while three Zaditorians or Friends stood by, supervising.

Something moved in my periphery, and I turned to see Zelda bounding over the snow down a path toward me like a deer. When she saw the Zaditorians at the gate, she stopped fifteen yards from me and lay down.

Where is she? I said.

In the monastery with the rest of the mummers, Zelda said. *I told you not to come here. All you're doing is calling attention to yourself. Let me scout the place out first.*

Is she okay?

She's cold and scared, the poor girl, but otherwise healthy, I think.

How do you know it's her and not Blanche?

Because she's a lunch lady.

A lunch lady? I stared into Zelda's inscrutable fox eyes, trying to glean something.

Yeah. She's got a hairnet, apron, the whole thing. Don't you remember? She predicted this.

Em had told me once that we became lunch ladies when we died, but I'd dismissed the theory as the imaginative rambling of a child. I should have listened. Arashanikas with Ghost Heart vesseled in Mummers to escape the nightmarish whorls playing relentlessly in their minds. If the lunch lady at Em's school was a Mummer, maybe Em had vesseled in her before. Maybe when Blanche had infected her, Em had escaped and ran to the most familiar place, her lunch lady. All of this seemed possible and gave me new hope, which I desperately tried to temper with skepticism.

How do you know it's Em and not just some lady in a hairnet? I said.

Her walk for one, Zelda said. *She bounces on the balls of her feet just like Em. And she has an eraser burn on the back of each hand. Also, my nose tells me. Also, I heard one of the other mummers call her Em.*

The hope I'd been trying to hold back overwhelmed me. She really was alive. I felt a queasy mixture of sadness and glee hearing of that familiar self-inflicted wound of hers. My legs wobbled. I dropped to one knee in the snow, and a few tears sprang loose. I'd learned how not to cry when I was a kid, and now I remembered why. It was a habit that quickly got out of hand. I needed to control my emotions better if I was going to prevent the apocalypse, if I was going to save what was left of my family. I clenched my jaw, swallowed my tears, and stood up.

She's cold, she's scared, and she's probably hungry, I said. *If I put together a care package, can you get it to her?*

I can do anything, Zelda said. *But I told you, I need to scout the place out first.*

Okay, meet me at the house when you're done.

There's flour on the coffee table, Zelda said, overly nonchalant and obviously proud of herself.

Did you get it from the house on the corner of 4th and D?

How did you know that?

I chuckled, then briefly recounted my meetings with Meadow and Hugo. *Did you see a typewriter there?*

I wasn't looking for one. Zelda sounded dejected. *This changes everything. We need a plan, a good one. Don't do anything until we've talked.* She stood, shook the snow from her fur, and bounded off toward the monastery.

Inflated with a kind of giddy delirium, I floated back to

the house and lightly flitted about the kitchen from counter to cupboard to drawer, my thoughts happy, scattered, and fluttering. Biscuits. Em loved biscuits and gravy. That was one of her favorites. What else? French fries. What else? Could May be alive too, using a mummer as a sanctuary? I didn't even know if she was shaka or shanika, but maybe maybe maybe . . . .

Em was hungry. I knew that. And cold. And scared. She had spent the night in a strange body, alone, not knowing what had happened to her mom. Alone. Or was she? Did she have autonomy? Was the mummer present? No wonder she already had eraser burns on her hands. She was grasping for control, grasping for something familiar. And now she was being rounded up and contained like cattle.

I started on the biscuits. I could think while I worked, organize my thoughts. Or should I have started the french fries first? Potatoes always took longer than expected. But not if I microwaved them before frying them. I needed to microwave the potatoes, then attack the biscuits. But that required flour.

The coffee table!

There it was, tightly packed in a plastic bag like a brick of cocaine, what constituted contraband in a gluten-free town. I could use all I wanted now that I knew there was no way a new sourdough starter would be ready in time to stop Blanche. But I made some starter anyway just in case.

I worked with focus for forty-five minutes. When Zelda came back from her scouting expedition, the biscuits and gravy were done and cooling, and I was fishing french fries out of oil and dropping them on paper towels.

I found a way in, Zelda said.

"Good," I said. "Is there a way to get her out?"

There's always a way. I just need a little time to find it.

"Did you see Bruce and Pam?"

I did. Zelda sat on the carpet outside the kitchen, sphinx-like, watching me load fresh biscuits into a Tupperware container.

"What?"

Nothing, she said, and quickly changed the subject to my meetings with Meadow and Hugo. She wanted to hear about what was said in greater detail, and I obliged her while I finished packing Em's food. I even found a tiny container for ketchup. Em loved ketchup. I put all the food in a paper sack, then grabbed the second coat hanging in the front closet, folded it up tight, and stuffed it into a plastic bag, realizing as I did that Zelda would have to make two trips. I wrote a note telling Em I was close, I loved her, and would rescue her soon, but in the meantime trust the fox.

While you're at it, Zelda said, *write me a letter of introduction to my grandnephew.*

"Hugo?"

And tell him to provide me with pen and paper. I'll need his help planning our escape.

"I'll just translate for you."

No, you need to focus on one thing, and that's preparing yourself to ride the Ghost in Blanche's whorl. I stole you a trout test DVD. It's on the coffee table. Watch it at the bakery so the Friends think you're doing what they ask. And don't stop watching it until you pass the test.

"I need to help Em and Kaliah. I don't need to be watching trout all day."

Let me and Hugo worry about Em and Kaliah. We'll get you the totems, and we'll get all of us out of here, but there's no point in us escaping if you can't undo what you did, and you can't undo what you did if you can't even pass a simple trout test.

"I've tried already. I can't do it."

Yes, you can. You have to. Pain can be used to deny the truth, or it can be used to see the truth. Use the pain from the ice water to see the truth. Sometimes all it takes to achieve grace is another perspective. Remember that. Zelda snatched the coat bag in her jaws and trotted out. *I'll come back for the letter and the other package. You better not be here when I do.*

She was right, I had to admit. Escaping would be pointless if I couldn't bring myself to eat my way past that cheese danish in Blanche's sourdough whorl.

After finishing the letter to Hugo, I grabbed the trout DVD, put on my coat, and walked through town, back over the river to the little shopping center not far from the monastery. The sky was overcast, but the light reflecting off the new snow was bright and squint-inducing.

My bakery was between a coffee shop and a nail salon. Both were open. The workers and patrons inside stared at me through large windows as I walked up. I didn't bother to wave. The door to the bakery was unlocked. Inside wasn't much warmer than outside, but the lights worked. The dining area was cramped, with barely enough space for three small tables. There were a register and a modest display case. A narrow counter folded up, opening a path to the kitchen, which had a commercial Hobart mixer, a deep stainless steel sink, and a wood table with a pastry rolling machine on one end. I didn't see a TV or DVD player anywhere. As I turned to go back and grab the ones from the house, two Zaditorians—the originals, Baldy and Beardo—walked through the door, followed by my mother. I froze.

She held up her hands. "Hear me out and I'll give you back your shanika's personal totems—a paintbrush, a handsaw, an agate, and an old beer bottle if I'm not mistaken."

CHAPTER 24

S HE PULLED THE TOTEMS out of her coat pocket one by one, followed by what looked like a bottle of bloom, and set them on the counter between the register and display case, while I watched from the kitchen. I couldn't meet her eyes. They were full of sympathy, but also imploring, like she wanted sympathy from me. I couldn't. She didn't have the right to ask. If she started crying, I wouldn't be able to stand there and listen, or so I thought.

When her shoulders began bouncing to the beat of her sobs, I didn't leave. I stood there. And despite what I knew, what I'd seen, I empathized. Being raised by someone like Blanche could not have been easy. Maybe Mom was a victim too. But she had manipulated me, her own son, from an early age, baked in my neurosis, stood by while her daughter and granddaughter were murdered. Her childhood, no matter how bad, could not excuse that. But how bad had it been, her childhood?

I stifled the urge to comfort her, struggled to appear impassive. This could be just another manipulation after all. How had she taken those totems from Brad? Why was she giving them to me? Did she know I needed them? Had she been listening? If the Friends were fascist enough to make a whole town gluten-free, they were certainly capable of bugging the house, the library.

My mom took a deep breath, blew her nose, wiped her eyes, and gave me a sad smile, that imploring look still in her eyes. I looked away. "You don't know what it's like," she said, "being Blanche's daughter. She's a very powerful woman. Demanding. I gave her my life. I tried to keep my children free, but she came for you too, even though she promised she never would. I thought about killing you all as toddlers, I really di—" Her voice quivered as she held back tears. "Can you imagine that choice? For a mother? You were all so happy. I didn't want you to experience the pain I knew what she had planned for you. Can you imagine? But I didn't give in. I fought for you with the little power available to me. And I thought I'd won too. I thought we could all live here, in Arampom, together, as a family. That was the agreement. We could be here together while the whole world turned into Blanche, the whole universe. We could be here together. Who cared if we had to pay tribute to her? We would be ourselves. We could be happy. You have to believe me, Charlie. My plan was working. I had saved us all. Then you walked into that bakery, such a brave boy. A mother never felt such pride and disappointment at the same time. You ruined … . But it's not your fault. It's Blanche's. She's a disease."

"That wouldn't have saved Em," I said in a weak, wispy voice, then coughed and spoke up, "Blanche took Em for herself. Did you have a plan to save Em too?"

"Of course I did. I'm your mother. Who do you think I am? Em was meant to have a vessel. We had one all lined up for her, a cute little mummer girl, but then Naomi betrayed us. She tried to take you for herself and ruined everything. I tried to find another vessel but there wasn't enough time."

Naomi had told me the truth after all. She had tried to save me in her own twisted way. "Why are you giving me these totems?"

"I'm the mayor of Arampom now, sweetheart, much to the chagrin of the Prime Nabob and her spoiled son. But I earned this much, at least, for my sacrifice. With what life I have left, I only want to make you happy. I won't allow Brad to torture your shanika. No one should suffer that indignity, let alone my son."

"What's the trick?" I still avoided her eyes.

"Oh my son, that's a dagger I deserve. There's no trick. In time, I hope you'll see that everything I've done, I've done for my children. Free your bond. Free her from her suffering. Brad can't stop you. I made sure of that." She turned and walked out, leaving the totems and bloom on the counter. Beardo and Baldy followed her.

I stared at the objects on the counter. I wanted to believe my mom, but I didn't know if I could. The safest course would be to assume the worst, that she meant me harm. The bloom could be a cackle poison of some kind. The totems could be tainted in some way, have traps planted inside their whorls.

But I had to take the risk.

Every moment I was stuck here, more innocent people were being infected with Blanche. And I wasn't escaping this town without Kaliah, nor was I abandoning her again.

I decided to use the bloom Hugo had given me. I took it from my pocket, unscrewed the lid, placed a finger over the opening, and turned the bottle upside down.

The voices ushered in the pain, pain at a cellular level, swimming through me, disassembling and reassembling like a bait-ball of sardines. Zelda's voice was prominent, curious why I was on bloom. I ignored her, focused on the agate, picked it up, felt it against my skin, let it inspire my Pictionary poetry: Shipwreck Salami Sweat, Shark Tooth Treasure Chest, Corduroy Crab Hair.

I found myself in a Victorian beach scene. Wooden chaises were grouped under umbrellas. Changing tents were spread apart along a line parallel the surf. Some Brad corruptions were dressed for the drawing room—slacks, vests, watch chains—while others were dressed in old-timey bathing suits, striped, with short sleeves and short pants. Others, still, wore dresses.

I found a jagged rock, cut open my palm, and disappeared the Brad nearest me. The others all turned to me at once, then fled. I chased them around with my bloody hand—a perverse game of tag.

Straying from the whorls pain, I was filled with the narrative of Charlotte, the ancestor from the fighting whorl I'd entered, where I'd first been infected by the rekulak, Craig. I was alarmed. Had my mom given me the wrong totems? But after disappearing a few more Brad corruptions, the narrative changed. Charlotte became Kaliah, and the details became more intimate, more real, to the point that I felt embarrassed and ashamed, like I was reading Kaliah's diary without permission.

I tuned out the narrative as best I could by focusing on my hatred for Brad. He'd contorted and twisted Kaliah's mind to fit his fantasy, changed her name even. Disgusting.

After disappearing six Brads—there were two dozen, at least, when I'd started—the graft failed, and I left a corruption behind to return to the real world. My rekulak didn't appear to send me off as usual. I wondered why. Only one of Craig's infinite heads was trapped in Blanche's whorl.

I reentered the agate whorl five times before I cleared it of all the Brad corruptions. Each time I entered, the scene became more contemporary, until, when I slapped a bloody hand on the last corruption, the whorl consisted of a group of teenagers listening to a stereo, laughing and drinking rum on a secluded beach.

I grafted to the rest of the totems—paintbrush, antique beer bottle, handsaw—and cleared their whorls of every last trace of Brad, changing them from Victorian fantasies centered around Charlotte, back to Kaliah's painful and true memories. But I left twenty-five of my corruptions behind in the process. At around two hundred, Lou had said, I would start losing noticeable pieces of myself. My total was still far below that, but I couldn't help being concerned. I didn't even want to come close to that mark. I also worried about what my corruptions would do in Kaliah's whorls. Would they behave, or do something terrible in my absence?

Thirty minutes had passed since I'd entered the first whorl. I felt exhausted and exhilarated, like I was eighteen and had just finished pulling a double shift waiting tables. I gathered the totems, stuffed them into my coat pockets, and walked back to the house. The cold air was crisp and refreshing on my face.

Something black was lying in the snow in the front yard. As I came closer, I saw that it was a burnt dress, a burnt Victorian dress. Kaliah? I rushed into the house, minding the icy stoop steps along the way, and found her in the kitchen.

CHAPTER 25

S HE TURNED, WEARING THE men's clothes from my closet. They were much too big for her. I smiled wide and felt joy when her eyes lit up. I wanted to hug her, but I wasn't sure if she wanted that. She'd been abused, tortured by Brad for weeks. Maybe she wanted space. Then I thought of what Lou had said, that Kaliah was in love with me, and I became shy. I tried leaning against the wall, but that didn't feel right, so I put my hands on my waist, which felt worse. "You feel better," I said.

She smiled at me like she knew something I didn't. "Almost. Your mom brought me here. She seems sweet."

"Really? I don't trust her. She's . . . . Where's Brad?"

"At his house, stewing, cursing your mom, cursing Blanche."

"Why are they helping us all of a sudden?"

"I don't know." Kaliah crossed her arms over her chest, the sleeves of her brown sweater hanging down, and she took four, slow, rhythmic steps toward me in the style of a bride walking down the aisle. She stood in front of me, looked up into my eyes, her face inches from mine, and parted her lips slightly. "I need to punch you in the face," she said.

I raised my eyebrows. "Now?" She was so beautiful and serious.

"I need you to graft to the punch, to clear one more whorl for me. As long as Brad is in my cackle, I'm vulnerable to him. He'll do it again if he gets the chance. And I won't be able to stop him. There's too much of him inside me still."

For whatever reason, I didn't see the obvious until right then. Of course, the punch whorl was part of Kaliah's torture, most likely the beginning, a foul seed Brad had planted while he and Kaliah were still dating.

What had she ever seen in him?

I admonished myself even as I thought it. I knew better. I knew from my sister people could rarely be blamed for the partner they chose. Partners were experts at hiding their monsters.

I couldn't think about what Kaliah might have endured from Brad or rage would overwhelm me, and I might do something stupid, unhelpful. This monster would be waiting for an opening like that, and he would take advantage of her again, with pleasure, without remorse. I couldn't let that happen. I couldn't make any more mistakes.

I stepped back from Kaliah, took the bloom from my pocket, and dabbed some on my finger. "Fire away," I said as the voices rushed through my body.

Kaliah smiled. "Thank you."

Then she launched her fist into my mouth.

The voices exploded. I grafted to the pain, sharp, dull, and otherwise, and the voices took shape around me. I was back in the Lodge, a young girl in an old dress, the gallery of Brads watching me from beyond the crown molding. I found a letter opener, sliced my hand open like an old pro, and began chasing the corruptions around. I took satisfaction from the fear on the Brads' faces just before I eradicated them from Kaliah's life forever.

When the graft failed, my bloody lip healed, which amazed Kaliah. I told her I would explain later, although there wasn't much to explain, and she punched me again, this time with a shirt wrapped around her hand to protect her knuckles.

On the third time reentering the whorl, I chased the remaining six Brad corruptions down a hallway, where they disappeared, swallowed by air. When the graft broke, I told Kaliah what had happened, and her face fell like an over-leavened cake. "I'm going to bed," she said, and stood.

"What? No. Punch me again. I'll catch them."

"There are places you can't go. Even as my shaka. To follow those last corruptions you would have to mix your blood with mine. And you wouldn't like what that turned you into."

"Are you talking about the Dirge?"

She nodded.

Lou had told me about the Dirge, a cackle disease he'd contracted from his first wife, who was also his shanika. Whenever he touched something with his skin, a song unique to that thing played in his head. Everything had a song, his clothes, even the air. Otalith cackle silenced the songs, and when he ran out of that, he had methods, honed over the years, of coping. But not everyone with the Dirge was as lucky or as strong as him. Some heard the songs and were never themselves again. Left alone, they would go around touching things until they starved.

I tried to imagine what that would be like. If Lou could handle it, I thought, then so could I, for the sake of Kaliah, to rid her of Brad forever. "I'll do it," I said, and swallowed hard. My tone wasn't very convincing, and I'd paused too long before committing.

Kaliah tried to smile. "Thank you, but no. I'm tired. I'm going to bed. I'll see you in the morning." And she shuffled out of the room.

I sat on the couch, stewing over my cowardice. I could have convinced her if I'd really tried. Then I stumbled on a thought: Craig. He could do miraculous things. Maybe he could help with this. I still had the page I'd ripped from Lonnie's *Help Me Rhonda* book in my wallet. I could make a rekulak spell. As long as I didn't make too big a crack in the mirror, it could work. I just needed a typewriter. I could make several spells, one for Brad, one for Kaliah, and one for my mom, so I could know for certain if she was telling the truth, if she was just another victim of Blanche.

I grabbed what remained of the flour Zelda had stolen, and I left. I was sure it would be enough to buy a typewriter on this black market. I hoped the otalith had one. In a whole town, there had to be at least one or two typewriters lying around. *Be posigetiful.*

The light, evenly dispersed across the overcast sky, was fading as I walked to the house on the corner of 4th and D. I knocked on the front door, heard stomping from inside, then the largest woman I'd ever seen answered: the otalith that had threatened to kill me, the otalith I'd sprayed with a hose and told to accept Jesus into her heart. She looked at me with narrowed eyes, then curled her lip, grabbed me by the coat, and dragged me inside.

CHAPTER 26

MY SHINS SCRAPED AGAINST the threshold as I tumbled forward into the house. I spun loose from the otalith's grip, but before I could stand, she dropped a heel between my shoulder blades. My stomach slapped against the floor. I heard a crack as her knuckles made impact with the back of my skull. A sharp pain shot deep into my brain like a fracture in a half-split log. The otalith wore rings. But I stood the pain well. By now I was an old hand at being punched. I scrambled to my feet, bucking her off of me in the process. She hollered in surprise as she fell, then spoke clearly as I took my first step to run, "Stop, unless you wanna get shot."

I turned, looked down. The otalith was on her butt, eyes bulging with rage, pointing a revolver at my chest. The front door was still open behind her, framing the icy walk and empty street. The otalith lurched to her feet and shut the door while keeping her gun and eyes trained on me. She wore a blue Dallas Cowboys hoodie and grey sweatpants. "You're the bastard that hosed me down," she said in a husky voice, and smiled a crazy smile with her eyes and not her mouth. "You're not a Jehovah's Witness at all, are you, you little sneak?"

"I'm sorry I sprayed you," I said with my hands up. "I needed your cackle for my niece."

She frowned. "Cackle. I keep hearing about that crap. Your Prime Nabobber comes over every day with that Meadow douche, claims to be an Eagles fan, just straight talks smack. The second I see her without those bubble dudes, I'm going to beat her ass." She laughed and wagged the gun at me. "Look at your face. You came to the wrong house for a cup of flour."

"I don't want any trouble. I'm really sorry about hosing you. What can I do to make it up to you?"

She snorted. "I'll let you go if you tell me how to kill those bubble dudes. I keep waiting for them to put some probes in me, or some crap like that. You got some alien guns somewhere, cuz bullets don't do nothin' to them."

"Tuvan throat singing. It won't kill them, but they hate it."

"Never heard of it. Do it for me."

"I can't. It takes training."

"Do it." She put a growl in her voice.

"Okay, okay. I'll try." I cleared my throat and tried my best to replicate the song I'd heard Lou sing, but I ended up sounding more like Frankenstein having an orgasm.

The otalith cocked her head to the side and squinted one

eye. Then her face turned red, and she screamed, "You give me jokes!? Turn around!"

"I'm telling the truth!"

"Shut up! Turn around!"

She directed me down the hall, had me open a door. There were stairs on the other side. I hesitated before descending, and she jabbed me in the back of the head with what I assumed was the barrel of the gun. I went down the stairs.

The basement was well lit and crammed with stuff, like someone had bought out three garage sales and stocked their haul in here. With a quick scan, I saw a knife set, two mini-fridges, several bricks of cash, a blender, table saw, weed eater, motor cycle, tool cabinet, armoire.

In the center of the basement were three medieval torture devices: a wooden chair with hundreds of metal spikes poking out from the seat, arms, and back, a wooden block on a stand with one big hole between two smaller holes, and a metal cage, three feet tall and three feet wide. A chain ran from the top of the cage up through a hook in the ceiling, then back down again to a winch on the wall with a spoked wheel for a handle.

"See all this crap?" the otalith said. "Cash, antiques. It's a small fortune. Only took two weeks to get. People don't understand. I don't survive. I thrive. You can drop me in Iraq and I'd have a hustle before the sun went down. This freaky town is nothing to me. You're nothing to me. Flour is selling like crazy. People give their firstborn for it. I never had a product so good. See that chair over there? That's a torture chair from medieval times. Some guy gave that to me for a quarter pound. You people are freaks."

"What do you want from me?" I said, staring wide-eyed at the chair, telling myself this otalith wasn't crazy enough to strap me into it.

"Get in the cage."

I turned to face her, mouth dry. "No."

"I can shoot you in the head right now, or you can get in."

"Why? You don't have to do this."

"The way I see it, you got some cackle for free by riling me up. Now you get to pay. You mess with me, I mess with you. I told you I'd kill you the next time I saw you. This is me being nice."

"The world's going to end in three days if I don't get out of this town. You can't put me in that cage. You don't understand."

She shook her head, smiling. "All you people are crazy. The sooner you get in, the sooner you get out. And don't tell me you can't fit either. I've already had a dude bigger than you in there."

I pleaded with her, promised to kill the "bubble dudes," to take her with me when I escaped, but I succeeded only in reigniting her fury. When her face turned red again, I folded myself into the cage, my knees against my chest. Inside smelled faintly of urine. The otalith closed the cage door with a clang and locked it with a padlock, then went to the winch on the wall and began turning. With each click of the wheel, I was lifted higher off the floor, swaying. The ceiling was only eight feet high. She stopped turning the wheel when I was three feet off the floor.

My breathing was fast and shallow, stomach tight. How could I get out of this cage? Could I pick the lock? Break it?

Where was Zelda? How did that communication work? Were there distance limits?

I told the otalith about radar guns and where we could get one if she let me go, but she didn't fall for it. She advised me in her way to keep quiet, then climbed the stairs and shut the basement door behind her.

The bars of the cage were already digging into my tailbone and back. The cage swayed, the door rattled, and I grunted as I squirmed to reach the bloom in my pocket. I had very little room to move. After some effort, I managed to get both hands and the bottle above my knees, where I unscrewed the lid and dropped bloom onto my skin.

Nothing. No voices. No pain. I dropped more. Still nothing. Then I realized the otalith had been angry, which meant her cackle had spread and contaminated mine, stifling its spread, stifling the bloom. I was trapped here. Alone. I hadn't told Zelda or Kaliah where I was going. I couldn't even talk to Zelda. Fears snowballed in my mind: the world would end, Em would die, everyone would die, and I would be stuck in this cage, useless, the captive of a sadistic otalith.

I pressed my back and knees against the walls of my cage and shook my whole body. I couldn't straighten my legs! They were folded against my chest, stuck that way! Claustrophobia rushed through me. My muscles felt electric. I wanted to explode out of my confinement. Panic, for minutes, long agonizing minutes.

Panic like that could only last so long. When it had receded somewhat, I gathered my thoughts. I had to remove the padlock somehow. I looked around me at the loot the otalith had accumulated. The table directly to my left was cluttered with miscellaneous items. I squeezed an arm through the bars and sorted through the pile: a silverware set, cash, two framed paintings, a jewelry box. Under a stamp collection, I found a scrapbook with the words "First Sojourner" printed on the cover. I dragged the book nearer to me and was able to turn the pages without too much strain.

CHAPTER 27

EACH PAGE HAD A small piece of paper glued on top of it behind plastic sleeves. On these papers were words from a language I'd never seen before. The letters were white, surrounded by gray shading, like someone had copied a relief, or several reliefs, by pressing the papers onto them and rubbing a pencil over the words.

In the margins of some of the pages were notes, handwritten in English: "By all accounts, the First Sojourner could speak with her rekulak fluently, and without the aid of elaborate rituals . . . . The totem of the First Sojourner was considered sacred among the ancient sojourners. It was fabled to have unique properties . . . . Ancient sojourners could sense when their time of death was near and often organized and attended their own funerals, gathering their friends and family around and using the totem of the First

Sojourner in conjunction with a Nexus Whorl to give their body to their rekulak so that it could enter our stomach and choose its next host . . . ."

In the plastic sleeve of one page was a silver metal disc, thin and palm-sized, with an elaborate pattern carved into its face. It was old, the grooves stained black and the edges worn smooth. The note above it read: "Rekulak Coin, one of many made that was fabled to have the power to summon the First Sojourner."

That sounded useful to me, so I freed the coin from its clear plastic prison and nudged it into my pocket. I read on, all the notes, hoping to find instructions for the coin or something else that might help me, but I found nothing more promising. The scrapbook was empty after ten pages.

Resuming my search of the room, I turned my head, and out of the corner of my eye, I saw the tool cabinet a few feet behind me. The top drawer was a little higher than the bottom of my cage, and it was open. Inside was a steel hand vise, among other things. Hope sparked in me. I imagined using the vise to slowly, turn by turn, clamp the bars together until they either broke, or there was enough room to wriggle free.

I shifted my weight forward and backward, forward and backward, to get the cage swinging, and I reached behind me. My neck burned and my shoulder screamed with pain, but I didn't cry out or let the voices distract me. At the apex of my backward swing, I snatched the hand vise with the tips of my fingers. Carefully, I brought the vise around the front of the cage and grabbed it more securely with my other hand. I set the vise over the two bars on the front and turned the handle, tightening, tightening. The bars were about as wide around as my pinky. The tighter the vise got, the harder the handle was to turn. I was sweating, pushing, and pulling. The bars creaked and bent. I felt giddy.

Then I pushed the handle too hard, or at too odd an angle because the grip slipped, and the momentum of pushing the handle sent the vise flipping through the air, end over end. It caromed loudly off a metal shelf and hit a large, crystal punch bowl, which shattered with a startling crash.

There was stomping from the floor above. My stomach seized. The basement door opened, and the otalith tramped down the stairs, cursing. When she saw the vise and shattered bowl, she shouted, "I warned you!" Then she snatched a lance from one of the loot piles and charged toward me, teeth bared, eyes raging.

I twisted and shook in my cage, and it hopped around on the chain. I screamed for help.

The otalith jabbed the lance between the bars, cutting my shoulder, and she let out a maniacal laugh. I screamed again, and she cut me again, this time in the thigh. She faked another thrust, laughed at my flinch, tossed the lance aside, and went to the winch. She raised me to the ceiling, climbed the stairs, and turned off the lights, leaving me in the dark.

Blood poured from the wound in my shoulder. My sleeve and coat were sodden with it. I vacantly wondered when Craig would heal me. Despair and despondency were creeping in when I felt something hot touching my waist and noticed a yellow glow showing through the fabric of my coat pocket, also soaked in my blood. I reached in and grabbed the Rekulak Coin, which was glowing in the dark with rekulak bile. It burned my hand, and I instinctively dropped it. And I winced, expecting a clang that would attract the otalith again, but instead, the coin landed on the floor with a wet plop.

The bile on it increased, piling over itself like lava, only moving much faster, and making dry, sloughing noises. In seconds, the pile had grown three feet high. In under a minute, it was the size and shape of a human. Then the glow dimmed and extinguished. I heard steady breathing. *"Hello?"* I whispered. The human shape, a shadow, shrank as it walked away and up the stairs with soft footsteps. *"Hey,"* I whispered louder. *"Come back."*

The lights turned on, and a naked woman descended the stairs. She was short and old, with wrinkled, loose, tawny skin, long white hair, and a broad, flat face. Her eyes were pale blue, striking. She picked up the vise from the punch-bowl wreckage, walked over to my cage, and raised it over her head, exposing the hair under her arms.

"Thank you," I said, reaching down and grabbing the vise. I was confused and in awe. This was the First Sojourner if the scrapbook was to be believed. Was she a facsimile or the real thing? How had she been resurrected? By my blood? Just add blood? She seemed to want to help.

After handing off the vise, she walked behind me without saying a word. As I reapplied the vise to the bars, I heard her rummaging around. She made a satisfied grunt, then came back carrying bolt cutters longer than half her height. I almost dropped the vise again in my excitement, and I had to stifle a cry of celebration.

She went to the winch, and I cringed with every click as she lowered my cage to the floor. Her crotch was at my eye-level when she came back. I looked away as she readied the bolt cutters. I heard grunting from her, followed by a soft, satisfying snap from the lock. It was cut. I removed it and crawled/rolled out of the cage. I stood, then immediately sat. My legs were numb. But I could straighten them. The relief!

The First Sojourner didn't give me much time to recover, nor did I want it. She helped me to my feet, and I offered her my coat. She shook her head, pushed it away. I grabbed the lance the otalith had used on me, and the First Sojourner and I tiptoed up the stairs, me in the rear.

She inched open the door. The hall was dark, except for fluttering and trembling blue-tinted light coming from an open doorway ten feet to my left. A TV was playing, sounded like football analysts analyzing football. I heard raucous snoring over the TV—a good sign.

The First Sojourner led me the other way, past two other rooms, to the back door. She unlocked it gently, and we slipped out into the night. The air had changed. It was warm. There was a breeze. A storm was coming. I felt wonderful. But I knew I had to go back inside to check those other rooms for a typewriter. I needed to free Kaliah from Brad, and I needed to know for certain, for maybe the first time in my life, if my mother had my best interests at heart. And now, while the otalith was snoring away, was my best opportunity.

The First Sojourner stepped into the snow with bare feet.

"Aren't you cold?" I said.

"Wonderfully so," she said, eyes sparkling at the cloudy night sky. She could speak English.

"Stay here. I'm going back."

She gave me a stern look. "Don't"

"I have to. My house is two blocks that way, the one with the maple tree in the front yard. If I'm not back in a few minutes, go there. A fox will help you."

I snuck back into the otalith lair, TV noises and snoring still mixing. The rhythm of the snoring accentuated every eighth beat of my racing heart. I had no desire to be back in that cage. My legs felt shaky as I carefully took one step after another. The first door I tried stuck at first, then swung open. I had to catch myself on the doorknob to keep from falling. The lights were off in the room, but there was a faint green glow in the air, like the room was filled with radioactive dust. A table on the back wall supported stack after stack of white flour. There were also laptops on the table, a scale, and one small, vintage-looking suitcase. When I came closer, I saw the words "Montgomery Ward" engraved near the handle.

My niece's dream came back to me. In it, I'd fought a cowboy for Montgomery Ward. The dream had sounded like nonsense at the time, like any other dream, but now . . . . She had predicted this. She could tell the future. What else was in her dream? I tried to think back, to recall, but then stopped myself. I had no time for that now.

I set aside the lance and opened the suitcase. Inside was a vintage typewriter—more specifically, for those typewriter perverts out there, a baby blue 1966 Montgomery Ward Signature 510.

As I closed the case, I noticed the snoring had stopped. Fear jolted me. I turned around and saw the First Sojourner standing, backlit, silent, between me and the door. The light from the hall was now on. I opened my mouth to tell her to run as a huge shadow filled the doorway and three deafening cracks sounded. The First Sojourner collapsed to the floor. The otalith flipped the light switch on with her gun. My breath caught in my throat as she aimed the gun at me.

Then the room transmuted into a desert, I heard the

otalith scream in terror, and I knew the cavalry had come, that Kaliah was throwing the Ghost of one of her nightmarish whorls. I couldn't see the otalith in the whorl Kaliah was throwing for me, but I could see the First Sojourner. She was looking up at me with half-closed eyes. "Craig is disappointed in you," she said just before green rekulak bile rapidly spread over her body and devoured her.

CHAPTER 28

—————————————————————————————

DEBRIS FROM INSULATION RAINED into my eyes as I lifted a tile from the drop ceiling and moved it to the side. Blinking, I lifted the Signature 510 from the sink over my head and restored it to its hiding place, balanced on the metal scaffolding. After retrieving the trout test DVD nearby, I slid the tile back into place. The loose toilet seat slid and squeaked as I stepped down. I prepared a bucket of ice water for my hand, popped the DVD into the small TV/DVD combo set on the towel table, and sat on the toilet to watch.

For the two days since Kaliah had rescued me from the otalith lair, I'd been training in the bathroom at the bakery. It was the only safe place.

The Friends had somehow noticed I'd gone missing right

away and woken Kaliah up to interrogate her. They'd brought in more Zaditorians to search for me, summoning them somehow from Zaditor. After I'd returned to my assigned home and explained to them that I'd merely been drinking alone on the river bank, gathering my thoughts, they'd assigned Beardo and Baldo to watch me full time and kept the extra Zaditorians in town to watch everyone else. Beardo and Baldy had stayed in my living room at night and followed me wherever I went.

With threats, Meadow had encouraged me to work at the bakery fourteen hours a day. She expected the grand opening in an hour. If I didn't deliver, she would peel a strip of skin from my arm.

The whole town was being driven to exhaustion creating critiques and art in honor of Blanche's accomplishments. A musical tribute and a folk-art tribute had also been scheduled for today.

The Friends were in a hurry to present their offerings to Blanche before the high water swept away the town. The warm rain had not let up in two days. The snow in the mountains was melting. The river had overrun its banks and almost reached the school. Mummers had been put to work stacking sandbags to protect the school and other vulnerable areas of town. I hadn't had time to see if Em was among them, but Zelda had told me she wasn't. I suspected Zelda was lying to keep me focused on my training, but I gratefully believed her. I couldn't do what I needed to if I knew Em was stacking sandbags in the rain all day.

With all the added security, I hadn't been able to talk with Hugo, but Zelda had told me he was furious with me, and she was too. My stunt had compromised the escape and forced

Hugo and her to rework their entire plan.

I had done most of my training during bathroom breaks at the bakery, keeping the fan on so no one could hear the TV or my typing. I'd worked on rekulak spells, though Kaliah and Zelda had both told me not to. When I'd offered to use one to remove Brad from Kaliah's whorl, Kaliah had refused, became sullen. But for the most part, she had been in good spirits. When we would go over the escape plan, faking to work, she would tease me and play pranks. And despite the circumstances, I'd enjoyed spending the time with her.

Brad had hurt her so much. I didn't want to remind her of him with my sympathy. I didn't want to be callous either. But I'd been pretending she wasn't wounded, wasn't hurt. That seemed to be what she wanted, or so I thought.

In thirty minutes, Meadow, the Prime Nabob, my mom, and most of Arampom's Friend population would attend the grand opening of the bakery. It would be filmed for Blanche because she couldn't be here in person for fear of infecting her "last bastion of independent perspective." Though I wasn't one of the Friends, they treated me like royalty. I was Blanche's grandson. The opening of my bakery in honor of her was a momentous occasion for them.

I was expected to explain my menu choices and how the ingredients related to Blanche. If I didn't, Meadow would flay me. If I was insincere, Meadow would flay me.

Kaliah and I had baked snickerdoodles along with chocolate and vanilla sheet cakes—hardly the desserts for a burgeoning God. I hadn't prepared any remarks either. I didn't need to. In thirty minutes, when most of the Friends had gathered around to look at my underwhelming creations, a bomb would explode at the Monastery. The mummers would flee to the east, drawing the Zaditorian guards while Zelda led Em, Bruce, and Pam to the western border, where Rhonaya was waiting with her squad of specially trained Zaditorian fighters. The resistance Hugo had been cultivating over the last several weeks would attack the Friends at the bakery, allowing Kaliah and me to meet everyone on the western border of the valley, where Kaliah would topple the Wall of Blanche. By the time the Zaditorians realized the mummers were a distraction, we would be gone, and if we weren't, Rhonaya and her special soldiers would be waiting to hold the Zaditorians off. After escaping, we would find Naomi and give her Bruce and Pam in exchange for the sourdough-starter totem, and I would enter the whorl, free Craig, and ride the Ghost out, killing thousands in the process, but saving trillions across all seven stomachs.

The trout test DVD playing, I submerged my hand in the bowl of ice water I'd set on the sink. I only had time for one more attempt before people started showing up, but I was confident I would finally pass. Zelda and Kaliah had been coaching me, and the last time I'd played the tape I'd felt something new, something they'd called grace after I'd described it to them.

I focused on the pain, explored it, opened myself to it, and it became more. It was cackle, spreading cackle, potentiality. It shimmered, shivered, rumbled, and fractured. It was a new type of perception. I filtered my senses through it, let it react to the inputs, and I read its reactions. I closed my eyes and listened to the trout jumping and splashing in the riffle, and the sounds took shape in the pain. I'd felt this during the last test, and it had thrown me. This time, though, I kept my focus. The whispering shapes gained detail and distinction. I counted the distinctions, and when the video was over, I opened my eyes. The world was more vibrant but less fixed, full of oscillating energy that blurred and clarified the edges of things, blurred and clarified, blurred and clarified . . . . I was in a state of grace, mobiak grace.

I didn't have to ask Kaliah if my count was correct. I knew exactly how many cutthroat and rainbow trout there were in the video with a certainty that was intoxicating. The state only lasted a few moments, and after it was gone, I felt loss, but I was also jubilant. I'd passed. Finally. And just in time. I had hope now, hope that I could face the cheese danish.

When I left the bathroom, Kaliah was leaning against the work table, half a twisted paper napkin in her hands, the other half in tiny shredded pieces around her feet. She looked at me and smiled and relaxed her shoulders. She knew I'd succeeded without asking. "Good," she said.

I walked over and leaned against the table next to her, and we stared ahead at the oven, clicking as it cooled. Baldy and Beardo watched us from the dining area. The cakes and cookies sat on the table behind us. The bakery was ready for the grand opening, the bare minimum of work complete. I had two rekulak spells prepared, and I'd passed the trout test. There was nothing left to do but wait.

Anxiety quickly overcame jubilation. We were about to be in a fight for our lives and the lives of everyone in the world. I thought about taking up Kaliah's habit of tearing napkins to calm down. Instead, I consciously slowed my breathing.

"Here," Kaliah said, and handed me a small tincture bottle full of a dark liquid.

"More bloom?" I said.

"My blood."

"I thought—"

"I don't. But if Brad reasserts control, you'll have to. But only then. Promise me."

"I promise. But why not let me do it now and get rid of him forever? We still have time."

"Because he's been there for years. Because he's the devil I know."

"And I'm the devil you don't?" I said.

"No, I am." After a pause, she looked up at me with a mischievous and seductive smile. "But don't get me wrong, you're a devil too. The worst kind." She stared into my eyes with a challenge in hers. Her bold, open expression was beautiful. She wanted me to kiss her? Or maybe I wanted to kiss her. But I was a coward, and too slow besides. The door opened and the moment collapsed.

CHAPTER 29

THE FIRST PATRONS FILED into the dining area, among them, Meadow, the Prime Nabob, and my mother, who smiled and waved at me, bobbing her head like a parent in the audience of a school play. Who was this woman? I remembered how intense she'd been in the kitchen of my childhood. Now she was being supportive? I remembered the reverence with which my sisters and I had been expected to treat the sourdough starter and the bread made from it, the same starter that had become the instrument of my torment, and the seed for the death of the world. My mom had kept this thing alive, tricked me into keeping it alive. Could she be blameless? Could she be a victim? If only I had the grace to know for certain.

Beardo and Baldy began documenting the opening of my bakery with their camera phones. The Friends looked around the place, curious, muttering to each other. I hadn't put up any decorations. Meadow would know, if she didn't already, that I hadn't given my best effort to this tribute. Before she could flay me for my lack of creativity and deference, though, the bomb at the monastery was supposed to go off. I checked the clock on the wall: any minute now.

Kaliah and I brought out the lackluster baked goods and set them on the counter. I stood in the spot that Kaliah and I had previously worked out. More Friends arrived, but they couldn't fit in the dining area, so they waited outside, protected from the rain by two canopy tents we had set up earlier.

"Help yourselves," I said.

Meadow stared at the sheet cakes in horror. "This . . . . You've debased the Memoirist. You've debased our cause." She turned to Beardo and Baldy. "Take him to the school. Room thirty-two."

My legs felt heavy and light at the same time. I looked at the clock. The bomb should have gone off by now. What were Zelda and Hugo doing? Had they been caught? I needed to buy more time.

"Wait," Kaliah said. "You clearly don't know the art of baking." She scoffed and made a face like she was offended. "Minimalism is in fashion now. This is known as cookhouse chic, a movement in the baking community marked by nostalgic presentations that mask truly avant-garde, truly revolutionary flavors and techniques. Trust me, after tasting Charlie's desserts, you will never look at food the same again."

I would have laughed if I hadn't been so nervous. Kaliah was an artful liar. And how was she so calm? She hadn't stumbled on one word.

Meadow had hate in her eyes as she studied Kaliah's face, hinting at a history between them I could only imagine, but she waved the Zaditorians back. "And we serve ourselves?" she said with a sneer.

"The lack of presentation is the presentation," Kaliah said. "And there are no plates, either, only napkins. Surrender yourselves to the experience."

I provided a knife, and my mom stepped forward and began cutting the cakes into squares. As soon as someone took a bite they would know Kaliah was full of crap, and Meadow would take me away.

Hugo's resistance was waiting nearby for the explosion before they attacked. If they saw me being hauled off, would they intervene or abandon the plan? I wished there was some way I could signal them to attack now.

I cringed as Meadow took her first bite and chewed. She shook her head, clearly underwhelmed. I looked to my mom. Her face projected sympathy and resignation, as if to say, "I'm sorry. My hands are tied."

Meadow waved at Baldy, and he put away his phone and came toward me, bumping Friends out of his way. Explosion or not, we couldn't wait any longer. I looked at Kaliah. She nodded, and I turned around. The kitchen and bakery dissolved, replaced by empty bleachers on the other side of a football field as Kaliah threw the Ghost we'd been practicing with.

Around me now were happy, chattering, excited people. The sun shone above. On the field below was a stage with a podium. "Pomp and Circumstance" played over a PA. Beside the podium, an older man in a black robe gave diplomas to a line of young people in black robes, happy young people. Other young people waited in folding chairs, rows and rows of them.

I heard shouts of alarm from the Friends behind me who were trapped in some nightmare that wouldn't last much longer if Hugo's resistance didn't come to our aide soon. I walked out into the open air, above the crowd sitting in the seats below me, along the route I'd practiced. I fumbled around for the doorknob to the bathroom, found it, and went inside. I stepped onto the toilet, blindly, higher up into the air, and retrieved my typewriter from over my head, pulling it out of thin air like a magic trick. Then I heard an explosion go off in the distance, the one we'd been waiting for, and I almost dropped the typewriter on my head.

The sound of rainfall was abruptly louder as the bakery door opened somewhere inside the bleachers to my left, beneath the sun-soaked families in straw hats holding signs and noisemakers. Along with the cheers of joy, I now heard shrieks of rage and fear along with the sounds of fighting. Hugo's resistance was here! I took what felt like my first breath in several minutes.

When I turned to where the kitchen should have been, Kaliah was holding my mom by the arm, and they were standing in the air twenty feet above the robed college kids. "Hurry," Kaliah said. "You got five minutes."

I knew I had five minutes. She'd told me I would only have five minutes three times already today. We were supposed to be heading to the western border now. But Kaliah had agreed to help me with this personal matter and to keep it from both Hugo and Zelda, who would have certainly tried to stop me. But I had to know.

I strode over to them and set the typewriter on a work table that wasn't there.

"What's going on, Honey?" my mom said. She sounded nervous.

I ignored the question, pulled out a microwave owner's manual I'd found in a kitchen drawer back at the house, and I began typing. Either this new typewriter had special properties, or I was just getting better, because now, instead of taking three hours to summon the rekulak, I could do it in three minutes. I swept everything from my mind and lost myself in the transcription. When the smell of menthol and strawberries hit me, I didn't bother to watch the rekulak bile transform the words on the page into a homunculus diary. I just took out the Homunculus Totem, a five-bladed, stainless steel pastry blender that I'd prepared over the last two days using the methods Lonnie had taught me with the pencil, and I recited the spell:

"Dear Rhonda: I think the IT guy at my office is sabotaging my computer to have an excuse to flirt with me. My friend says I'm crazy, but no one else in the office has even close to as many problems with their computer as me, and it is so frustrating. He is always asking me what I did on the weekend, which I know everyone asks, but it's somehow different when he asks it. I was thinking of complaining, but I don't have any proof. Also, my boss isn't very good at being confidential, so word will get back to him, and then who knows if I'll even be able to use my computer after that?

Help me Rhonda,
—Unlucky in I.T."

My mom looked confused. She was trying to tell me something, but I ignored her, pointed my Homunculus Totem at her, and finished the spell, "This pastry blender inspires you to answer my next question truthfully" The pastry blender erupted with yellow bile and dissolved in my hand.

I had thought a lot about what I was going to ask my mom over the last two days. I knew I wouldn't have much time, so I got right to the point: "Mom, do you love me?" The words had almost caught in my throat. I was embarrassed by the sincerity of the question, but I needed the answer.

Her expression became cold, impassive. "No," she said, her mouth opening just enough to let the word escape.

I groaned involuntarily and searched the air with my hand for the work table to lean on.

Kaliah's voice, solemn: "Let's go, Charlie."

My mom was no longer compelled to answer truthfully, but another question came to mind, and I blurted it out: "Why did you give me Kaliah's totems?"

"Because I wanted you to think you could escape," she said, almost hissing. The hate in her eyes was agonizing to see, but I couldn't look away. "Then Blanche would finally see how dangerous you are and let me kill you. You had always been her favorite. She was the one who sang to you before bed, through my lips. So many nights. She was your mom, not me."

I heard incongruous applause and cheers beneath me from the graduation audience, then spinning black graduation hats flew up all around us like a fountain. They reached the peaks of their flights and paused for a moment, reflecting sunlight. As they fell, I saw Brad walking out of the bleachers and through the air toward us. Kaliah controlled who walked in her projected whorls, except for him. He was a trespasser.

CHAPTER 30

H E WORE BOARD SHORTS, a tank top, and a black, down parka. He waved and tapped a staff in front of him like a blind man as he navigated Kaliah's whorl. He had a black eye. He smiled at Kaliah and said, "There's my little Testarossa. I missed you. Can't wait to have makeup sex."

My mind had been flailing, trying to process my mom's betrayal until I saw Kayak Brad and heard the disgusting words out of his mouth. Rage gathered and swaddled my thoughts, pinning them comfortingly to a single purpose. I took the three strides separating Brad and me in such a way that I was swinging when I reached him.

"Charlie, don't," Kaliah said, but she was too late to stop me.

My knuckles smacked against the side of his head. I'd

been aiming for his chin but he ducked at the last moment. As I threw the left, he knocked me square on the nose with his staff. I stumbled back, eyes watering. Taking advantage of my temporary imbalance, he swiped my legs out from under me with his staff. My head and back slammed onto the concrete floor. As I scrambled onto my feet, Kaliah's projected whorl failed, and we were in the kitchen of the bakery again.

Brad turned and sauntered toward Kaliah, who backed into a corner, slid down, curled into a ball, and began crying like a frightened child.

"No," I said, realizing the stupidity of what I'd done. By punching Brad, I'd opened the gates for him to reenter Kaliah's whorls.

I took the two bottles from my pocket, drank Kaliah's blood from one, and dropped bloom on my skin from the other. Then I punched myself in the face and tried to graft . . . but failed. I punched myself harder. This time the graft caught, and the voices in the cackle formed the Lodge around me and put me in Kaliah's twelve-year-old body.

Already, Brad had inserted seven corruptions in this whorl that weren't here when I'd last visited. As long as he had a foothold in Kaliah's cackle, he would never leave her alone.

As I deviated from the path of pain and reached for the familiar letter opener to gash my hand, the Brads scattered like crows that had seen a gun. I chased them down the hallway where they'd disappeared before. But because I'd drunken Kaliah's blood, they now remained visible to me. And I was able to follow them into a dining room where people sat in groups of two to five, drinking mimosas and eating omelets at tables with white tablecloths. The Brads screeched and made a mess and a racket trying to escape from me, but I tracked them all down and purged them from Kaliah's whorl.

I'd strayed from the pain of this whorl longer than I ever had before, but my graft remained strong. I wondered if drinking Kaliah's blood had anything to do with that.

Just as the whorl's loop was restarting, I went through a series of foundation gestures and found the path of pain again next to a boy standing just outside the dining hall, peering in. Filtering my senses through the cackle, applying what I'd learned while taking the trout test, I found that I was no longer following the whorl's pain, but riding it.

The boy looked up at me. He was maybe nine. I recognized Hugo's features in his fresh face—certainly not in the nose, but in the eyes and mouth. The skin around his glossy eyes was red and puffy from crying, eyelashes still wet. His mouth twisted as he bravely fought off a rising sob.

"Did you tell her?" I said.

He nodded.

"What did she say?"

"She told me to stop complaining and to go away."

Still riding the Ghost, I hugged him, and he gave up fighting the tears. I hugged him for a long time. Then I marched back into the dining room full of eating, talking adults. No one was dressed in Victorian garb anymore. They wore dated, modern clothes. I snatched a steak knife from a table I passed, then stabbed it into the thigh of a well-dressed, well-postured middle-aged woman eating a poached egg. Her leg jerked away reflexively, and she punched me in the face. I fell back into a diner who yipped as his chair scraped across the floor a few inches.

The well-dressed woman did not reach for the knife stuck in her thigh. She did not express pain or fear on her face or with speech. She only let out a disdainful snort and looked down on me through her nose. Then she motioned to someone across the room.

A teenage girl sat at the same table. She glared at me. Kaliah's narrative bubbled to the surface—*sister*—before I pushed it back down.

A man came and led me by the hand to a room with a piano. I didn't fight him. He left me there alone. I sat for a few minutes, then the door opened. Karen and Melissa, wearing jeans instead of dresses now, looked both ways before they entered and quietly shut the door.

We fought as we had before. I rode Kaliah's movements. I felt the movements drawing cackle voices into my body from the ancestors of Kaliah's line who had mastered martial arts. The whorl became a Kaleidoscope of flashing images of other opponents, other places, other and mismatched body parts—a hairy arm attached to a small fist slamming into a Picasso-like face—from countless fighting whorls entangled through grace in movement, until the graft succeeded, and I was back in reality, back in the kitchen, with the combined knowledge of fighters who had lived years, centuries, millennia ago. Their voices whispered, argued, shouted inside me. I gave them my intentions—*hurt Brad*—and I rode my body across the kitchen, moving in a foreign way. I felt separate but in charge, like the captain of a ship.

Brad must have heard me grafting moments earlier, muttering my Pictionary poems to myself, because he'd turned from Kaliah to face me in a defensive stance, staff ready. He raised his chin and puckered his lips in an expression of supreme confidence. Now that Kaliah's whorls were completely free of him, I could punch that face all I wanted and he wouldn't be able to get inside her head anymore.

I took the giant whisk from the giant mixing bowl and hurled it at Brad. He batted it away and swung for my head, but I hopped back, and his staff clanged into the proofing rack, sending metal trays clattering to the floor. He advanced, his staff a blur of swings and thrusts as I ducked and weaved and used the confined space to my advantage. I was amazed and exhilarated by my speed and skill. A gleeful laugh escaped my lips. This was fun.

But after several seconds of not landing a punch or a kick, worry crept into my mind. Brad was quick and relentless with the staff, and probably riding a Ghost of his own.

"Time to go to bed, Charlie," he said. "The grown-ups want to play."

Dodging a swipe at my shins, I briefly slipped on one of the trays scattered about. As I recovered balance, Brad jabbed the end of his staff into the tender spot just beneath my sternum. I crumpled over in pain, struggling to breathe, unable to move in any kind of effective way. And I braced myself for a blow to the head.

The gravity of my failure seized me like a frozen hand. After all this work, after passing the trout test, after riding the Ghost, how had I let this happen? Em and Kaliah were doomed, at the mercy of the Friends, at the mercy of this sick, sadistic freak, this brociopath. The horror and agony of it were annihilating. I disassociated. I was no longer there.

But then the blow never came . . . and I returned.

Brad was on the floor, scooting backward away from me, a look of terror dancing on his face as he screeched in higher and higher pitches. Kaliah stood over him, watching him try to escape something she knew he couldn't, her eyes sparkling with fury, half her upper lip slightly arched. A dark stain emerged and spread from the crotch of Brad's shorts as he peed himself.

The pain in my diaphragm subsiding somewhat, I straightened my spine and placed a hand on Kaliah's elbow. "Come on," I said between Brad's screams. "Let's go." When she didn't respond, I gently shook her elbow.

She jerked her head up and gave me a glare that promised violence. I put my hands up and backed away. "Okay, okay," I said, and she returned her focus to Brad.

In the dining area, a bizarre sort of brawl was taking place, opponents stepping carefully about, jumping for no apparent reason, eyes darting this way and that. I saw one person kick the air, another punch a wall.

When mobiak pairs fought, the shanikas projected whorls, attempting to control the reality of the battleground, while shakas rode Ghosts and struggled to determine which reality would lead them to victory.

I saw flashing green bubbles outside in the rain where Beardo and Baldy were fighting a group of Hugo's resistance fighters.

I looked around for my mom, but she was gone. She must have slipped away while I'd been fighting Brad. I didn't know what I would've said to her even if she was there. I'd stupidly wasted a rekulak spell on her, as well as time. We should have been at the town's western border by now, meeting up with Em and Zelda and the rest. How long did

Kaliah want to torture Brad? If she gave him nightmares for the next week, that still wouldn't be enough to punish him for what he'd done to her.

I gathered the typewriter and paced in front of the bathroom, trying to tune out Brad's screams. I nervously watched for a turn in the strange battle waging in the other room and outside until I couldn't take waiting anymore.

"Kaliah!" I said. "We have to go."

She stomped on Brad's testicles. Hard. He shrieked. I winced. She stomped again.

"Kaliah!"

Without acknowledging me, she tramped to the back door and threw it open. I followed her outside into a rain that was eerily warm for winter. We climbed over sandbags and sloshed through the now flooded streets, the water up to our ankles. Still riding the Ghost, my muscles were full of energy. I felt I was cutting through the water like a clipper.

The rain sounded like a storm of cicadas combined with a million dogs lapping up water. Still, I was able to hear sloshing noises behind us. Ten yards down the street, the otalith ran toward us, pushing a shopping cart full of the contraband she'd accumulated while here. Chasing after her was a Zaditorian with tape-worm arms that slithered through the air.

On top of the pile of stuff in the shopping cart was a samurai sword.

The otalith didn't deserve my help. But otaliths were rare. If the world survived this, mobiaks, including Lou, myself, and my niece, would all need a steady supply of her cackle. I couldn't let a Zaditorian kill her.

Still high off riding the ghost for the first time and

brimming with irrational confidence, I sprinted to the otalith, ignoring Kaliah's protests. I was already muttering my Pictionary poems as I grabbed the samurai sword. I hoped there was enough bloom left inside me for one more ride.

I entered the whorl with the campfire and the rapey ranchers, and I followed the pain, killing over and over, riding through loop after loop until—one with the whorl's Ghost—I returned to the flooded streets of Arampom.

I spun around the cart, putting myself between the otalith and the Zaditorian, whose unearthly appendages attacked with alarming speed. I severed the small, fanged heads in bunches with a master's skill and agility, sending the bodies spurting and wriggling back inside their bubbles. In seconds, the fight was over, and the Zaditorian ran away, screeching.

The otalith grunted at me and held out her hand.

I gave her back her sword and said, "You owe me."

She grunted again, then walked away, pushing her cart off the road and through a flooded pasture toward one of the surrounding mountains.

"Why are you just standing there?" Kaliah said. "Let's go! I can't believe you did that. You feel tough now?"

"Yeah," I said.

"I'm happy for you."

I smelled the western Wall of Blanche before we reached it—the sweet, nauseating smell of fresh carrion. Fewer birds flew overhead since the rains came, and their cries were fainter. Where there was higher ground, the wall was marked by a six-foot-wide band of sodden bird carcasses and the occasional concrete building housing a former monastery warden whose infected cackle spread out and combined with the next warden and the next, forming the invisible wall that would turn anyone who tried to cross it into Blanche.

Hugo and Rhonaya were waiting for us beside an army transport truck. The special squad of Zaditorian fighters sat in the covered bed, two large speakers at their feet, pointing out. Hugo gave Kaliah and me rain ponchos.

"Where's Em?" I said. "And Zelda?"

"We don't know," Hugo said. "Something went wrong. We should go while we can. It will mean finding the sourdough totem without your mummers, but I think it's our best course of action."

I clenched my jaw and stared at him.

"That was the plan," he said. "If something went wrong, that was the plan."

Too disgusted to respond, I turned my back on him, shoved a hand in my pocket, and felt around for the tack I'd put there. After escaping from the otalith lair, Zelda had explained to me the limitations of our unique connection. If we were near each other, within one to two hundred yards, depending on certain factors, I could speak to her with my mind. But whenever I was in pain, whenever my cackle was spreading, our connection had no distance limits, as long as there wasn't an angry otalith around.

I plunged the tack into my finger and reached out for Zelda with my mind.

She won't come, Zelda said, frantic.

Em? I said.

She says she won't leave without the rest of the mummers.

What? Why?

Hardship has bonded her with them. She says she's sorry.

I turned back to Hugo. "We have to go get them."

"No," he said. "We leave now."

"Then good luck. Because I'm not leaving without Em."

He threw his head back dramatically and shook his palms at the sky, then walked away from me, climbed into the driver's seat of the truck, and fired the engine.

CHAPTER 31

HUGO'S ELITE SQUAD OF Zaditorian fighters was comprised of barbershop singers, or more precisely, those that could ride the Ghost of ancestors who were barbershop singers. Kaliah and I sat in the covered bed with them, seven in all, as the truck roared down the flooded streets of town. The singers had just finished grafting to their totems: straw hat, red-striped vest, a bowtie, one guy even stroked his mustache to enter the right whorl. They sat with thousand-mile stares, poised for battle, gripping their microphones tight.

Rhonaya stood in the rear, looking out, holding a radar gun.

We crossed the raging river that was threatening to overtake the bridge. Branches and small logs were entangled around the pilings like beaver dams. Driving around the battle outside the bakery, Rhonaya popped Baldy's spider-head bubble with her radar gun. Emboldened, the resistance fighters pressed the attack and knocked him to the ground.

The gates at the monastery were open and unguarded. As we barreled down the driveway, one of the singers turned on the PA and adjusted its knobs until the screeching feedback stopped.

We found the mummers and Zaditorians fighting in a field around back. An entire wall of the monastery had been blown off, black smoke billowing from the wreckage, exposed wiring and insulation hanging from the interior walls and floors. Green, purple, yellow bubbles expanded and popped, expanded and popped as the Zaditorians released horrors from the other stomachs—fanged tentacles, flat, spiked tails, grotesque flaps of skin that twisted and folded and whipped around—onto the mummers, who fought back with rakes and shovels and rocks. Hundreds of mummers against a dozen Zaditorians, and the Zaditorians were winning. Fallen mummers littered the battlefield, and six more were added to their lot just as we pulled up.

Rhonaya jumped down from the back of the truck and started popping bubbles with the radar gun while the singers sang "Mr. Sandman" into their mics. Their harmonies blasted through the speakers, and the Zaditorians stumbled, fell, and flickered, then became transparent. And the physical attacks from the mummers passed right through them.

Zelda bounded over to me, fur plastered to her sides with rainwater. *Follow me!* I ran into the melee, among the confused and frustrated mummers who couldn't land a blow to the enemies standing right in front of them, enemies presumably waiting for the singing to stop.

There, Zelda said, nodding her head at a woman swinging a knife through one of the transparent Zaditorians. The woman yelled and swung and swung, apparently unable to accept that her opponent, in its current state, could not be hurt. The woman was approaching middle age, and she wore an apron and a hairnet. Zelda had warned me Em would be wearing these things. They had become something like security blankets for her, ties to the mummer host who had comforted her when she was afraid and confused and alone, a host that still comforted her now. I felt uneasy that Em had formed such a bond with a mummer, a creature that as far as I could tell was parasitic at best. But at least she was alive.

"Em!" I yelled over the sounds of rain and battle.

Her head jolted up, and she turned to me, her face simultaneously hopeful and on the verge of tears. I pushed mummers aside to get to her, and we hugged. "I'm so sorry," I said. "I'm so sorry."

"Where were you?" she said, breaking my heart.

"I came as soon as I could. I'm so sorry."

She breathed out and rested her weight on me, as if she'd fallen asleep watching TV with me. But she was so much heavier now as a woman, and I had to brace myself not to fall.

"Is Mom dead?" she said.

Just to hear the question hurt, brought back pain. "I hope not," I said, telling myself that I wasn't lying, that anything was possible now. "We have to go."

She stood back from me. "I'm not leaving without them."

"Who? These *mummers*?" I said with disgust.

"They're my friends." She looked hurt. "They helped me. I'm a mummer now."

"Don't say that."

"I'm not leaving without them. Suzanne has been good to me. You should talk to her."

"Who's Suzanne?"

"The lunch lady."

I shivered at the thought of my niece sharing her mind with a grown woman, a stranger I knew nothing about. "We can't stay here."

"I'm not leaving without them." Her face was not hers, but it wore her expressions. She gave me her stern, determined look, the one she gave when she was pointing out some adult hypocrisy, some fundamental unfairness like bedtime. "There are school buses. We have the keys." She pointed to the ghostly Zaditorian she'd been trying to kill. It stared at us without expression. "Now that these things aren't stopping us we can use them."

"Then let's do that. But we have to hurry."

She smiled, then put some bass in her voice and shouted over my shoulder. "Let's move out." She walked back toward the monastery, motioning for others to follow, and they did, hundreds of mummers following my niece. They gathered their wounded as they came. We marched between buildings to the front drive, where four yellow school buses were parked, and the mummers filed in.

Hugo drove the army transport truck alongside as I stood by Em/Suzanne, who was watching over the retreat like a sergeant, helping and spouting orders when needed.

"What in the seven stomachs is this?" Hugo shouted from the driver's seat.

"We're gonna have a convoy," I said.

He frowned and looked away, his head shaking with

frustration as if he had palsy. I couldn't blame him. I felt much the same way. But if this was what it took to get my strong-willed niece to come, then this was what it took.

I found Bruce and Pam in one of the lines and stopped them. They seemed happy to see me, like we were old friends. When I told them not to try any metaphors on me, they looked hurt and promised to do no such thing. They claimed they were only trying to save me per Naomi's instructions, but now that we were all doomed there was no need for that anymore. They just wanted to get back to Naomi, the love of their lives, before the end.

I convinced Em/Suzanne to ride in the back of the truck with me, Zelda, Kaliah, Bruce, Pam, Rhonaya, and the singers. The convoy rolled out, the four buses in front, while the singers launched harmonies at the Zaditorians, who had lost their transparency and were following at a distance. The bubbles on their extremities produced long animal legs, allowing the Zaditorians to lope unnaturally on all fours at great speed.

Bruce nudged Rhonaya with his elbow, pointed at me, and shouted over the barbershop singing, "This guy doesn't like guacamole. Can you believe that?"

Rhonaya looked straight ahead, taciturn.

Bruce shrugged, smiled, and shook his head at me. "I still can't believe it. Cracks me up. You're a piece of work, you know that?"

"Back at you, Bruce," I said.

Zelda shook herself off, sending water flying all over, and everyone but the singers squawked in protest. *Sorry,* she said.

"She says she's sorry," I said.

"Is she your pet?" Bruce said.

I laughed as Zelda jumped onto Em/Suzanne and curled up in her lap.

"No," Em/Suzanne said, defensive.

Bruce smiled and shook his head again. "This guy. Some piece of work."

As we came to the edge of town, approaching the Wall of Blanche, Kaliah grabbed my hand and closed her eyes, and the landscape outside the truck transformed into a high desert with tumbleweed, sand, and a sun shining high in a blue sky, incongruous with the sounds of rain still pattering on the canvas cover over our heads that we could no longer see. I'd been in Kaliah's projected whorls several times now, but I still wasn't used to the experience. Seeing a bleak, grey, flooded town turn into a desert was uncanny, especially knowing that it was the only thing protecting everyone from the Wall of Blanche, the only thing protecting us all from having our thoughts, our minds given over to a woman obsessed with her own "journey."

When the desert scene dissipated, we were climbing out of the valley. The border of dead birds, the white houses, and the flooding river were all behind us. We had escaped Arampom, but the Zaditorians were still following just out of range of the time-collapsing notes of the barbershop singers.

CHAPTER 32

KALIAH SLUMPED, TEETERED, THEN fell against me. I put my arm around her shoulder. "Are you okay?" I said. She didn't respond. I shook her.

There's nothing you can do, Zelda said. *Let her rest. She'll either wake up on her own or she won't.*

What do you mean? I said.

She's spread herself too thin getting us past the Wall of Blanche. She's trying to gather herself now. I can't explain it better than that.

There has to be something we can do. What about Craig? Or otalith cackle. I used that the last time this happened.

Far away, I heard a rustling noise, like a tarp being dragged across concrete. It grew louder and louder until I couldn't hear anything else, then it dipped and was silent, only to come right back, softer and in a halting rhythm—rustling sounds producing various notes and tones, playing together to make a song. The notes were coming from my clothes. I could hear where they originated on my body.

This was the Dirge I'd been warned about. The bloom must have worn off. I was no longer riding the Ghost.

More sounds jumped in from where my hand touched Kaliah, where my skin contacted the air. They merged and flowed together with the barbershop singers, making beautiful and unique music. I was entranced by it. Why had Kaliah been so afraid for me to catch this cackle malady? It was wonderful.

Fight it, Zelda said, almost singing herself.

Why? I smiled at her.

Because it's one of the songs of death. I know it well. You're not ready for it. Rhonaya has otalith cackle for you. Tell her to give you some.

I tried to speak, but when I opened my mouth, air made music on my tongue, and I made gargling sounds that Rhonaya couldn't hear over the barbershop squad. Zelda jumped down and pawed at Rhonaya's leg, then ran over to me, just like Lassie would have done. I made more gargling sounds, and Rhonaya got the gist, pulled out a small bottle, and sprayed me in the face. In moments, the Dirge went silent. All I could hear now was "Mr. Sandman" for the second time today.

"Thank you," I said to Rhonaya.

Her only reply was to toss the bottle in my lap.

"Are you okay?" Em/Suzanne said.

"I just needed some medicine," I said, not wanting her to worry. "I'm okay now."

"I'm cold," she said.

"Me too. Come sit next to me."

She did, and I put my free arm around her broad shoulders. Zelda jumped onto her lap and curled into a ball. Even though we were all wet, our combined body heat soon warmed us. Em/Suzanne and Zelda fell asleep. My eyelids grew heavy. I hadn't slept much the night before, knowing what was coming. I was tired but anxious. Would we find Naomi? Would I be able to eat the cheese danish? Why had Zelda called the Dirge a song of death?

Despite the worries swimming around in my head, I dozed off.

I don't know how long I slept, but I was startled awake by sustained and otherworldly shrieking. I looked out the back and we were still on the mountain road that ran along the south fork of the Eel River. The Zaditorians were still loping after us with their long limbs, but now they were closer than they had dared to come before. I heard off-notes from two of the singers and realized they were getting tired.

The two reserve singers across from me were rushing to graft to their totems, but they had cumbersome techniques. One attempted to paint a watercolor on her lap as the truck shook and swayed, while the other molded something from modeling clay.

The Zaditorians shrieked and drew closer.

I tensed, wondering if I should drop more bloom and punch myself in the face again.

But then the reserves put their art projects down, apparently riding their Ghosts, and took the mics from the failing singers and belted out the shielding harmonies, barely missing a beat.

The three Zaditorians in the lead stumbled and fell, rolling back, then regained their feet and continued following at the distance we were all more comfortable with.

I looked away from their frightening spider heads to the exhausted singers slumped across from me, sweating and breathing hard. Rhonaya, who was as much their handler as their leader, put the art supplies in a case and gave her spent soldiers each a thermos. Steam rose from the contents as the singers drank, and new worries added to my list. How long could the barbershop squad keep this up? What would happen to us when their voices failed? The Zaditorians didn't seem to be tired at all.

The excitement dying down, I noticed Em/Suzanne was no longer keeping my left side warm. She was in the far corner by the cab, sandwiched between Bruce and Pam, who whispered to her.

"Hey," I said. "Get away from her."

Bruce and Pam turned and gave me their best *who-me* faces.

"They have a body for me," Em/Suzanne said with a youthful and excited smile that was jarring to see on such a weathered face. "Suzanne's daughter is with Naomi. She's my age. Naomi can put me in her."

"What?" I said. "No. We're going to get your old body back."—I hoped we would anyway—"Don't talk to these mummers anymore. They're parasites."

Em/Suzanne stomped her foot. "They are not. And they don't call themselves mummers either. They're Terwer."

"We are definitely not parasites," Bruce said in a huff. "What an extremely racist remark. You're really showing your true colors, sir."

"Shut the hell up, Bruce," I said. "Go eat some guacamole."

"I'm not going back to my old body," Em/Suzanne said,

more forlorn than indignant now. "I don't want to have the nightmares anymore."

"You're not having them now are you?" I wished Kaliah was awake to help me with this.

"Suzanne protects me from them."

I didn't know how to feel about that. I was glad Em was no longer experiencing the unbidden and unfiltered memories of our ancestors, but I didn't know Suzanne. How could I trust her? She voluntarily, as far as I could tell, took a backseat to my niece in a mind they shared. What if Suzanne decided to take the front seat? Would Em be trapped behind her without a voice?

As I tried to think of what May would do or say here, the truck lurched to a sudden stop. We all slid a foot or so along the bench seats toward the cab. Poor Zelda, lighter and with less traction, hit the cab wall, but not too hard. There was a brief hiccup in the singing but the barbershop squad recovered nicely.

The Zaditorians paced in the road fifty yards behind us, their multicolored bubbles bright against the mountainside.

"What's going on?" Kaliah said, sitting up, squinting.

"You're okay," I said, surprised to hear her voice. "We were worried."

"Keep singing," Rhonaya said to her squad with a booming voice.

Zelda darted outside. After telling Kaliah to rest and Em/Suzanne to stay put, I followed, jumping down from the back of the truck and scampering around the side as fast as I could to get away from the blaring speakers pointing outward.

The culverts were overflowing. Sheets of water ran across

the road. I jogged ahead, around a bend. Beyond the lead school bus, the road had been consumed by a mudslide four stories tall with regolith and trees poking out like bones, and some trees still standing on the top.

I heard someone behind me yell, "Noooooo," and I turned to see Hugo crouch and put his face in his hands. For a moment, I shared his sentiment, but then Zelda said, *Go get your typewriter,* and I remembered I had one more rekulak spell. I patted Hugo on the shoulder and told him we weren't dead yet, then jogged back to the truck.

CHAPTER 33

THE ZADITORIANS WERE STILL pacing. They'd been waiting for something like this. We were like castaways on a leaky raft, in the open ocean, and they were the circling sharks.

"What's going on?" Kaliah said when I climbed in out of the rain.

"Mudslide. We need to get on the lead bus." I went to Em/Suzanne and put my hands on her shoulders, looked her in the eyes. "I don't know if we're going to make it." My voice faltered a little. "But we have to try. We can't stay here. The world ends if we stay here." I turned to Rhonaya and told her what I was planning, that she would have to stay behind and hold off the Zaditorians as long as she could. She had an intimidating stare that made me feel a little uneasy telling her how things were going to be, but she listened and nodded and said, "Good luck."

Em/Suzanne, Kaliah, Bruce, and Pam jumped out of the truck. I grabbed the signature 510 and followed. Hugo was still crouched where I'd left him. I told him what I'd told Rhonaya, and he stood and raised an eyebrow at my typewriter. Then he hugged Kaliah, who ordered him not to die. A solemn smile dimpled his cheeks before he turned and headed back to the truck.

The doors to the lead bus opened with a hiss. Em/Suzanne, Kaliah, Zelda, Bruce, Pam, and I climbed inside. The engine was off, and all the windows were fogged up. The mummer passengers silently stared at us from their seats. Water dripped from our rain ponchos and pooled on the floor. I gave a brief speech explaining what was about to happen, during which I felt oddly at home, like I was back on a tour bus, pointing out the sites.

I took the driver's seat, fired the engine, and blasted the defrost. As the condensation cleared, I summoned Craig by creating a gap in my choices, which I accomplished by transcribing the user manual for a vacuum cleaner I'd found under the sink in the Arampom house. Following Lonnie's teachings, I'd chosen a totem and a dilemma, and I'd posed all the different uses I could come up with for that totem as solutions for that dilemma, thereby mutilating a choice and making a common reference point that could be used to communicate, to trick the god-like creature that preyed on me.

When I smelled menthol and strawberries, I stopped typing and pulled out my prepared totem—a lemon zester— and I recited the spell before Craig could fill the gap in my choices with a homunculus diary:

Dear Rhonda: I recently developed an appreciation for yodeling and signed up for classes to learn. When my husband found out, he insisted on coming with me so we could learn to yodel together. But I told him yodeling was my thing and he couldn't come, which made him very offended. It's been two months since then and I haven't gone to one class yet because he is still sensitive about the subject and I am afraid of causing a rift in our marriage. Am I being selfish for wanting yodeling all to myself?

Help me Rhonda.

—Desperately Seeking Lederhosen

I held up the Homunculus Totem and said, "This lemon zester made a large tunnel for *this* part of *this* road."

Yellow rekulak bile devoured the lemon zester from my hand as more bile swarmed on the face of the mudslide, then dissipated, leaving a large tunnel through the heap of mud and rock and trees. I could see the road on the other side. I heard gasps from the mummers behind me. Em/Suzanne said, "Whoa."

I jammed the gearshift into drive and stomped the gas pedal. If Lonnie was to be believed, the destruction wrought from rekulak spells was permanent, because of the arrow of time, but the creation wrought from the spells was temporary. But how temporary? Lonnie had said seconds, but he hadn't specified how many. There were four buses and a truck in our convoy.

We drove into the dark tunnel. There was no concrete or

anything visible between us and the slide. The mud was smooth, as if behind glass. Whatever homunculus structure that held it out was invisible to the naked eye.

I counted twelve seconds before we hit daylight and were clear, rain once again hammering on the metal roof. The mummers cheered and clapped. I took a deep breath and brought the bus to a safe stop two hundred yards from the tunnel. The other buses were right behind us. I turned to Kaliah. Her face was pale, tight. Her brother was sacrificing himself so we could go on. She didn't know what the Friends would do to him. She didn't know if she'd ever see him again. I went to her, put a hand on her shoulder. She grabbed it and lowered her head.

A horn blared, and I looked up to see headlights in the tunnel. "Something's wrong," I said. "They're coming through." I watched the tunnel in horror, expecting it to collapse. What was Hugo thinking? They're going to be crushed.

But the tunnel kept its shape, and the truck came barreling out on our side. This time I cheered, along with Kaliah. But then I saw a green glow on top of the slide. A Zaditorian was bounding over it toward us. Somehow it had slipped by the barbershop squad.

Rhonaya came around the back of the truck—now stopped—and pointed her radar gun at the advancing Zaditorian. Its bubbles collapsed, and its momentum sent its now entirely human body flying into the street and sliding to a stop by the bus behind us.

Rhonaya turned away and pointed the radar gun back at the tunnel, where the rest of the Zaditorians were, clustered just inside, clamoring over and around each other with their spindly and freakish bodies, trying to escape, reforming bubbles almost as fast as Rhonaya popped them.

Something was off about the barbershop squad's singing. It was quieter, less dynamic. I realized more singers had lost their voices.

Hugo backed the truck closer to the tunnel, and the Zaditorians backed further inside.

"Collapse!" I said as if I could make it happen with my words. What was taking so long? Collapse!

The bus door slapped open, and I turned in time to see Em/Suzanne stepping out. I called after her, but she ran toward the fight. A few mummers were right behind her, others were already standing, lining up in the aisle, and filing through the door. I wedged between two bodies, pushed my way outside, and sprinted to catch up with Em/Suzanne, shouldering mummers out of my way. She was heading straight for the Zaditorian that had climbed over the slide.

He stood now, scraped bloody—my old friend Beardo. Bubbles formed all over his body in a variety of colors. Nightmarish body parts sprouted from the bubbles: a hairy leg thicker than a tree trunk, a tentacle with spiked feathers, a car-sized torso oozing a viscous substance with corral-like rocks tearing through the skin along the spine, a head that looked like a neon shrub with a beak, a head with a spear-length proboscis and a forehead piled high with orange eyes like salmon roe, a head that was a gigantic, wrinkled blue worm with a mouth like a monstrous sea anemone.

An arm with red, flaking skin and dozens of purple vines for fingers swung toward Em/Suzanne. The vines wrapped around her waist and lifted. She screamed. I was ten yards away. She was a foot above the ground when Zelda darted past me, leapt through the air, bit the arm, and latched on, her body hanging as she shook and tugged. The vines let go of Em/Suzanne, and the arm whipped sideways, sending Zelda hurtling over a bus toward the cliff.

"No!" I cried. Then my feet flew out from under me, and my shoulder slammed into the road. A mummer had been thrown at me and was under my legs, hurt. I stood and ran to Em/Suzanne. Mummers were charging the beast only to be tossed back by its flailing limbs. The worm head was slowly eating some pour soul with its writhing mouth.

When I reached Em/Suzanne, she was hurling rocks at one of the heads. Mummers all around us were either doing the same or attacking one of the seven legs with the yard tools they'd hung on to from the battle at the monastery. They were all mad, suicidal, and my niece appeared to be one of them.

"Em!" I shouted. "We have to get out of here."

Purple flashed as vine fingers flicked and curled around me. The vines pinned my arms to my side and squeezed the breath from my lungs. My stomach dropped and the world blurred by as I was lifted into the air. Then I was stationary, looking down on the street, the parked buses, the fighting mummers, and the raging river below. Then I was being lowered into a green, lily-shaped flower bigger than a kiddy pool, with boiling red liquid inside. Then the flower disappeared. I smelled ozone and fried onions. Bubbles collapsed below me. I caught a glimpse of Hugo out of the truck, a radar gun in hand. Then I was falling, but only for a dizzying moment. I landed hard on the roof of one of the buses. My shoulder, ribs, guts screamed with pain. I writhed and groaned and struggled to breathe until I smelled menthol and strawberries—my old friend, Craig—and the pain was gone.

Rolling over to the edge of the roof, I saw Beardo's last bubble burst. He was the shape of a man again. The mummers swarmed him, knocking him to the ground, beating on him, beating on him.

I hung over the side of the bus and dropped to the street. A gravelly, crackling, whooshing sound filled the air. The tunnel was gone in an instant, crushing the remaining Zaditorians. The mountain above it flowed down, swift and fluid, catching the army truck, which spun, teetered, and was swept over the side. The cab was empty, but the barbershop squad was still singing when the slide hit, and there was no time for them to get out.

"Did you see where she went?" Em/Suzanne said, walking over to me, worry painted on her face. I knew she was talking about Zelda. I shook my head, and we went to the edge of the road, calling Zelda's name. I poked myself with a tack and called out to her with my mind. No response.

Em/Suzanne's voice broke. She and Zelda had become close during Em/Suzanne's imprisonment. Zelda had brought her care packages and kept her company through the nights. I began to feel frantic, darting this way and that, my head on a swivel, calling, searching. I loved this little fox, almost from the first moment we met. She had shown me compassion, given me love in the darkest moment of my life. And now she was special to my niece. Our broken family needed her.

Em/Suzanne had stopped calling. Her shoulders and chest heaved with sobs. I put my arm around her and looked down the embankment, hoping. Part of the army truck was submerged in the river. Above it, a patch of mud was moving slowly up the slide. I squinted at it and almost cried out but sucked the words back in before they could escape. I didn't want to get Em/Suzanne's hopes up only to dash them away.

A few moments later, I made out the shape of a snout and two pointy ears. "Look! Look!" I said to Em/Suzanne, and we ran to the slide. Zelda was shivering, trudging up and over the moved earth, her fur caked in mud. I had to hold Em/Suzanne back from going down to meet her. When Zelda reached the road, Em/Suzanne scooped her up, and Zelda licked Em/Suzanne's face. Shivering, pressed against Em/Suzanne's chest, Zelda said, *I'm here. I'm here.*

CHAPTER 34

THE LAST BUS OF Mummers volunteered to stay behind and help Rhonaya rescue the barbershop squad, if any still lived, but Rhonaya turned them down, despite assurances from Bruce and Pam that they wouldn't harm the singers. Like all mobiaks, Rhonaya was distrustful of mummers.

Hugo told her to come with us now, that we needed her abilities, that our mission was more important than a few lives. Of course, he was right. Six lives were nothing compared to the trillions Blanche was set to take, but leaving Rhonaya alone to rescue the singers who'd just saved all of us felt wrong, horribly wrong.

While Hugo and Rhonaya argued, mummers walked over to the slide and began forming a daisy-chain down to the wreck, most of them sinking deep into the mud. When

Rhonaya saw what they were doing, she shouted at them to stop. The mummers continued making the chain. She told them they better not expect anything in return for their help and declared she would kill the singers before she would let their cackle be taken.

"They're not going to hurt anyone," Em/Suzanne said to Rhonaya with scorn in her voice. "Only some are like that."

Rhonaya ignored her, raising her chin and looking away, like a dog bothered by the antics of a puppy. Then her eyelids peeled back, and she pointed her radar gun up at the slide. I followed her line of sight. Four Zaditorians were climbing over the mud and regolith to get at us. They must have hung back while their brethren were crushed inside the false tunnel.

"Go," Rhonaya yelled. "Go now." She began throat-singing, but I could barely hear her over the rain.

"Run," Hugo cried.

I grabbed Em/Suzanne's hand—I wouldn't lose her again. She held Zelda under one arm, and we scrambled over and around the twisted bodies of the mummers who had died fighting Beardo. Hugo was already in the driver's seat when we reached the lead bus. Kaliah, Pam, and Bruce climbed in after us, and the bus was moving before we found our seats, before the door was even closed.

"Stop," Em/Suzanne said. "We can't leave them."

Hugo stared straight ahead as if he hadn't heard anything, and we accelerated.

"Stop," Em/Suzanne said.

Pam crouched down in the aisle beside her, put a hand on Em/Suzanne's arm. "It's okay," she said.

"We have to go back," Em/Suzanne said. "We have to save them."

Pam shook her head. "This was the plan all along, Little Bear. Remember?"

"But they don't have to stay behind. We can all make it."

Pam's face expressed pride and sadness. "We can't all make it. We tried. And that was very brave of you to insist that we did. But they have to fight now so that we can go on, so that we can save the universe."

Em/Suzanne's face pinched as she began to cry. Pam hugged her and rubbed her back.

Little Bear? I didn't trust Pam, and I didn't like her comforting my niece, but I kept my mouth shut this time. Em/Suzanne had clearly bonded with her and the rest of the mummers during their confinement and deprivation. I couldn't break a bond formed under those circumstances with a few words. And if we managed to save the world, there was a scenario in which Em/Suzanne spent the rest of her days in a mummer's body. Pounding my prejudices, earned or not, into her head would only drive a wedge between us.

Hugo drove us around the mountain, along the river at a decent but safe pace. The rain fell, slamming against the roof. The windshield wipers flapped back and forth. No cars approached from either direction. We were the only ones on the road. We came across three more slides, but they were small and only blocked part of the road, which was lucky because I was out of rekulak spells.

Bruce tried to make small talk with me, asking about the cheese-themed dates Naomi had taken me on. After I grunted a few terse responses, Kaliah came to my rescue and spun a yarn about why cheddar was orange. I had to smile as she went on about the Protestants bringing the practice over from Ireland, where they'd developed a secret code using shades of cheese to send messages to each other during their war with the Catholics. Bruce dimpled his chin with a frown and nodded while he listened, as if he were learning a truly interesting historical tidbit.

As we neared the highway, the road dropped in elevation. Large sections were flooded, but the water never came more than halfway up our tall wheels. When we reached the highway, Hugo stopped the bus, turned around, and said, "North or south?"

"North," Pam said. "To the DMV in Eureka."

Bruce smiled at me and said, "Naomi will be delighted to see you again."

"Good to know," I said.

Hugo turned north and got the bus up to highway speed. Eureka was about forty minutes away. Shortly, we crossed the bridge over the confluence of the north and south forks of the Eel River, but I couldn't see the forks or the river, only a muddy body of water sprawled across the land. Giant trees sprouted from it like reeds.

As we drove, I worried again about how many people, mobiaks and barrens alike, Blanche had infected, how many people I would have to kill to save the universe. I pictured Craig the way Zelda had described him, as a string through all seven of Arawok's stomachs. As long as Blanche was attached to that string, she couldn't be regurgitated into the void, the way my sister had been. I wanted to ask Zelda how the void was different from regular dying, but I was afraid of the answer, of knowing what my sister had experienced in her last moments and for the rest of eternity, what the Blanche-infected people would experience when I excised them from Craig.

I thought back on my kidnapping, on meeting Kaliah for

the first time, on everything that had led to this point. I made myself nauseous gaping at the constellation of misjudgments and poor choices that had coalesced into this disaster. If I'd only done this, said that, gone here . . . .

"She's a lot like you," Kaliah said, her chin resting on the back of the seat in front of me.

"She's like her mom," I said, looking over at Em/Suzanne, who was sleeping in Pam's arms now.

"You both want to save everyone."

"Isn't that the plan?"

"You have to play with the money you have left. Don't think about the hands you used to have or the ones you could've had. That's how you go on tilt."

"What is this? Are you quoting Kenny Rogers now? Just say what you're trying to say."

I caught a glimpse of hurt in her eyes as she turned and sat back down, and I felt instant remorse, but before I could apologize, the brakes screeched, and I had to brace myself to keep from sliding off my seat.

The bus stopped, and I looked ahead to see the north- and southbound lanes, four in all, congested with empty parked cars. I'd seen no vehicles traveling south since we started this journey, but there had been plenty passing us. And they'd all ended up here. There was no space for the bus to get through.

We were on a small hill overlooking Scotia, the mill town where I'd drunken the Zaditorian milk that had saved my life. The rows of nearly identical houses reminded me of Arampom. This town, though, had a working mill. The buildings were weathered, but not falling apart, and there were stacks of fresh lumber and mountains of logs and sawdust in the yard.

Its sister town, right across the Eel River, was Rio Dell, where Blanche's celebration of the 1964 Christmas Flood was being held. The festivities looked well on their way.

Three cars pulled up behind us. Twelve people got out of them, mostly men, a few of which wore skirts and V-neck sweaters. Everyone in the group carried an umbrella and a gargantuan purse. And they all had bleach-blond hair.

Blanche!

CHAPTER 35

A S THE GROUP WALKED down the highway, approaching the bus, I crouched between the seats and said, "Everyone get down." If any of the Blanche's happened to be a shanika spreading cackle, they would inadvertently infect everyone in the bus but me.

I watched my skin for circulating blue scrill.

Other than an umbrella scraping against the outside of the bus that made me jump, the group of Blanches was silent as they walked by. After a while, I poked my head up and sighed relief. They were gone. We'd dodged a bullet. I could have easily lost Em to the Blanche infection just as I'd gotten her back.

I went to the front of the bus and made a little speech: "Looks like Blanche is still gathering her army to invade all the stomachs," I said, "which means we're not too late. Since

I'm the only one immune to Nemaloki poison, I'm going to scout ahead to find a path through that's safe for all of us. After I go, turn the bus around and park at the south end of the mill, away from the people arriving. I'll come find you there."

I looked down at Hugo in the driver's seat, and he nodded.

I'm coming with you, Zelda said.

No, I said, *you're hurt.*

I'm feeling better.

Em needs you.

Em needs you.

I knelt next to Em/Suzanne, put my hands on her broad, working-class shoulders, and said, "Take care of Zelda while I'm gone."

Em/Suzanne narrowed her eyes in determination, nodded, and wrapped her arms tighter around Zelda. Through my connection with Zelda, I felt her warmth and love for my niece.

I stood and looked at Kaliah, who was staring fiercely at something out the window, jaw clenched. She was mad and hurt, more than I'd suspected.

"I'm sorry," I said to her.

She didn't turn from the window or change her expression.

Hugo opened the door, which I took as my cue, and I hopped off the bus. I skulked from parked car to parked car until they ended at a long, two-lane concrete bridge. More cars were parked on the other side, but on the bridge itself, there were only three vehicles, an RV, and two trucks. Throughout the length of the bridge, dozens of people performed various tasks: some unloaded from the two trucks, others set up stages, others erected canopy tents.

Directly to the west, adjacent to the bridge, was its sister, also concrete, also two lanes, but for southbound traffic. An RV and two trucks were on it, too, along with dozens of people working setting up stages and tents. Further west was a steel truss bridge, painted green, that connected Scotia to the town of Rio Dell. It was the bridge from my dream in the deprivation tank, I realized for the first time.

This was the place where Blanche and her followers had died forty-nine years earlier, which had resulted in the creation of a Nexus Whorl. She was gathering her army in the same place, during similar conditions, so her soldiers could graft to the new flood, enter the Nexus Whorl, and invade the seven stomachs.

I'd crossed all three bridges many times, taking tourists to and from the Avenue of the Giants, sometimes stopping in Rio Dell for lunch. During a typical winter storm, forty feet separated these bridges from the Eel River below. Now, less than ten feet separated them, and the water had risen above the tree-covered bluffs on the north bank and spilled into Rio Dell. The north- and southbound lanes of 101 on the other side were dry but surrounded by water, like two spits running parallel.

We couldn't swim across in current like that, and I didn't see any boats handy, but even if we found one, I would be afraid to launch in these conditions. The bridges were the only way across, but they were teeming with Blanche's worker bees, who were preparing for a mass grafting to the flood. They would sound the alarm as soon as they saw me.

Squatting behind the wheel of a truck, I brooded over

how to get across unnoticed: lure the workers away somehow, create a diversion . . . . If I hadn't used that rekulak spell on my mom, I would have it now, to use in any number of ways. I had wasted it. Why? I shouldn't have needed a spell to figure out she was lying. A lifetime of experiences with her should have made that clear from the beginning. I shook that train of thought out of my head.

What did Blanche want, besides to become a god? What could I use? She liked being interviewed. She liked her exploits to be filmed. She had set up a whole town to create art in her honor. She was a narcissist. She wanted to control the whole universe, literally turn it into her, but she had tucked a select few of us away in Arampom so that we would be around to notice her achievements. Who was she trying to impress? Her dad? If so, could I use that somehow?

I was getting nowhere until my thoughts swung back to the flood. It was the totem that led to the Nexus Whorl. If I could corrupt that totem, make it somehow different than the flood forty-nine years ago in a significant enough way, it would no longer work as a totem. Blanche's followers wouldn't be able to graft to it, and she wouldn't be able to spread herself throughout the stomachs. I wouldn't need the sourdough starter totem to stop that. But how could I alter the totem of a whole town, of a whole flood?

Fire.

The bridges were evidently a crucial part of the flood totem, which meant this place was crucial. Neither Rio Dell nor Scotia had burned during the '64 Christmas flood. If I set one of them on fire, it might corrupt the flood totem, change the grafting conditions just enough to prevent Blanche's army from making a clean graft and marching into the Nexus

Whorl. And it might also create enough of a distraction to allow me to get the others safely across.

I quietly opened the door of the car I was crouched next to and searched inside for a gas can or a tube to use for siphoning. Nothing. I popped the trunk. Nothing. I went to the next car, and the next, and the next. Nothing. Ten minutes passed of this fruitless search.

I traveled down the onramp from Scotia, checking each car along the way. I hid from more groups of Blanches bleach-blond and dressed in vintage clothing. I was soaked through, despite my rain poncho, and frustrated. There wasn't one work truck among the parked vehicles. Did Blanche have some kind of aversion to them?

Despair crept into my mind. Even if I managed to start a fire, would that change anything? I imagined the world as I knew it ending. I imagined Blanche preserving the charred remnants of my feeble rebellion as an art installation, something inspired by her greatness, something for her to cherish—a monument.

But I had to do something. I couldn't give up.

The longer I kept rifling through the cars, the more I risked being discovered. I had already had one close call.

Scotia had a gas station. If the pumps didn't work, they also had a market.

Scotia's Main Street started where the bridge ended. It was packed for several blocks with rows of parked cars. Christmas lights, glowing dimly in the gloomy half-light of the storm, hung from the facades of the businesses that lined both sides of the street. Green and red garlands were wrapped around every lamppost.

Knees bent, back hunched, head bowed, I shuffled down

the middle of Main Street, keeping below the car hoods, out of sight of the infected.

The sidewalks were congested with them, all dressed like they had traveled through time from the early sixties: suits and fedoras, tucked-in white shirts and jeans, brown wool skirts and collared long sleeve shirts, high heels, horn-rimmed glasses, crew cuts, pipes, cigarettes, more cigarettes. Some men wore dresses. Some women wore suits. They opened and closed umbrellas as they traveled in and out of storefronts pointed to by A-frame signs.

The signs closest to me read:

"Sounds of the Flood: A Marimba Remembrance," "Quilt Deluge," "Flood Scenes: A Diorama Spectacular," "Flood Fashion."

The whole thing reminded me of Arampom, but instead of creating art in Blanche's honor, these people were creating it to better graft to the flood.

I came to a narrow stretch where the cars were parked too close. Afraid of bumping into one a little too hard and setting off an alarm, I flattened my body and was sidestepping along when I heard someone whisper, "*In here.*"

Startled, I flinched and banged my head against a fender, then froze and held my breath, terrified an alarm would go off, but no horn sounded, no lights flashed.

"*In here.*"

I looked up. A woman with her head and one arm out the back window of an SUV was waving me over. "*Hurry,*" she whispered. Her tone sounded conspiratorial, like she wasn't one of the others, like she hadn't been infected by Blanche. But then why was she here, in the middle of this? And why did she have bleach-blond hair?

I thought about running, but that would attract the whole town's attention. At the least, the woman was being discrete, and if she turned out to be another Blanche, she had already seen me and the option of running would still be available.

The woman cracked the door and scooted over while I squeezed in out of the rain. She wore a blue wool dress with a collar and large black buttons.

Two men sat in the front seat, also dressed from the fifties or early sixties. Three small screens, one embedded in the back of each front headrest, and one hanging from the roof over the rearview mirror played the opening credits of a movie. The title appeared: "The Thousand-Year Flood."

"It just started," the woman said. "'You didn't miss anything. I wish we could see this in the theater. I personally don't think this was the best way to handle the overflow."

She didn't appear to recognize me. "Why are you here?" I said.

"To celebrate the forty-ninth anniversary of the 1964 Christmas Flood," she said, a little confused by my question. "What part of the documentary do you identify with the most so far?"

"Uh," I said, scanning the sidewalks to see if anyone outside had noticed me in here. If Blanche was inside this woman, she hadn't come to the surface yet for whatever reason, and I didn't want to raise her from the depths. I answered the question: "The font choice?"

The two men in front turned in their seats and grinned at me. "How exciting," one said.

"I identify most with the picture of the house," the other said. "It reminds me of my grandma's house."

The woman slid close to me so that our bodies were

touching, and she placed a hand in mine. "I like your answer the best," she said.

"That's nice," I said, taking my hand away. "I've actually seen this movie before, so I'm going to go. Goodbye." I cracked open the door and slipped out into the rain, then almost shut the door on the woman who was scrambling out behind me. As I crouched down, she opened up her umbrella. "Go back inside," I said. "You're going to miss the movie."

"I find you stimulating," she said. "An estimated seven thousand head of cattle met their demise in the 1964 flood. What part of that do you identify with the most?"

"The part where you get back in the car."

"Interesting."

"No, wait." I remembered the other guy's answer that she'd found so unremarkable. "My grandma's house. It reminds me of my grandma's house."

"Oh wow." She opened her eyes wide and let her chin drop. "You're the performance artist, aren't you?" She turned and shouted at her fellow umbrella-toting revelers on the sidewalk, "Hey everyone. The performance artist has finally arrived." She pointed down at me, and I peered through the windows of an empty car to see people stepping out into the street with excited smiles.

No point hiding now, I turned and sprinted down the middle of the street. I reached another narrow stretch, leapt onto a hood, and stomped over the roof, denting sheet metal. I leapt to the next hood, then the next, while the infected kept pace, occasionally peering up at me from under their umbrellas with grotesquely exuberant faces, like children experiencing a trampoline for the first time.

Then my feet slipped out from under me, and I landed on

my back with the wobbly smack of denting metal. Faces crowded over me. They gave me compliments: "Amazing!" "Great job!" "Revelatory!" "An inspiration!"

Then they went silent for a moment before all speaking in unison, "Hello Charlie."

CHAPTER 36

I WAS TAKEN NORTH, equal parts dragged, carried, and shuttled in a golf cart out of town and over the bridge, up Rio Dell's Main Street, which mirrored Scotia's Christmas decorations identically. They took me through a group of flying, hopping crows and pigeons into a green and beige building, where I was set on my feet in the middle of a party. Forty or so people in vintage clothes, with vintage hairstyles, talked in small groups or danced in front of a jazz band playing in the corner. A Christmas tree stood in the other corner, lights fuzzy around the edges from the haze of cigarette smoke that filled the room. Garlands hung from the ceiling. Food and alcohol sat on tables against a wall.

I tried to run, but my minders grabbed me. "Be still," they said as a chorus.

A thick layer of blue scrill sprang from my skin and

circulated in on itself. I felt it all over, but could only see it on my hands, which glowed faintly in the dim light.

A group of talking, drinking, smoking people parted, and Em's old body walked between them toward me, wearing pearls and a green dress with a matching jacket. The band stopped playing.

This was no longer my little niece. But part of my mind couldn't comprehend that. Seeing her, conjured memories and feelings in me—love. I felt love for a vessel that held the monster that had killed my sister. It warred with the molten hatred flowing through my mind.

Blanche. She smiled up at me through Em's darling face. "I am so surprised right now. How did you get here?"

"Does it matter?" I said, looking at the finger sandwiches on the table, the first gluten I'd seen in days, and wondering if I could successfully graft to them

She frowned. "To me it does, but I guess I'll have the answers soon enough." She waved at the tables. "Do you want a drink? It's Christmas Eve after all."

The whole party looked at me like I was an especially adorable act in a children's talent show. They horrified me. What about a defeated man touched them in that way? I'd failed Em and Kaliah and Zelda, the only people left in this world I cared about, and these people thought I was cute.

"What are they?" I said, curling my lip in disgust and indicating the party with a sweeping gesture.

"People," Blanche/Em said. "From all backgrounds. Just people."

"Infected by you."

"With my cackle, yes. But they still have agency. I've just given them . . . perspective."

I snorted.

She frowned. "Truth is relative, Charlie. It is only universal when perspective is universal." Her lips tightened around her teeth, and she furrowed her brow. "That is what true grace is. And I will bathe the seven stomachs in it. And it will be glorious."

"Truth is truth."

Blanche/Em's expression relaxed and turned doleful, and she shook her head. "Hardship has made you cynical. That's a shame. You can be so much more."

"Oh? You mean like a baker who puts your face on cakes?"

She clicked her tongue, then said, "The flood is already here and you're still moored to the past. Let go and you will rise to heights you've never imagined. Cling and you will drown. You have so much to live for. You have no idea. Your mom was much more fertile than I ever was. You have brothers and sisters you've never met."

I stared at her. She was playing some new game. I couldn't trust anything she or my mom said.

"It's true," she said. "If you don't want to be a part of this, if you don't want to be a part of something great, you can live in Arampom with them, as a family. I'm shipping them there now. They are so much like you. You'd be surprised."

I didn't have the energy or desire to ponder the veracity of her claim. I was exhausted, defeated, dejected. Blanche had won and could do, say whatever she wanted. Eventually, Em and Kaliah would come into town looking for me, and Blanche would have them too. I wanted to lie down, give up, stop thinking. I almost wished I could be infected by Blanche.

But then a sound came through the PA speakers and filled the room: *tink tink tink tink tink tink.*

I looked over to the stage, where a man was tapping on a champagne glass with a fork in front of the microphone. Though he wore a gas mask around his mouth and nose and had blond hair now, I recognized him immediately by his square head and the way he stood, weight on one foot, head held high, exuding attitude. He wore a gray suit and fedora he probably thought made him look like Frank Sinatra. I was so surprised to see him I said his name out loud, "Lou!"

"Merry Christmas everybody," he said, his speech muffled a little by the mask. "I'd like to propose a toast to a very special lady, Blanche Duluth, who's made this a very special Christmas for all of us. Who needs Santa Claus when you got her, am I right? Ho ho ho everybody."

Lou gestured with his hands while he talked as he always did, but something was different about his gestures now. They were enthralling. I followed his hands as they changed shape and darted around like I was a kitten following a string dancing in the air. I was overcome with the sudden urge to attack his hands, to make them stop moving, to eat them.

"And don't get me started on the decorations," he said. "Come on. They're gorgeous. Are ya kiddin' me? The frickin' wreaths. But I gotta say, you're missing one thing. Lucky I never leave home without it. No applause, please. Just think of it as my humble contribution."

I literally drooled as I watched his hands open a box, pull out a black cylinder the size of a soda can, attach it to a stand, set it on the floor, and press a button on it.

A light show erupted onto the wall, green and red stars zipping around. I rushed toward them. I wanted to kill them all, but so did everyone else at the party, and many of them were closer and reached the wall before me. From two rows back, I had to watch their impotent attacks, pouncing on the stars, leaping after them, batting, swatting, cupping, biting, but the stars kept moving, moving, unwounded. I could do better. Desperate for the chance, I pressed into the people in front of me.

Then two arms wrapped around my waist. I pushed and pulled at them and tried to wriggle free, but they didn't budge. They lifted me off my feet and carried me outside, back to the rain and daylight, and set me down on the sidewalk. Away from the stars, I forgot about them. Dead leaves floating on the water rushing down the street gutter caught my eye now. I instantly wanted to kill their movement. I tensed, ready to pounce, but then more leaves floated by, and more, and more, and my head snapped from side to side, and I didn't know which leaf to kill first.

Lou ducked his head into my line of sight. He no longer wore the gas mask. "Relax pup," he said. "You'll be cured in no time." He brushed scrill off my face with his hand. Something wet but too warm to be rain touched my cheek, and a moment later I lost interest in the leaves. My brain felt like it had been released from a clamp. My obsession with movement was gone. I had my mind back, my reason, and I realized that Lou had just poisoned everyone at that party and given me the antidote.

"What was that?" I said.

"I call it Go-Fetch," he said. "It heightens the prey drive. Come on."

He marched up the sidewalk, and I followed him into a flower shop next door. No one was inside, I was surprised to see, and the flowers were all dead, naked stems in pots, brown petals strewn across the floor. An open duffle bag full of clothes and blond wigs was on the counter. Lou rifled through it and handed me a wig, a short-sleeve collared shirt, and a gas station attendant's jacket with a patch sewed into the right breast that read "Doug."

"Put these on," Lou said.

"Why?"

"Blanche has infected the whole county and more. But she can't be everyone at once, not yet anyway. Think of the population as her brain. Most of it is subconscious. If we dress like her, don't draw attention to ourselves, she won't see us."

"The whole county?"

Lou nodded. "And more. She ran through the Coast Guard and the National Guard when they came to bring aid. Those guys could've taken shanikas all over the country by now, spreading her cackle."

I hung my head. Humboldt County had a population of 135,000, all infected in a week, and there could be at least that many infected outside the county. If I succeeded in my mission, they would all die, all be regurgitated into the void. I would be a mass murderer. That many people, that many lives, were unfathomable to me, but sickening.

I drug my rain poncho over my head, slapped it onto the floor, and said, "Why aren't you infected. That party was loaded with Blanche's cackle."

Lou pointed to a clump of scrill that had fallen off my body and splatted on the floor. "All that gunk I collected from you came in handy. After I lost you guys, I started noticing everyone suddenly had blond hair and wore old clothes. They smelled real strange too, so I checked some of my whorls. Turns out the smell was nemaloki. Not to mention everyone started acting like it was *Invasion of the Bodysnatchers.* I put two and two together and mixed your gunk in a spray bottle and boom, I got armor."

"Do you have any more?" I finished putting on my disguise and transferred the bloom and otalith potion to my new pockets. "Em and Kaliah are waiting for me. I need to get them over the bridge somehow."

Lou grinned, turned up his palms, and shook his shoulders. "Already done, Doughboy. They're waiting for us on the north end of town. They told me the plan. Don't worry. I can get us to the DMV, and you can do what needs to be done."

"Do you know what that is?" I said. "It's murder."

"Hey, we can't be having a world of bodysnatchers. You gotta do what needs to be done."

"Do you have an empty bottle or a jar?"

Lou squinted one eye. "Who are you talking to? Do I have a bottle?" He scoffed, pulled an empty bottle from the duffle bag, and handed it to me.

I scooped scrill off my neck and plopped it into the bottle, took off my coat, and scraped the scrill off my arms. "This cures Nemaloki poison, right?" I said, holding up the blue substance. "We just kidnap a shanika infected by Blanche, put her in a room with me where Blanche can't find us, and we harvest the scrill that pours off me, and we save everyone one by one with it."

Lou shook his head as I filled the bottle. "Unfortunately, we don't have time for that. In less than an hour, she'll be invading the other stomachs. We gotta think about those people. They got lives too." He took the bottle from me.

"This will save one person, though, and I'll make sure it does before this is over."

He was right. Even if I ignored the plight of the other stomachs, Blanche would always be able to infect people faster than I could cure them. I looked at the bottle, enough scrill to save one person. I wondered if Lou would choose someone randomly to save, or if he had someone in mind.

"I didn't want to ask Em," Lou said, lowering his voice almost to a whisper. "But I gotta know. Where's May?"

"Dead," I said, looking him in the eyes. "Regurgitated."

Lou took a long breath through his nose, looked up at the ceiling, then growled as he breathed out through his mouth. He did this two more times, and on the last one, his growl sounded more like a moan. His eyes shone with tears, but none spilled out. Seeing his emotions brought mine to the surface, and I had to fight back my own tears.

He put a hand on my shoulder. "I know I was tough on you, kid. But that's because I knew what you were up against. These are the most twisted people I've come across, and I've tangled with the worst. This whole thing, it's not your fault. You understand? It was a setup from the beginning. This isn't your fault. You're a good kid." He patted my shoulder.

"Thanks." I turned away to keep from crying. I put my coat back on, and we left the flower shop and walked up the increasingly crowded sidewalk. We squeezed between bodies, against the current, a canopy of umbrellas over our heads. We literally rubbed elbows with Blanche's subconscious, relying on some old clothes and bad wigs to conceal us from her. Fear dried my mouth. I tried to relax my body and appear nonchalant, but I kept expecting to hear someone say, "Hello Charlie" in Blanche's sing-songy way.

After a short while, the infected became so numerous Lou and I could barely move. Everyone was waddling from side to side like penguins and getting nowhere. Blanche was packing the entire population of the county into these two little towns separated by the Eel River.

We dipped down an alley and turned up a much less crowded street, although it, too, was lined with exhibits commemorating the '64 Flood. We moved swiftly now, but not enough to draw attention to ourselves.

Lou abruptly joined the back of an audience standing on the corner watching a puppet show being performed on the other side of a shop window. For a second, I feared he'd been infected, but then Kaliah turned around and shined her eyes on me, stepped close, rested her umbrella on my shoulder, raised up onto her toes, and kissed me. Her lips were soft and wet and vaguely sweet.

As I reached to put my hand on her waist, she withdrew, smiled up at me, and said, "In case the world ends."

Em/Suzanne turned around at that, followed by the rest of our party, all wearing vintage clothes and blond wigs. Zelda's snout peeked out between the buttons of Em/Suzanne's trench coat. I was happy to see them all, even Bruce and Pam, though I was still flustered from Kaliah's kiss.

"I told you you were in trouble," Lou said.

"Why's he in trouble?" Em/Suzanne said.

Kaliah still smiled at me. I couldn't help smiling back. My eyes must have shined as bright as hers. Giddy little sprites danced in my stomach. I forgot all my troubles. I'd felt awful for hurting her feelings earlier, but now I felt buoyant and volatile all at once, and grateful that this beautiful and enigmatic and strangely funny woman had chosen me to be the home for her affections.

"There isn't much time left. Let's go," Lou said, calling me back to our plight, but not breaking the spell completely. As I and the rest followed him, I bounced along, stealing glances at Kaliah like a junior high kid. *This is nice,* Zelda said.

This is mine, I said, appalled.

This is the universe's. Get over yourself.

When we reached the north end of town, we climbed up the last highway onramp, past parked cars and crowds walking in the other direction. Our disguises were still working. No one gave us a second look. On the highway, the cars stretched to the north as far as I could see. One of the southbound lanes had been left clear to shuttle people from their parking spots to town on golf carts with long bench seats in the back. The high water was lapping at both sides of the road.

Lou slid on his gas mask and approached a cart that had just unloaded its passengers. He sprayed the driver in the face with one of his poisons, then pointed a pocket laser at the ground and swirled it around. The driver jumped out and ran after the red dot with a single-minded intensity. I almost felt sorry for the guy. That had been me not much earlier.

"Get in," Lou said, leading the driver farther down the road with the laser.

We piled onto the bench seats, and Lou drove us off as the next shuttle arrived, our tires momentarily losing traction on the wet concrete, the electric engine whirring. Feeling the wind against my cheeks, I gazed at the tree-covered hills looming over us from the east, their tops hidden by the clouds and rain-haze, and I felt hope.

Then a seagull flew up next to us, keeping pace at eye-level. Another joined it, and another. They called. I looked ahead. Two more seagulls flew above an oncoming shuttle.

"Lou!" I said, but I was too late. The oncoming shuttle veered for us at the last second. Lou wrenched the wheel to the left, and we plunged into the flooded ditch between the roads.

CHAPTER 37

I was tossed violently forward. My ribs slammed into something hard. Then I was cold, wet, underwater. I kicked my legs and hit the bottom. I stood. My head broke the surface, and I swallowed air. Water had gone up my nose. I coughed.

Heads popped up around me and on the other side of the sinking cart, taillights pointing to the sky. One, two, three, four, five, six heads—we were all still alive. Hugo scrambled out of the water first, then Lou and Em/Suzanne, who grabbed me by the armpits with her powerful hands and pulled as I climbed and pushed and slipped and climbed until I was back on the road.

There, I noticed a thin layer of blue scrill over the skin on my hands, pocked by raindrops. A shanika infected by Blanche's cackle was somewhere near. We had to get out of here fast. I looked up from my knees at Em/Suzanne. She stared down at me, mouth flat. "It's over, Charlie," she said. And I knew that Em was gone. Again. The scrill Lou had sprayed on her to protect her from Blanche's cackle had been washed off during the dip in the water.

Blanche/Warren walked toward me from the shuttle that had swerved at us. She pointed a handgun to my left. I turned to see Zelda shaking her fur dry. Before I could move, I heard the shot. Zelda yelped and fell, tried to stand, and fell again. I leaped between her and Blanche/Warren. Blanche/Suzanne grabbed one of my arms, and Blanche/Hugo came and grabbed the other, and they dragged me away as Zelda crawled back into the water, whimpering.

Zelda! I cried in my mind. *Zelda! Run!* But she wasn't in my mind, like she was shielding her pain from me.

Blanche/Warren strode to the water's edge and fired down. I couldn't see Zelda on the surface. Was she still alive? Could foxes swim underwater? Blanche/Warren unloaded her clip. I watched the surface of the water, waiting for Zelda's head to pop up, her little snout, or her dead body, but I saw no sign of her.

Bruce, Pam, Lou, and Kaliah took their seats in the shuttle like the obedient subjects they now were. Seagulls perched on the roof above them. Blanche/Caroline, Warren's bond, sat in the driver's seat, talking to herself: "You have to tease it through the wood. You wrench on it like that, you break the blade. That's why I put this reinforcement bolt in, to keep the blade steady. See? Just tease it through the wood."

Blanche/Warren holstered her gun and walked over to me. Warren's signature smirk was gone. Blanche was making the faces for him now. She pulled a small bushel of zip-ties from her coat pocket and doled them out to Blanche/Hugo and Blanche/Suzanne, who used them to bind my wrists and ankles. Still in shock from the crash, from losing Em again and Kaliah, from seeing Zelda shot, I offered no resistance.

After binding me, Blanche/Hugo and Blanche/Suzanne went to the shuttle and took their seats with what was left of our band of would-be world-savers, and Blanche/Caroline drove them off, still talking to herself, back to Rio Dell, back to the festivities.

Blanche/Warren crouched in front of me and leaned in so that her face was inches from mine. "I will be a benevolent god," she said, voice low and rumbling, eyes bulging with rage. "I will be a personal god. When people pray, I will answer them. I will bring peace to the world. What about that don't you like?" She slapped me hard enough for my head to whip to the side. My cheek stung. "You killed my Zaditorians," she said. "I know everything your friends know now, all your plans. You've been a busy busy busy boy." She slapped me again. "You put a Ghost in a fox? I've never seen that before. Your mother was right. I should have killed you. I laughed at her when she wanted to make Arampom gluten-free, but she was right. Clearly, you're more dangerous than I thought. You have no idea how much killing you is going to hurt me. Special little Charlie, you had so much potential, so much. Now all of your misguided energy, all of your plans have come to nothing." Spittle sprayed from her mouth. "I'm on my way to the DMV now. That little duckling, Naomi, thought she could hide my own breadcrumbs from me? She will find that I can also be a wrathful God."

The words "duckling" and "breadcrumbs" stuck out in my mind like seagulls in a duck pond. She had not used them accidentally. Naomi's spell was somehow still alive in Warren, despite Blanche's occupation of him. But how much power did it still have? By breadcrumbs, I assumed she meant the sourdough totem. The last time I'd seen Naomi, she'd given me a rushed tutorial on how to use her spells: repeat the metaphor before the command.

A lust for vengeance as strong as my grief overcame me. If I couldn't save the people I loved, I would ruin Blanche and her plans, and send her back to the void.

Blanche/Warren's face softened. "Oh Charlie," she said. "As angry as you've made me, I still wish I could end your life in a gentler way, but you sojourners are hard to kill. Burning, beheading, drowning, these are the easiest ways. Drowning, I believe, will be the most pleasant of the three. And it's not like we have a shortage of water." She shrugged, then stood, grabbed the zip-ties around my wrists, and tugged.

I relaxed my whole body, let it go limp, which wasn't easy after Blanche/Warren had filled my head with the prospect of drowning.

Grunting, she pulled me closer to the edge of the flooded ditch. "Really, Charlie?" She breathed heavily. "Try to die with some dignity. After tonight, the whole universe will share this memory. Doesn't that mean anything to you? Try to think of some last words, at least."

"When the storm comes," I said, "the ducks will have to share the duck pond with the seagulls."

Blanche/Warren stood. Her eyes glazed over.

There was still power in the metaphor.

I thought back on my experience under the influence of Naomi, how I'd been plunged into a new reality, how I'd participated in it, shaped it, fleshed it out, like I'd been implanted with an end and given the tools to manufacture and rationalize the means to that end. Warren's end, according to Naomi, was to help me, but that was vague. Maybe he had several ends, each one designed to help me differently, and I just had to set him on the right course, one that brought me in contact with the sourdough totem—breadcrumbs—and massive amounts of Blanche's Cackle—seagull feathers?—so that I could enter the sourdough whorl and end all of this. But how was I supposed to relay these needs to Warren? I could spend all week and not get through, and I only had an hour at the most before the county grafted to the flood, and probably a lot less than that before Blanche discovered I wasn't dead yet.

The last thing Naomi had said to me was, "Remember our picnic in Sequoia Park." At the time, I'd thought she was using sentiment and nostalgia to mess with my head, but she could just as easily have been giving me the final instruction in her tutorial.

I waded through the memories of that day, of our picnic: The sun was out. Summer was almost over. We had errands to run in Eureka, and as a treat for finishing, we picnicked in the park. We walked down a trail, through giant redwoods that blocked the sun, and we sat at a picnic table by a pond. I didn't remember any ducks in the pond, but there were turtles and a couple of swans. That was close enough to get me excited. I took a stab:

"Swans protect ducks from seagulls," I said.

Blanche/Warren didn't move or change expression. A shuttle drove slowly by. The passengers looked past us. I waited a minute—still no movement. Maybe something was happening internally, the way a duck appears calm on the surface while underwater their legs are pedaling ferociously. I waited a little longer before realizing the metaphor was having more effect on me than Blanche/Warren. I took another stab: "When the storm comes, the ducks will have to share the duck pond with the seagulls. Turtles and ducks work together to hide breadcrumbs from seagulls."

A high-pitched moan slowly seeped out of Blanche/Warren like air from a balloon, and she began squatting, standing, squatting, standing, over and over. She seemed distressed, tormented. I could only imagine what was spinning around in her mind. I preferred she be motionless like before rather than doing this and drawing attention to us. Another shuttle was coming from up the road. Worried the spell would break if the passengers saw Blanche/Warren in her current state, I dipped back into my memory. What else? What else?

Crayons! That was it! It had to be. After our picnic, I'd tossed some leftover potato chips into the pond for the swans. In a hurry to eat the chips, the swans also ate some crayons floating nearby that a kid must have thrown in earlier. Feeling responsible, I considered calling the city to get the swans' stomachs pumped. Naomi just laughed at me and told me they'd be fine.

The shuttle was twenty yards away. This had to be what she was looking for. If not . . . .

I repeated the metaphor and followed it with a new command: "Crayons! Crayons in the duck pond. Crayons and potato chips. Crayons aren't poisonous to swans."

Blanche/Warren stopped squatting, reached into her back pocket, and pulled out a wallet with an envelope sticking out the top. She handed the envelope to me. After the shuttle passed without Blanche taking notice of us, I hunched over the envelope to shield it from the rain as I opened it. My fingers were wet, pruney, shaking. I found a letter inside. Drops fell onto it from my jacket, running the ink as I read:

"Dear Charlie,

I know that secret tests are frowned upon by relationship experts, but I've been alive a long time. Fashions come and go. Anyway, you passed. You remembered a day that is very special to me, the day I fell in love with you. Your concern for those swans was so sweet, so cute, so emblematic of your nature, that I couldn't help but risk everything to keep your light in this world.

"It took all of my skill as a wanda to prepare Warren for you, and to keep that hidden from Blanche. Now that you've given him the key phrase, or at least an approximation of it, you no longer have to speak metaphorically. He will now translate your commands into my metaphor so that you don't have to, but because of the strain this puts on the spell, you will only have fifteen minutes before it wears off.

"Good luck, and I love you. Always, Naomi"

Old feelings I had for Naomi breached in my mind and made a huge splash. I dropped the letter in the water behind me and scooted back as if from a snake, afraid Naomi had somehow laced it with her cackle. Though I was grateful for her help, and my judgment of her had softened, I had no desire to join her harem.

"Tell Blanche I'm dead," I said to Blanche/Warren, testing Naomi's claim.

"The swan swallowed too many crayons," Blanche/Warren said, and I hoped that meant the command had been followed.

"Free my hands and feet,"

"Plastic six-pack rings can be deadly to wildlife." Blanche/Warren crouched in front of me, took out a pocket knife, and cut the zip-ties.

CHAPTER 38

MY FIRST IMPULSE WAS to get a car and get to Naomi and the sourdough totem before Blanche. But the DMV was a thirty-minute drive away, and Blanche could be anywhere, in anybody. The whole county was either here or coming here, but that didn't mean there weren't stragglers passing through Eureka right now, trying to kill Naomi right now.

My only hope was to find Blanche's portion of the sourdough totem and graft to it using Blanche/Em's cackle deluge. I figured chances were good that the totem was nearby. It was Blanche's link to Zaditor, and now that a lot of her Zaditorians were dead, she would want to send for more.

I told Blanche/Warren to lead me to Blanche's nearest sourdough totem without giving us away, and she replied, "A powerful mothering instinct will express itself between species," then walked off the road and waded into the flood.

I followed her, swimming part of the way to a frontage road. My clothes suctioned to my skin as I climbed out of the water. We crossed the road and entered a neighborhood with narrow gravel streets.

"Faster," I said.

Blanche/Warren muttered something and began to jog, and I jogged after her. I had maybe twelve more minutes before the metaphor wore off. She led me south, above Main Street, four blocks from the festivities, where the streets were empty, where there was a view of the three bridges, now packed with people, the big brown water churning beneath them, all around them.

We turned a corner, and Blanche/Warren's jog abruptly became a casual stroll. I almost ran into her back. A few houses down, a line of infected stood in front of a garage, holding umbrellas. They didn't look over at us. They stared straight ahead and shuffled forward.

Stomach clenched, movements stiff, I followed Blanche/Warren to the back of the line, trusting she knew what she was doing, trusting the metaphor. I had no choice, really.

The line moved swiftly. At the head, inside the garage, a man in a white apron and chef's hat stood behind a table ladling what looked like sourdough starter—gray, stretchy goop—from a giant stainless steel pot into mugs, which he handed to the next in line. A pile of short, black, leather cattail whips sat next to the pot. After the infected took a mug of goop from the chef, they exchanged their umbrella for a whip and filed into the house through the garage, holding the sourdough starter to their nose and whipping their own back.

Blanche was using the pain from the whips to implant whorls tied to the sourdough totem into the cackle of the infected, but to what end?

Three of the infected walked up from the direction of Main Street. I readied to make a dash for the pot, but they just took places behind me and Blanche/Warren in line and remained silent as we moved forward.

My command to tell Blanche I was dead had worked. Blanche didn't appear to be actively searching for me. But that didn't mean she wouldn't discover the ploy before the spell wore off if I did something to draw attention to myself.

Coming to the head of the line, I stepped just inside the garage, out of the rain. The chef slapped some totem in a mug and handed it to me. I lifted the mug to my nose, as the others had done, and I smelled the familiar yeasty fermentation of my family's most precious heirloom, then I moved on, took a whip from the pile, and began pretending to whip myself with it.

After following Blanche/Warren, who appeared to be flagellating herself for real, around the table, I leaned forward and whispered, "Take me to Em."

At a volume that made me want to shush her, she said, "The seagull with the loudest call is always at the center of things." Then she broke from the line, and we walked out of the garage and toward Main Street. No one stopped us or even looked at us.

"Why are they making whorls with the sourdough?" I said.

"A single quack can have various meanings, depending on the tone," Blanche/Warren said. "The Alocril invasion force requires special training."

I asked where Em was, how far? Blanche/Warren made another remark about the loudest seagull, then answered, "The green bridge."

That wasn't far. The metaphor had around eight minutes of life left. I had time. I could still stop this. I stuffed the mug inside my coat, under my arm, to keep the starter from diluting in the rain, and said, "Faster."

We ran downhill for two blocks before hitting the crowd. Not wanting to barrel through and attract Blanche's attention, I instructed Blanche/Warren to slow down, be discrete, and we weaved through the bodies, careful not to bump anyone too hard. Following Blanche/Warren's example, hoping to fit in, I occasionally tapped my back with the whip.

At first, we were surrounded by a group of what could only be interpretive dancers, moving like puppets made from wet noodles. We had to be light on our toes not to disrupt them. Blanche's army was already grafting to the storm, entering the Nexus Whorl.

Further down, I passed young and old quilters sewing soggy patches together, bearded men with keening chainsaws carving sculptures out of burl, austere painters in front of easels painting with meticulous strokes only for the rain to run the colors. All grafted in the open, exposed to the storm. The scene was dreamlike, almost nightmarish. The faces of the infected were sincere, focused.

A thin film of blue scrill spread over my hand. A shanika must have been nearby. I briefly tried to graft to the storm, muttering a trio of Pictionary poems, but there wasn't enough of the infected cackle to get past Craig.

The crowd was thickest on Main Street, slowing our progress even more. I had five minutes left. But I could see the green trusses of the bridge, where ravens, seagulls, pigeons, and ducks were perched, only twenty yards away.

A mad circus of self-expression swarmed around us, and I pretended to whip myself, pretended to participate. We walked by more sculptors—some molding clay, others welding steel—and more dancers—ballet, pop and lock, swing, salsa. We cut through a troupe of histrionic actors performing clashing soliloquies at the top of their lungs. Beyond them, we ran into a wall of photographers taking pictures of bone-thin men and women in gaudy outfits, strutting up and down a catwalk running across the roofs of the parked cars. Blanche/Warren tried to clear a path, but the photographers were huddled together tighter than penguins in a polar storm. As I searched for a way around, I heard in my mind:

Wait.

Zelda! I said.

I'm here. Her love suffused my body.

How bad are you hurt? Can you walk? Where are you?

I'm close, and I'm fine. I was healed by Craig. I'm pretty sure he has a thing for me.

I let out a celebratory "Ha" out loud. Then, back in my mind, *I have the totem. I'm on my way to Em now.*

You have to wait. Blanche is more present on the bridge. I can smell her. She's performing her one-woman show there right now, and also watching from the audience. You'll never make it through, but there's another way. Do you see the last house before the bridge?

Just past the scrum of photographers, to my right, was a one-story white house with north- and south-facing gables and a porch packed with infected, all looking in the same direction. I followed their eyes to a small stage standing where the bridge met Main Street. On the stage I saw a dresser, a bed, and Blanche, wearing a young woman's body and a retro prom dress with billowing shoulders drooping from the rain. Dozens of people were crammed around the stage watching her. Blanche was moving her mouth, but I couldn't hear what she was saying over the birds and the heels knocking on the catwalk and the soliloquies behind me.

I see the house, I said. *And the one-woman show.*

Good, Zelda said. *On the other side of the house is a trail leading below the bridge. From there, you can crawl along the steel girders running underneath until you get to Em. She's at the center of the bridge.*

Fear surged through me at the thought of clinging to the underside of a bridge in a rainstorm.

Don't worry, Zelda said. *I'll be with you. You can do it. Go now, while we still have time.*

The wall of photographers extended up a side street, blocking the front and side of the house. But behind them, I could see, through a more diffuse group of infected grafters, a backyard fence and gate.

Afraid of the metaphor wearing off at the worst possible time and having to fight Blanche/Warren while clinging to the underside of the bridge, I ordered her to stay put.

Then I strode around the photographers and stepped gingerly between another group of infected who were employing some kind of culinary grafting method—standing around, holding plates of food and glasses of wine, eyes closed, lips pursed, chewing, sipping, and making rapturous *mmm* noises. A skinned and roasted goat, head and hooves still attached, ribs splayed and picked clean, lay on a table against the fence.

I pulled a string on the gate and entered the backyard,

where there was another group of grafters. They stood facing the same direction, holding oversized colorful drinks with umbrellas in them. There were tiki torches planted into the lawn and a tiki bar next to the house. Through crackling speakers, someone was croaking out an awful rendition of Creedence Clearwater Revival's *Who'll Stop the Rain*. Between nodding heads, I caught a glimpse of Lonnie in the corner of the yard, wearing a Hawaiian shirt, singing into a mic while reading from a karaoke prompter.

I ducked my head and worked my way across the yard. There was no gate on the riverside of the fence. I would have to climb over it. But then Lonnie would see me. Maybe if I waited for the chorus, or waited—

No, Zelda said. *We don't have time.*

A few fence boards shuddered, and I looked down to see the little fox wriggling through a small hole by my feet, her fur caked in mud. I smiled, despite the circumstances, and reached down to pet her, then stopped myself when she said, *I'm not a dog, Charlie . . . . You can hug me though.* I kneeled, put my arms around her, and squeezed.

When I pulled back, she looked up at me with half-closed eyes. *Be ready to run.* She darted from my arms into the audience, disappearing into a forest of legs. A moment later, a piercing yowl crackled through the speakers, followed by cries for help.

As the audience leaned and pushed forward, distracted, I leapt onto the fence and looked out above their heads. Lonnie was on his back, flailing his limbs like an overturned beetle, while Zelda bounced around him snapping her jaws.

Go! she said.

I flipped my body over the top of the fence and dropped.

When I landed on the other side, my legs buckled, and I slid downward, over rocks and through brush. I swung my arms about wildly, grasping at branches, at dirt. I spun onto my belly and spread out my arms and legs to slow down. My foot caught in something hard, swinging my body sideways. My ankle cracked. Pain wailed through me like a siren, like sound on fire. Voices, voices, voices. Then Zelda. Then calm. *Be calm. You'll be okay.* My ribs slammed into a small tree, and I was still.

Get up, Zelda said. *No time for pain.*

I think my ankle's broken.

Keep moving. No time.

I held my breath and growled as I sat up, grabbed my ankle, and twisted it free. My toes pointed inward ninety degrees. Bone protruded beneath stretched skin. My stomach flipped at the sight.

Get up!

Grimacing, I swiveled on my butt, planted my good foot downhill, shifted my weight to the other knee, rose, and hobbled toward the bridge, dragging my useless foot behind me, grabbing onto branches, rocks, roots, chunks of sod to keep myself from sliding further down into the muddy, churning river below. The roar of the rushing water drowned out my moans and cries and whatever was going on above me. The terrible scale and power of the flood were frightening and exhilarating to see up close.

When I reached the path that led under the bridge, I found I was able to put my weight on my ankle. A tingling sensation mixed with the pain now, and yellow scrill glowed through my skin. Craig was healing me. Still, I limped to the bridge, wincing and letting air out in hisses.

I hiked up a short but steep and slippery slope to where the bridge met land, and I pulled myself up onto the wet and cold steel girder on the western side, hidden from view of the other two bridges. I crawled on my hands and knees out over the water. The lip of the girder was only two feet wide. My knees knocked as I inched forward, and my right shoulder and hip scraped against the concrete of the deck as I leaned as far from the ledge as possible. Wind whistled through the steel. A rusty, metallic smell filled my nostrils.

Water rushed around the concrete pilings below. A tree floated swiftly downriver with a live black bear on it. With wide eyes, I watched the wild creature hurtle by, balancing for its life.

Out of everything I'd seen in the last few days that might have been the most alarming. I truly felt at that moment that the apocalypse was here and now. I started shaking and had to pause, relax my stomach, and slow my breathing before I could move on. The water was close and moving fast. One slip and I would be worse off than that bear.

Ten yards in, I had to scramble through a large bracket to move forward. The mug fell out of my coat, and I almost slipped trying to catch it. I wasn't quick enough, and it shattered on the girder. Pieces of the mug tumbled down and were swallowed by the river. A large dollop of the glutinous goo jiggled on the girder where the mug had hit. I carefully, slowly gathered the dollop and put it back into my coat pocket, hoping it would be enough.

I crawled on. Pigeons shared the girder with me, some so tame or lazy I had to bat at them to clear the path. For a moment, a seagull hovered in the air beside me, its wings twitching small corrections with the wind.

A massive, floating nest of debris that included logs, a

large stump and root ball, two dead cows, and the remains of a house was being pressed against the second piling by the careening current. The bridge moaned here. I resisted the urge to crawl faster—slow and steady, slow and steady.

When a thick layer of blue scrill sprouted on my hands and circulated in on itself, I knew Blanche/Em was close. I carefully reached out above my head and grabbed onto the vertical bars of the short pedestrian fence. Tensing the muscles in my arms, I lifted myself off the girder, feet dangling over the water, and pulled myself up, up, then clambered over the fence and landed on the deck, thankful for all the workouts I'd done at Lou's house.

The pain in my ankle was gone.

I was amongst a group of large opera singers who belted out notes with emotion, sustain, and tremolo. They didn't even know I was there. One inadvertently slapped me in the face as she spread her arms and sang to the turbulent clouds above.

Parked a few feet to my right was the old truck with a camper shell my mom had been driving back when I thought she was just a drug addict. To my left was another stage. This one held mimes and people who, by their clothes and handwork, appeared to be magicians.

I broke through the opera singers toward the camper into a small, unoccupied space. The scrill circulated thicker and faster. Breathing heavy from exertion and fear and relief, I plunged my hand into my coat pocket, into the totem that squished around my fingers. I cupped what I could and held it up to my nose. I took in the smell, the look, the feel. I put a pinch in my mouth, and I grafted:

"Dust Mote Guillotine, Tinsel Kitchen Crucible, Oven

Air-Karma Dance."

The camper, the opera singers, the bridge, the storm faded into a large, familiar room with a view of the ocean. I was in the sourdough starter whorl. I was Blanche, wearing a pink polka dot dress, sitting in a leather chair with a Tupperware bowl of starter in my lap. The corruption I'd left behind on my last visit was busy typing at the desk, while Craig's head peeked out from a large pool of scrill that spread backward from the fireplace, through the wall, and into other rooms. Craig was trapped watching my corruption, transfixed like a cobra in a basket.

A cheese danish sat on the end table next to me. It was a wall, a mote full of crocodiles that had prevented me from grafting to the whorl the last time. I could've picked up the knife next to the danish, cut myself, and freed my corruption, freed Craig right then, and exposed all of the Blanche-infected to Arawok's vomit reflex as I'd planned. But seeing the cheese danish there angered me.

What was Blanche hiding from me?

What was beyond the cheese danish?

I wanted to know. I could always come back and free my corruption after I rode the Ghost. So I began tapping the quick I knew was on Blanche's heel, and I fell into the track of this whorl's pain.

A young Lonnie came into the room. "Why are you tapping the Quick?" he said.

"Partly a backup plan," I said, tapping, tapping, "in case you fail me. And partly because I want to preserve the look on your face for my future selves."

"What look? What are you talking about?"

"How did you do it? Some sojourner trick?"

"How did I do what?" Lonnie crossed his arms over his chest and rocked from side to side as he widened his stance.

"We searched that whole tomb. We found the totem, but no book." I frowned. "Odd. So odd. We even searched you. Remember? Where did you hide it? Did you go back for it later?"

"I can't hide something that doesn't exist."

"Denial is such a powerful tool if you have the gall for it. People want to believe people. I'm sure it's been useful for you your whole life. But I had you followed. We found the book. Has anyone ever told you you look like a rat?"

Lonnie's face twitched, and I smiled and reached for the cheese danish on the table. The pain was worse than I remembered—crawling fire, burrowing thorns.

I recalled my lesson from the trout test: explore the pain with new eyes. I regarded the cheese danish with the knowledge that my mother had always hated me, that she had used a pastry as an instrument of torture on her own child.

That pain was fresh.

I focused on it and let it in, let it spread and react. It became visible, a halo of bright and colorful particles around all things in the whorl. The beauty of the pain made it bearable. As I moved, I was able to twitch corrections, like that seagull in the wind, by watching the pain react.

"Did you think you could stop me?" I said to young Lonnie as I cleaned the danish from my teeth with my tongue. "Did you forget about your brother?"

"No," Lonnie said. "I didn't forget, and I'm not trying to stop you."

"Then why did you hide the book from me?" I smirked.

"I can trap my rekulak. It will work. But becoming the

rekulak is a bad idea. I'll lose it, and so will you, and we'll both have nothing."

"I will lose nothing." I raised my voice. "I have only to gain. With your rekulak, my victory over the other stomachs is certain. Without it, my victory is slightly less certain, as it was before I discovered your treachery. You, on the other hand, you will be losing your rekulak. That is my guarantee. So say goodbye if you can. The only choice left to you is this: Do you want to lose your brother as well?"

Lonnie stared down at my tapping foot while clenching and unclenching his jaw. "Rekulak scrill cures nemaloki poison." He spit out the words in breathless succession, like a child telling their parent about the injustice their sibling committed. "The totem of the First Sojourner will be in the Nexus Whorl. If you carry it through the portal to our stomach, you will come back as your rekulak and you will be able to undo whatever damage Blanche has done."

I had stopped tapping my foot partway through his hurried instructions. "Who are you talking to?" I said, smiling. "Was that a cry for help to future generations? I assure you they will not receive it. My power in the realm of whorls is beyond your imagining. But what has made you so bold? Is there some gambit I am not aware of?"

Lonnie and the room faded as the graft took. The bridge and storm—reality—materialized into the foreground. Clashing arias boomed from the tenors, sopranos, and contraltos at my back as the significance of Lonnie's outburst dawned on me. I could cure the infected without relinquishing them to the void. I could bring them back, Em and Kaliah and Lou, the whole county, by becoming Craig in this world and spraying everyone gathered here with his vast supply of healing scrill. I could minimize the damage wrought by my mistakes. Lonnie's younger self had shown me the way.

My perception of him flipped. He was another one of Blanche's victims, or at least he had been. Likely, he had played a part in the undoing of Blanche's plans the first time around in 1964. And now he was playing a part again. He'd left a message in a bottle, a lifeline through time and space, for Blanche's next sojourner to find: me. I understood now why Blanche and my mom had worked so hard, done so much to keep it from me.

Wherever Lonnie ended up after this, I hoped he would have access to as many nudey channels and mai tais as he wanted.

Blanche/Em walked out from behind the camper, followed by Blanche/Lonnie, the karaoke singer, and Blanche/Warren. Blanche/Lonnie held a long pole with a noose on the other end tightened around Zelda's neck. Zelda was attempting to walk with her head held high, but Blanche/Lonnie kept jerking the pole and making her stumble. My hatred for Blanche intensified.

Blanche/Em looked at me like she knew I would be there. "I'm glad you still have some spirit left. Drowning in a river is a much more respectable death than drowning in a ditch."

"I ate the cheese danish," I said, giving her a nasty smile.

Blanche/Em looked confused.

"I ate the cheese danish," I said again, louder.

A look of surprise tinged with curiosity colored her face. I was disappointed. I had hoped for fear.

I opened my arms, looked up, and grafted to the raging storm: "New Year's Aviary Escape, Saltine Confetti Dance,

Purple Rain Dove Tears."

The world decayed into a kaleidoscopic fog of luminescent particles. There was silence. There was stillness. Then shapes emerged through the fog, of the fog. I was on the same truss bridge, but the two highway bridges downriver had not been built yet. The water was even higher than in my time. There were no vehicles or stages or mimes or opera singers around, only a group of thirty or so people kneeling before me in a semicircle. They looked up at me, their faces expressing admiration and awe. This was the moment Blanche first took nemaloki cackle, in 1964, when she and her Friends had been regurgitated into the void.

The glowing particles drifted through the air like sparks from a bonfire. They clung to, moved through, and swirled inside objects and people. Everything was beautiful and true.

I held a small stone disk with a spiral of hieroglyphics carved into its face. Flush with the grace from riding the sourdough Ghost, I knew it for the totem of the First Sojourner. The fog of particles took on the shape of the hieroglyphics, and they swayed around me.

I was reminded of the program from the poetry reading at the coffee shop. It called the patterns from my old shower curtain seeds in the language of the gods, seeds that needed only thought to sprout and grow. I pictured the shower curtain from Kaliah's apartment, and it appeared in the fog before me with all its familiar patterns, patterns that were the key to travel between the stomachs. Avoid the pink polka dots, the program had warned, they lead to the void. Instead, I focused on the argyle, the pattern that corresponded to Crolom, our stomach.

Wait, Zelda said, and then she was sitting at my feet, her fur glistening with vibrant, changing colors. *Give me the stone.*

Why?

If you do this, you will die, and Craig will be trapped in Blanche's whorl forever. You may save people now, but Blanche will just come back later and reinfect them. Give me the totem and I will bring Craig back and save as many as I can.

But you're not a sojourner.

Am I not partly you? I will get the job done, but you must return to the sourdough whorl and free Craig.

A woman blinked into existence in front of me, standing among the supplicants, taller and thinner than my mom, but with the same eyes and nose. She wore what I currently wore, black gloves and a black double-breasted raincoat.

Hurry, Zelda said. *Blanche is sending corruptions to stop us. Don't let them go through the portal with me.*

I held out the stone disc, and Zelda took it gently in her jaws. Argyle patterns ran through the fog in front of us, quivering and spinning into a vortex. Blanche and the supplicants blurred and fragmented, then erupted like dandelion seeds blown for wishes. The particles they were once made from were sucked into the vortex, now ten feet in diameter. A larger circle of blue scrill dilated behind it, and Craig peeked his head through and unhinged his maw, stopping short of swallowing the vortex.

Glowing argyle patterns swam through Zelda's fur like water snakes. As they grew brighter, they multiplied and seemed to seer into and through her body, which blurred. Two more Blanche corruptions popped up beside her. I leapt over Zelda and crashed into them, diverging from the whorl's path of pain. One corruption tripped and dragged me to the ground with her. I swung my elbows wildly and connected, freeing my arms to latch onto the leg of the other corruption before they could dive into the vortex and Craig's open jaws.

A stream of glowing, three-dimensional, multi-colored argyle was running from a faint outline of Zelda into the vortex.

Then the graft failed.

The whorl collapsed into a single point, and reality flooded in around it, leaving me dizzy and unsure on my feet. A tenor behind me belted out a high note and held it.

I had left my corruption behind, and I had no idea if Zelda had been sucked into the portal before the graft had failed.

Everything back in reality seemed dull and grey compared to the beautiful fog of the Nexus Whorl.

Blanche/Em curled both sides of her upper lip at me while Blanche/Lonnie lifted his long pole and swung it between the trusses out over the water with Zelda on the end, dangling by her neck, her body squirming, feet dancing in air, eyes bulging. Blanche/Lonnie dropped the pole.

Zelda fell.

I ran to catch the end of the pole, but when I reached the guardrail it was over the edge. As I watched Zelda descend into the rushing water, my arms and legs were grabbed. "Now it's your turn," Blanche/Em said.

I love you, Zelda said. *I will see you again. Tell Em I will see her again.*

Swim to shore, Zelda. Swim to shore.

Please don't mourn me. I can't die. I'm already dead. Don't be silly about this.

Swim to shore!

She did not speak to me again.

I resisted Blanche/Lonnie and Blanche/Warren and was about to break free, but then the opera singers all stopped singing and attacked me. There were too many of them, wrenching, lifting, and pushing, trying to get me over the side.

I wanted to get to my coat pocket, to where there were still remnants of the sourdough starter, but if I let go of the railing, I would be tossed into the flood. *Maybe there would be enough time to graft on the way down,* I thought.

Then a shimmer of blue appeared in the water between our bridge and the newer, highway bridges. It spread to the size of a square city block and brightened, boiling with texture, bubbling above the water now. Zelda/Craig rose from it, gigantic, awesome, the girth and height of a skyscraper. The swirling scrill beneath her armored plates lit up the dark and overcast day with blue light and reflected off the waterfalls rushing down her body. Trees and roofs and other debris caught in her plates or fell, flipping through the air and splashing back into the rushing river.

I am here, Zelda/Craig said, and her voice boomed through my mind with power and terrible love. Craig's inscrutable presence was in it.

A loud and deep whirring noise resonated in my ears, tickling the little hairs, as Zelda/Craig spewed blue scrill down on the town of Rio Dell, a thick plume, like a river in the sky. Zelda/Craig swiveled her head, sweeping the plume through the town, down Main Street, leaving all the infected caked in scrill. Zelda/Craig skipped our bridge, swept back around and over the highway bridges, then onto Scotia, blanketing the town in blue snow.

Distracted, the opera singers' grip on me loosened, and I let go of the railing, retrieved what was left of the sourdough starter from my pocket, and grafted to it once again.

Back in the leather chair with the view of the ocean, I picked up the knife leaning against the plate that held the cheese danish. A dozen Blanche corruptions now stood between me and Craig and my typing corruption. Blanche had anticipated me coming back. As they moved to restrain me, I sawed at my neck with the knife, crying out in pain, until I severed an artery. Blood hissed from the gash and shot across the room in a fine mist, spraying the corruptions, including my own, and making them disappear, freeing Craig to remove himself from the whorl by unceremoniously submerging back into his pool of scrill.

The graft failed, and I was once again on the bridge, between two towns blanketed in blue snow, above a raging river. I heard Zelda/Craig's cascade of scrill slapping against the concrete deck as it advanced across the bridge.

But it was too late for the poor souls around me. Blanche/Lonnie, Blanche/Warren, and the opera singers tumbled around me, regurgitated into the void. I hadn't been able to save them.

I stepped over and around them and found Em's lifeless body as the scrill rained down on us in clumps, hot and steaming, the pungent smell of menthol and strawberries clearing my sinuses. I kneeled beside Em and held her in my arms and wiped the blue grit from her face, and I kissed her on the forehead. I hoped that she had survived somehow in the lunch lady again. In truth, that hope was the only thing keeping from turning and jumping off the bridge. But I mourned this Em. This Em was dead.

As my face clenched and tears sprang loose, Em sat up, wide-eyed and screaming. All at once, I was startled, confused, gleeful, and concerned. I tried to comfort her. "It's okay. It's okay," I said, but she wouldn't look at me. She just kept screaming, like I wasn't there. It was the same way she'd screamed when Warren had first infected her with Ghost Heart. I fumbled around in my pockets and found the otalith potion Rhonaya had given me to stave off the Dirge. I sprayed Em with the medicine, and in moments she calmed and focused her eyes on me. I smiled, so happy to see her in her own body, but she began to cry.

"What's wrong?" I said, hugging her. "We're safe. It's over. Blanche is dead."

"The nightmares," she said between sobs, and I felt that weight inside, that dreadful pressure that comes when a loved one is hurting. I'd been lying to myself. I would never be able to keep her nightmares away, not all of them.

CHAPTER 39

ZELDA/CRAIG DESCENDED INTO THE scrill pool, and Em and I walked back into Rio Dell and searched for our people, calling out their names: "Kaliah! Lou!"

I didn't know why or how Em had been returned to her body, but I liked to believe Zelda had convinced Craig to do it somehow.

Rain washed some of the scrill off of the would-be grafters, but many faces were still obscured by it, making our search more difficult. Most people, free from Blanche's cackle, were either rushing into buildings to get out of the rain or to their cars to get home. There were shouts and honking as people drove down the sidewalk around the gridlock. I wondered what they thought, how much they remembered, if they feared they were going insane. What were the ramifications for the cackle races after this? Was the secret out of the bag, or would Lodges come together to contain this disaster? Did mobiaks have their own version of FEMA?

I found everyone together, Kaliah, Lou, Hugo, Suzanne, Bruce, and Pam, all covered in scrill, a block up from where the foodies had been gathered. The street was mostly clear. They had heard me calling them. Their eyes and smiles were white chasms in the blue. Em ran to Suzanne, and they embraced.

Kaliah's smile was so bright and beautiful. We hugged.

Hugo broke up the moment by asking what had happened since the golf cart crash. I told him and everyone about Naomi's metaphor spell, which made Bruce and Pam nod and smile with pride. I told of the secret beyond the cheese danish, and of Zelda's sacrifice. They had all seen the rekulak, along with everyone else gathered here.

Em mourned Zelda, and Suzanne comforted her.

After I finished answering a few more questions, Lou and I went back to the bridge and carried the bodies of the mimes and magicians and opera singers out of the rain to a half-empty carport, and we laid them down in a line, then found blankets to cover them with.

Our group spent that night in Rio Dell, in an empty apartment above where Blanche had held her Christmas party. For Christmas Eve dinner, we ate the leftover snacks—chips and dip and finger sandwiches and canned oysters and sardines on crackers. We drank the leftover liquor as well. Lou even found some eggnog for Em. At some point, the rain stopped rapping on the roof. I didn't feel right about celebrating, but I couldn't help doing a little of it. Despite the lives lost on the bridge and among those outside the county who had been infected, and the lives lost in the other stomachs, I was happy to be alive, happy I had people to love, people that loved me.

On Christmas morning, the clouds were not as thick, not as dark. No rain fell. The river had gone down. Coast Guard and Army helicopters flew overhead, searching for survivors and delivering food, I presumed. Most of the people in the two towns had left, taking their cars with them. The people that remained moseyed up and down Main Street in heavy coats exchanging stories about the day before and the giant centipede beast that had risen from the river. I overheard a few comments about never swimming again, and more than a few about moving and all-night packing sessions. Rio Dell's volunteer fire department had suited up and found the bodies Lou and I had placed in the carport. They were putting them in body bags as our group walked onto the bridge.

We returned to our school bus and drove to Eureka, Hugo in the driver's seat. Part of the way we listened to emergency broadcasts on the radio reporting power outages, road closures, evacuation zones, and the location of shelters. We reached the south end of town in thirty minutes. Elk River was flooded, but we were able to drive through. Eureka was far enough away from the larger rivers to be affected too much.

Only a few cars were on the road. The town was empty, eerie. The DMV sparking lot was abandoned. I didn't know why Naomi was there, or why she'd chosen this place to meet. I didn't care. I was tired.

Bruce poked me in the ribs before exiting the bus and made a cryptic comment about me facing my fears. Naomi walked out of the DMV and greeted Bruce and Pam with hugs and kisses and face strokes.

I turned to Em. "I understand if you still want the body they're offering," I said. "I'll support you. I'll love you no matter what."

Em looked at me with resolve in her eyes. "Mom would've wanted me to get back on the bike," she said, calling back to the story I'd told her about breaking my arm when I was a kid.

"Okay." I thought about the power of metaphors, even the ones without magic entwined in them.

"If I'm not in this body, I can't help you," she said.

"This isn't about me. This is about what's best for you. You don't need to help me."

"Can Suzanne stay with us? She helps with the nightmares."

"Okay," I said, looking at Suzanne, who looked down at Em with tender eyes.

Then I stood and went to the door of the bus.

"Don't," Hugo said, wary of Naomi.

I stopped at the bottom of the steps and looked through the glass at my ex-girlfriend, who stared back at me from five yards away. The streets were quiet. She could hear me through the door.

"Thank you," I said.

"I will always protect you, Charlie," she said, placing a hand over her heart. "I will never let you die."

I shuttered a little hearing that, then Hugo clunked the bus in gear and we lurched out of the driveway back onto the road. We passed old Victorians with Christmas trees in the windows. I wondered what the people inside were talking about, if the children thought the rekulak had something to do with Santa Claus, if the faithful thought it was a sign of the end times.

After dropping Hugo off at the Lodge, Lou got in the driver's seat, and we got back on the highway heading north. At my direction, we stopped at the Mad River Inn. I wanted to know what became of my sister's body. The parking lot there was empty as well. Not knowing what I would find, I said to Em, "Stay here. You don't want to see this."

"I'm going," she said. "I've seen worse."

I had to accept that she was telling the truth. I had to stop deceiving myself about her so that I didn't feel like I was falling off a cliff every time I was confronted directly with her loss of innocence. She was no longer the child I had known, though she looked the part now.

Kaliah, Hugo, and Suzanne stayed behind, while Em, Lou, and I left the bus. I noticed what looked like a new bronze plaque bolted to the stucco wall by the front doors, and I stopped to read it: "In memory of those who lost their lives to the void so that Blanche could be reborn." Lou and I exchanged looks of disgust at this, then the three of us walked inside.

A man in a mauve collared shirt stood behind the front desk, unmoving, unblinking. His clothes, skin, and hair all glistened. As I came closer, I saw he was covered evenly in a shiny, thin membrane, as if he'd been dipped whole into a clear glaze and left there to dry. At different angles, the faint outline of small yellow scales caught the light.

"I recognize this," Lou said. "It's a Zaditorian ritual, a way of honoring the dead."

The drinkers that had been in the lobby bar the day May had been killed were honored in the same fashion, glistening statues, preserved in different poses, most watching a TV that wasn't on.

The elevator didn't work, so we climbed the stairs. My stomach constricted as we approached the room. Lou went in first and hung his head. May was standing with one hand encased in a black bubble. She was still. She was shimmering, lifelike, gone, preserved in some strange Zaditorian substance.

Em walked out of the room. I went after her, but she told me she wanted to be alone, and I listened.

Lou and I wrapped May's stiff, preserved body in hotel blankets and carried her down the stairs and past the other honored dead. She was lighter than I would have thought. Outside, Em was beating on the bronze plaque with a hammer she had found. The plaque wasn't budging. I didn't try to stop her. But after Lou and I set May's body down in the aisle of the bus, I went back and held out my hand. Em gave me the hammer, and I chipped away at the stucco around the plaque with the claw end, then I pried and pried at the plaque. After several minutes of work, it loosened, and I gave the hammer back to Em. She smashed the plaque off the wall.

In silence, we drove to Lou's house. I dug a grave in his backyard. The work was restful for my mind. We buried May's stiff body in the grave. Em talked about making a headstone. I encouraged her.

Lou's fridge was full of rotten food, but the sourdough starter my sister had made to cheer me up so many days ago was still alive. I made bread from it, two loaves, and we ate it for dinner, hot and fresh with butter.

OTHER BOOKS BY COREY MARIANI

STRANGE TOTEMS SERIES

The Mind-Warper Special (Book One)

SCIENCE FICTION

Silicon Moon & Other Stories

Portrait of a Time Tourist

MYSTERY

The Death of July
Co-written under pseudonym, Waylon Joshua

ACKNOWLEDGEMENTS

Thank you to the first readers: Martin Fusek, Davenzane Hayes, Natasha Mariani, and Crystal Watanabe of Pikko's House. Your time and thoughts are appreciated. Anything wrong or unsavory found in this book is the fault of the author.

COPYRIGHT

This is a work of fiction. Names, characters, places, and incidents are products of the author's imagination or are used fictitiously and are not to be construed as real. Any resemblance to actual events, locations, organizations, or persons, living or dead, is entirely coincidental.

Copyright © 2021 Corey Mariani

All rights reserved. No part of this book may be reproduced in any form on by an electronic or mechanical means, including information storage and retrieval systems, without permission in writing from the publisher, except by a reviewer who may quote brief passages in a review.

First edition March 2021

Cover by Geoffrey Bunting Design

Published by Widow White Books

ISBN: 978-0-578-85353-6

www.ingramcontent.com/pod-product-compliance
Lightning Source LLC
Chambersburg PA
CBHW021105110726
47900CB00007B/2033

DEDICATION

To Caleb

ABOUT THE AUTHOR

COREY MARIANI was born in Bridgeville, California, the first town to be sold on eBay. He is a graduate of McKinleyville High School. He has traveled extensively throughout Humboldt County. His short fiction has appeared in *Lightspeed Magazine*, *Kaleidotrope*, and *Lore*.